Much Ado About Jack

Christy English

sourcebooks
casablanca

Published by Sourcebooks Casablanca, an imprint of Sourcebooks,
Inc.
P.O. Box 4410, Naperville, Illinois 60567-4410
(630) 961-3900
Fax: (630) 961-2168
www.sourcebooks.com

Printed and bound in the United States of America.
VP 10 9 8 7 6 5 4 3 2 1

For Amy Smith Pierce, Marianne Nubel, and Ellen Seltz:
I was not given sisters at birth, but
I'm grateful I was given you.

Author's Note

Gentle reader, *Much Ado About Jack* begins one month before the action of my previous novel, *Love on a Midsummer Night*. Most of this book follows the timeline of *Love on a Midsummer Night*, culminating in the same week in June 1818 when Raymond Olivier plays Oberon in Titania's production of *A Midsummer Night's Dream*.

ACT I

"Sigh no more, ladies, sigh no more.
Men were deceivers ever,
One foot in sea and one on shore,
To one thing constant never."

Much Ado About Nothing
Act 1, Scene 3

One

ANGELIQUE BEAUCHAMP, COUNTESS OF DEVONSHIRE, found a hulking Scot standing on the deck of her ship.

Her kid leather slippers whispered against the damp oak planks as they would have on a ballroom floor. She glided across the deck strewn with vats of tar, coiled rope, and unattended brushes.

The crew was supposed to be preparing her ship to go back out to sea, but she could only see Willy, the ten-year-old boy she had taken on last year, perched in the rigging high above. He waved to her, and she waved back, but after that, she kept her eyes on the man in front of her.

The Scot was as tall as a Viking. His broad shoulders were barely contained in a coat of black worsted, hard worn but well mended. He wore his auburn hair long, tied in a queue at the back of his neck.

Angelique was tall for a woman, but beside him, she felt delicate, like one of the china doll beauties so popular that season on the Marriage Mart.

"Good day, sir," she said. "May I ask what you're doing skulking about my ship?"

He smiled, and she caught the light of genuine humor in his eyes. He was a man who did not take himself too seriously, then. In spite of his military bearing, she might be able to deal with him.

"Good day, madam. I have come to speak with Captain Farvel."

"You won't find him. He deserted yesterday."

She spoke with confidence, as if she had not come down to the docks to speak with the erstwhile captain herself. She simply assumed that Farvel had deserted, from the state of the ship and from the absence of her crew. If she got her hands around her captain's neck, she would throttle him. Farvel had better stay hidden away, wherever he was.

The Scot's blue eyes did not take on a gleam of avarice to hear of her misfortune, as some men's might have done. He did not give the appearance of looking upon her staffing problems as an opportunity. He frowned, seeming almost concerned for her. "And the rest of the crew?"

"I assume they are in the stews of Southwark."

He laughed then, and she was tempted to laugh with him. For the first time since her man of business, George Smythe, had told her of the cargo of rotting cotton that Farvel had brought back from Charleston, her temper ebbed a bit, and she felt almost human.

Like all things, her good humor did not last.

"I understand this ship is for sale," the Scot said.

Angelique felt the dark of her temper rising like a summer storm, and she clamped it down. "You heard wrong."

She could count on the fingers of both hands the

number of men angling to get the *Diane* away from her. It was a good ship, her only ship, and would make a charming addition to any fleet. And if she sold it, the West India Company would no longer have to deal with her. In spite of their drawing room manners and open courtesy, they did not like doing business with a woman.

"Well," he said, "perhaps I might speak with the owner about that."

"I am the owner. And I can assure you, the *Diane* will never be for sale."

The deck lurched beneath them in the wake of a passing barge, and he reached for her, catching her arm.

Angelique had spent her childhood on this vessel. She had kept to her feet in storms off the coast of Africa, in the gales that blew north of Scotland. She could keep her footing without help in the midst of the Thames. She felt her mask of glacial calm come down as she drew her arm out of his grasp.

"I would thank you not to touch me," she said. "I would also thank you to let it be known among your acquaintances that the *Diane* belongs to me."

"Does it indeed?" He seemed not at all offended by her ire, but amused. The blue of his eyes reminded her of the sky on a clear summer day: guileless, open, hiding nothing. But she knew better than anyone how quickly such a sky could change. Beauty and serenity like that was an illusion, the kind of deception she would never be taken in by again.

"She is a beautiful ship," he said. For the first time, she heard a hint of his brogue, a shade of Aberdeen thickening his voice as his eyes ran not over the deck beneath their feet, or the furled sails above their heads, but over her.

Angelique felt the old telltale heat of desire rising from the center of her belly. She had not felt the lick of a flame like that, nor even smelled the smoke of lust, since Anthony Carrington had left her over a year before. She had taken one or two lovers since, of course, but with neither had she felt this warm beginning, this caress of craving.

She clenched her stomach against the onslaught, against the traitorous heat that rose to consume her. She tamped it down, just as she had tamped down her temper. When she raised her eyes to meet his, the man facing her smiled as if he knew her struggle and welcomed it. As if he knew that he had already won.

She meant to leave the insolent man standing where he was. Since Farvel was nowhere to be found, she would have Smythe start looking for a new captain at once. But before she could take another step, the ship lurched again, and this time her choice of shoes betrayed her and she lost her footing.

Her slippers slid out from beneath her, and she flailed, trying to catch hold of the rigging behind her where it was tied to the mast. Her hands touched not well-oiled rope but a burly, masculine arm. The man laid his hand over hers and drew her close.

His hands were strong and calloused. He no doubt spent a great deal of time on a ship at sea, for in spite of the rocking of the deck beneath their feet, he did not sway, but held himself and her as steady as if he stood on dry land.

As Angelique stood close to him, her cheek pressed

against his chest, she caught the scent of leather and spiced rum. The scent of that man brought the peace of her childhood back to her, layered over with the heat of lust.

Angelique closed her eyes and took in his scent, relishing the strength of his arms around her and the illusion of safety they gave her. The ship rocked again, and she came to her senses. Dear God, had she lost her mind?

She stepped away from the man as if nothing out of the ordinary had happened, straightening her gown and pelisse, smoothing her skirts. Two curls had escaped the prison of her bonnet and had fallen across her breast. The man reached for them, gathering them at her throat, lingering over their softness.

She jerked back reflexively, and he released those curls. The tendrils of her hair clung to his fingers like limpets, as if they would tether him to her. Her hands shook as she slid them back beneath her bonnet.

The blue of his gaze was no longer amused. The planes of his face were hard with naked desire. His need called to her own, a siren song that would draw her onto the rocks. The ship of her reason would splinter, and she would be left to drown.

"Good day," she said again, turning to flee from her own ship. She crossed the swaying deck to the narrow gangplank, certain that she had escaped, but when she raised her gloved hand to steady herself against the railing, he laid his hand over hers, capturing her so that she could not move.

"What is your name?" he asked.

The wind was strong, and a piece of his auburn hair

had come loose from the queue at the nape of his neck. Angelique felt an almost overwhelming need to reach for that strand and to draw it back from his face just as he had touched her errant curls. She held herself very still until the longing passed.

"Angelique Beauchamp, Countess of Devonshire."

If she had thought that her title might discourage his advances, she was mistaken. She saw the definite light of challenge in his eyes, as if by running away from him, she had thrown down a gauntlet at his feet. He smiled as if he had taken it up.

She had not been conscious of issuing a challenge. Her battlefield was a ballroom—her adversaries, mincing gentlemen of the *ton* who would inevitably bow to her will. This man was not one of those. She found herself grateful that she would never see him again.

Forcing herself to rally, Angelique walked down the plank from her ship without faltering. She allowed her footman to assist her into the carriage that bore her crest, a phoenix rising from the ashes, flames falling from its wings. William's gloved, indifferent hand felt nothing like the hand of the stranger.

She did not allow herself to look back. She could still feel the heat of the man's gaze on her skin, coupled with the overwhelming rise of her own long-banked need. She shook with that desire still, pressing her hands together, forcing them to lie docile in her lap.

She had skirted danger, but she had avoided it in the end. That man's touch would steal her reason; lust like that would take over her life, as Geoffrey had when she was a girl, as Anthony once had done. She would never allow any man such power over her again.

Fortunate then that a nameless ship captain would never be allowed entrée into the world she had built for herself so carefully.

She laid her head back on the soft velvet squab of her well-sprung carriage, not noticing the jolt of the cobbled streets as her driver took her home.

Two

THE SCUTTLEBUTT WAS THAT OLD DUKE OF HAWTHORNE had died, leaving his money and his estate in his nephew's hands. William Darlington, the new duke, had called a special meeting of the Hellfire Club to celebrate.

Captain James Montgomery heard something of this when he visited his father's club in Mayfair, but he listened to the speculation with only half an ear. In spite of the food and the women that were bound to be on offer, James would not be joining his fellow Hellfire members for the party in the new duke's honor. He had never met him and did not much like the idea of celebrating another man's death.

He was determined to track down the Countess of Devonshire instead.

James wore his Navy dress uniform though he had sold his commission the day before. He had been so certain that he was ready to settle on land, but that morning he had found himself back down at the docks, this time not at Greenwich but in London proper, where some of the smaller merchant ships came into port. He had found one almost completely unattended, save for a lone boy in the rigging, when Angelique Beauchamp had shown up and changed the course of his day. Perhaps even the course of his week.

James was a man to enjoy a pretty face. Even more, he was a man to enjoy the fine turn of a blushing cheek, the swell of full breasts beneath a silk gown, the curve of a woman's hips as she walked away from him. He had seen little of the last in his twenty years at sea. Always, since the age of twelve, women had been walking toward him. Angelique Beauchamp was the first to walk away.

He drank his whisky while sitting in a deep leather armchair. Raymond, Lord Pembroke, sat across from him, slumped over his own brandy, half-drunk though it was barely five o'clock in the evening.

He and Pembroke had come back to England from the Continent two years ago on the same ship and had struck up a friendship of sorts. Pembroke had been his guest for dinner in his captain's quarters and had brought James into the Hellfire Club, where it seemed a man of certain appetites was always welcome.

After only a few meetings, James had found the Club tiresome, almost as mundane as White's. Though the food was always good and the whores varied, James had spent too many years sampling the women of the world to let another man do his selecting for him.

And now, once again, he had his sights on a woman. A woman who, it seemed, might even be a challenge to get.

"Angelique Beauchamp," James said to Pembroke. "Where can I find her tonight?"

Pembroke's sky blue eyes were bloodshot. He rubbed one thumb against his temple as if trying to alleviate a headache, and failing.

"Why do you ask?"

"I want her."

Pembroke laughed, one bark that turned into a guffaw. The men around them turned to stare, and a waiter came by to stand silent at Pembroke's elbow. For a moment, James was sure his illustrious friend was about to be asked to leave, but the footman only poured him a fresh brandy.

Pembroke dried his eyes on a fine linen handkerchief drawn from his coat. He folded it again and set it aside before he fixed his gaze on James.

"Every man in London wants Angelique Beauchamp."

"I'm going to have her."

Pembroke leaned back in his chair, his fresh brandy untouched beside him. "That woman is trouble, Montgomery. That's all I'm going to say."

"All women are trouble," James replied. "Only some of them are worth it."

His friend sighed. "I have it on good authority that she is a lovely woman. Intelligent, well-spoken, a woman who makes her own way in the world. But I would not recommend her to an adder."

"Why not?"

"Some women are complicated. Angelique is one of them."

"Maybe I like complicated," James said.

"Since when?"

James ignored his friend's question and posed one of his own. "Where can I find her?"

"I don't keep her diary about my person. Perhaps if you inquired at her town house in Regent Square, her butler might assist you."

"Regent Square? Perhaps I will."

"I was joking. For God's sake, Montgomery, I don't know how you came to know Angelique, but I recommend you have a drink with me and forget about her."

"Angelique Beauchamp is a woman a man cannot forget."

"I agree completely."

A man with dark brown hair and a hawk's gaze sat down across from James. The stranger drew his leather armchair closer so that they might not be overheard. Pembroke took one look at the man and groaned, rubbing his temples again. James ignored his friend and nodded to the stranger.

"The Countess of Devonshire will be at the Duchess of Claremore's ball tonight. Number 5, Grosvenor Square," the stranger said.

James waved the address away with one hand. "I'll find it. My thanks."

"Happy hunting. I await the tale of your success with interest," the man said, rising once more to his feet.

"I don't carry tales of women," James answered.

He saw the first gleam of respect in the other man's eyes, but it might have been a trick of the firelight. "That's just as well, because you won't succeed. If the Duchess of Claremore doesn't turn you away at the door, Angelique will."

James smiled. If there was one thing he was good at, it was getting a woman to do what he wanted and thinking it was what she had wanted all along. "We'll see."

"Indeed," the stranger said. "We will."

Pembroke groaned again as the man walked away. James wondered if he should offer his friend a head-ache powder. His mother always favored willow bark.

"You are a damn fool," Pembroke said.

"Is that so?" James leaned back in his chair, satisfied. "It seems that I have discovered where Angelique Beauchamp will be this evening. I fail to see what's foolish about that."

"You're a fool because that's her ex-lover, the Earl of Ravensbrook."

"The man who saved your life twice at Waterloo?"

"And a hundred times before that."

James craned his neck to see if he could find the man in the room, but Ravensbrook had already left. "I wish I'd known," James said. "I would have thanked him."

"For telling you where to find Angelique?"

"For saving your hide."

Pembroke drank deep, as he did anytime anyone said anything remotely truthful or kind.

"Do you think he'll shoot me?" James asked.

"He might. He loves his wife, no doubt of that, but he just might shoot you."

"For making love to his mistress?"

"Ex-mistress. No. For asking about her in a public place."

"Hmmm," James said. "I'm not brilliant with a pistol. If he calls me out, it'll have to be rapiers."

"Oh, Anthony won't call you out," Pembroke said. "He'll just shoot you in the street like a dog."

James laughed and downed the last of his whisky. "I look forward to it."

James Montgomery forgot about Ravensbrook then. He couldn't care less how many lovers Angelique Beauchamp had, or who they were. He only cared that the next man in her bed would be him.

Three

ANGELIQUE STOOD IN FRONT OF HER FULL-LENGTH mirror as she dressed for the Duchess of Claremore's ball. Lisette fussed with one errant curl that refused to lie in submission along her neck. Only a few tendrils fell against Angelique's throat to frame her face and to lead a man's gaze downward to her deep décolletage.

She wore the gown that had been delivered from the dressmaker's just that morning. Instead of her usual shade of midnight blue to match the indigo of her eyes, Angelique dressed in a clear sapphire that made her eyes seem to sparkle even when she was not smiling. She wore the set of diamonds and pearls Anthony had given her the first year they were together. So much time had passed that no one save he and a few old dowagers, and perhaps Prinny himself, would remember.

"*Zut alors, Madame la Comtesse, je ne comprends pas le beau monde à London.*"

"English, please, Lisette. The war is barely over. I do not want someone spreading lies about you, saying that I harbor a French spy in my household."

Angelique had rescued the girl when she was on the Continent years before, meeting Anthony between battles for the supremacy of Europe. She had celebrated with the victorious allies in Paris during the heady days before Napoleon had escaped from Elba. She had returned to London as soon as hostilities began again in earnest, at Anthony's insistence, and she had taken Lisette with her.

After years in London, the girl was still as thin as a whippet, not a spare ounce of flesh on her bones. Her piercing green eyes were as cynical as her politics, for she loved nothing in the world save for Angelique and her lost emperor.

"*Madame la Comtesse*," Lisette began.

Angelique raised one curved eyebrow, and Lisette caught sight of its reflection in the silvered looking glass. She tried again, her voice still thick with the shadow of France. "My Lady Devonshire," she said. "I do not understand the paranoia of the ruling class of the British aristocracy. They have won the war. What do they care what a maid says in the privacy of your boudoir?"

Angelique smiled, taking a seat in an armchair upholstered in watered silk, inclining her head so that Lisette could weave a rope of diamonds through the darkness of her curls. "I do not know why, Lisette. I know only that they do."

"*Vive l'empereur*," Lisette muttered under her breath.

Angelique caught the girl's eye in the looking glass, and Lisette fell silent for the length of a breath, obediently arranging her mistress's hair. But when Lisette saw her mistress's lips quirk in a smile, she began to hum "La Marseillaise."

ॐ

At the Duchess of Claremore's ball, Angelique went straight to the font of all gossip, Anthony's aunt, Lady Westwood.

"My lady," Angelique said, offering a curtsy, her inherent grace making the older woman smile. "I am happy to see you here."

"And I, you, my dear. No need for such formality between us. We've been allies far too long for that."

"It gives me pleasure to show you respect," Angelique said.

"You outrank me, my dear."

"No one outranks you, Lady Westwood."

Her old friend took her hand and squeezed it. "It seems Arabella Hawthorne needs our help."

"The rumor about her taking a lover is absurd," Angelique said.

"Of course it is. That is why it makes such a lovely *on-dit*. Fortunately, this rumor has not caught fire yet, though someone has been spreading it assiduously. I will call on my friends in the old guard. We'll put a stop to that nonsense."

Angelique smiled, relief coursing through her. She had not realized how worried she was for Arabella until Lady Westwood offered her a remedy. If the old cats of the *ton* joined in full support of Arabella, no one would stand in their way.

Two more unlikely friends could not be found in the London *ton*. Arabella, a quiet, biddable woman who had married the Duke of Hawthorne in secret over ten years before, left her town house only to go to church. Angelique, on the other hand, traveled as she pleased and slept with any man who caught her fancy. She and Arabella were nothing alike, which was why their friendship flourished. The idea that sweet, almost silent Arabella had ever been unfaithful to her husband was ridiculous.

Arabella was a kind woman, at the end of a hideous marriage. She did not deserve to have her reputation shredded on the eve of her freedom.

Angelique, a widow for more than ten years, knew just how sweet that freedom was.

Satisfied that all was well in regards to Arabella, Angelique left Lady Westwood's side and caught the eye of her last lover from across the ballroom. Victor Winthrop, Viscount Carlyle, smiled at her from his post by the doors that led out into the garden. Her old paramour looked as if he hoped to flee through them, leaping over flower beds in an effort to escape, as if he wished to take wing and fly above the city, far away from his debutante fiancée.

Angelique knew that he would do nothing of the sort. He needed her money too much to risk running away.

Victor moved through the dancers with an unstudied grace, almost as if they were not there, as if she and he were the only two people in the room. She remembered now why she had kept this man as her lover for so long.

At first, she had taken him as her lover because he was Anthony Carrington's mortal enemy. She had kept him because of his lack of interest in anything but himself and his soft smile. Victor, Lord Carlyle, loved nothing and no one, which made it impossible to love him. But he had been a very easy companion in the dark reaches of the night.

Angelique wondered if she would ever feel an honest emotion again. Since Anthony left her, she had felt the sharp dagger of betrayal, the pain of lost love, heartache, headache, and all the rest. But now, for the last six months or so, she had felt absolutely nothing. Not even amusement, unless her maid was close by, spouting her treasonous twattle. Angelique wondered if she had lost the capacity to feel.

Earlier that day, on the deck of her ship, the tall, auburn-haired stranger had held her in his arms. She had felt something then. All was not lost if she could still feel desire, even for a common sailor.

Victor was at her side. He did not speak, but took her hand, and she stepped into his arms as he drew her into the fluid movements of the waltz. The rest of the *ton* drew back to watch them, the mother and aunts of his fiancée murmuring in quiet protest from the side of the room.

"Do I see the ring you once offered me on your girl's finger?" she asked.

Victor smiled and drew her closer. The sensuous warmth of his touch on the dance floor was an illusion. In the bedroom, with the curtains drawn, he was as selfish a lover as any she had known. Occasionally he had bothered to pleasure her, but like so many men of wealth and status, he had thought it her business to please him. She had done so, if only to make Anthony Carrington squirm.

"You refused me," Victor said, his lazy drawl surrounding her, cocooning her as the music did, the strains of the waltz drawing her into another world.

Against her will, she moved for a moment into

the bliss of the first days of her marriage to Geoffrey Beauchamp. A world in which everything was beautiful, an enchanted place where men said the words *I love you* and meant them.

She forced herself to push away the memory of Geoffrey and that first betrayal. She came back to the here and now.

Victor was amusing, but he was her opponent, as was every other man in that room. She tossed her head back, knowing that the diamonds at her earlobes caught the light from the chandeliers when she did, sparkling with cold fire.

"You might have bought her something more suitable, instead of handing over one of my castoffs."

Victor laughed. "She's good for bedding once or twice and breeding my heir, but little else. Once she's tucked away in the country, I'll be counting her money here in town."

"No doubt the whores of Cheapside will welcome your wife's gold," she said, her eyes roving over the crowd around them as if she were bored with the conversation.

Victor laughed again. The waltz ended, and he escorted her back to the edge of the ballroom, where she had been standing alone.

Angelique looked down at Victor's golden hair as he pressed his lips to her gloved hand, bowing over it as over some great treasure. "You have only to change your mind," he said, "and that sapphire is yours."

She forced herself to smile, though the sight of him suddenly wearied her. "You honor me," Angelique said. "But let us keep the sapphire where it is."

Victor stepped away from her and went to meet the

girl in question. His pretty fiancée smiled brightly at his approach as if he were a hero in a fairy story, come to change her life for the better.

Angelique sighed and turned away. She had loved Geoffrey with just such blind devotion. She hoped Victor would have a little more compassion for the girl than Geoffrey once had for her.

The gong for dinner sounded, banishing her thoughts of the past, and Angelique felt some of the tension in her shoulders melt away.

By now Lady Westwood no doubt had squelched all rumors that Arabella Hawthorne had ever been anything but a faithful wife. With her friend's reputation being protected by that great she-cat of the *ton*, Angelique could leave.

She had no idea whom the duchess had assigned as her dinner partner, and she did not care to find out. She wanted only to go home to soak her feet, which had been pinched for too long by the new dancing slippers she wore.

She turned to slip away just as the rest of the company began the precession into the dining room. False laughter mingled with the sound of tinkling crystal, and Angelique nodded once to the Duchess of Claremore across the ballroom. Isabelle Claremore had married the same year Angelique had, but the duchess's marriage had lasted a good deal longer. In spite of his advancing age of seventy-two, the Duke of Claremore seemed in no hurry to die.

Angelique was known among the *ton* for her eccentricities as much as for her prowess as a lover, so no one would think much of the fact that she had left before supper had been served. She slipped along the edge of the ballroom, nodding to acquaintances when she could not avoid them, smiling absently and moving on steadily whenever it looked as if someone might try to stop her. She had almost reached the doorway of the ballroom and freedom when a masculine hand caught her arm.

She stared at that hand, shocked that someone would be so bold as to touch her without permission. Angelique opened her mouth to rebuke the offender only to meet the blue gaze of the man who had tried to buy her ship that morning.

Dressed in the dark-blue uniform of a captain of the line, her Scot stood in front of her, the navy wool of his coat stretched across his broad shoulders, a vibrant contrast to the gold braid on his lapel and the white breeches that encased his powerful thighs. Her words of censure died in her throat, unspoken.

The auburn-haired stranger from the wharf did not speak to smooth over the moment, but seemed to enjoy the fact that the sight of him in uniform had managed to fluster her. He simply smiled.

Four

ANGELIQUE WAS FORCED TO TAKE A DEEP BREATH AT the sight of him, her stays suddenly too tight along her rib cage. The scent of cloves caught her, and the scent of cedar. His auburn hair gleamed in the candlelight, and his smile made her feel as if she were the only woman in the room.

Whatever else he was, whatever he pretended to be, he was certainly a beautiful man.

"How did you come to find yourself at the Duchess of Claremore's ball?" Angelique asked, allowing her mask of control to slip just enough to reveal a little of her inner fire, the sight of which never failed to draw a man in. It brought this handsome man a step closer to her. "Perhaps you are acquainted with the duchess herself?" she asked.

The stranger in the naval uniform found his voice at last. His eyes still lingered on her lips, rising to caress her face as if he would drink her in. But his voice was smooth and cultured, with only a hint of Aberdeen buried in it.

"It turns out that I am acquainted, very distantly, with His Grace, the Duke of Claremore."

"How charming for you," Angelique said. "You have your evening free then, for I have not seen the duke all night."

The man smiled. She felt certain that at any moment he would begin to peruse the curves of her body beneath the sapphire silk of her gown, but for now, he kept his eyes on her face. "I did not come here for His Grace. I came here for you."

Angelique laughed outright at that, not her practiced, seductive laugh but a burst of genuine mirth. The naval stranger did not seem to think her uncouth in spite of her sudden lack of polish. His eyes lit up as with a victory.

"You don't know me," she said.

"But I will," he answered.

She thought to leave him where he stood, but his hand was on her elbow, and she found that she could not slip away.

"I hope you will let me partner you at dinner," he said, steering her toward the dining room.

"I was just leaving," Angelique said.

"And now you are not."

Angelique thought about making a scene, pulling away from him and leaving him flat, but then she realized that they were making one already. Not only had they missed the procession into dinner, but also it went against all etiquette for a naval captain to escort a countess at a duchess's ball.

As soon as she heard the hum of horror fill the room around her, Angelique decided to let the stranger do what he would.

Everyone watched as her partner seated her at table. People stared openly, speaking about her and the man they took to be her new lover in sinuous whispers. Angelique did not look at her new dining partner, but smiled as if the only reason she had come to the ball at all was for him.

It always amused her to set the *ton* on its ear. And if tonight was any indication, the captain had provided just the fodder she needed. If anyone had thought to give credence to the rumors of Arabella's supposed infidelities, surely her own antics would distract the gossipmongers until they found a fresh tale to spread in the morning.

So Angelique sat where he bid her and decided to enjoy herself.

She picked up her fork to sample the light halibut, carefully breaded and roasted so that the white flakes of fish nearly fell off the bone. One of the benefits of the war with France had been the influx of French chefs into London and the subsequent rise of London cuisine. Angelique savored the salty flavor of the halibut before taking a sip of cold white wine.

The man beside her still had not spoken or touched his own food. He simply watched her eat as if nothing on Earth might give him greater pleasure, a soft smile on his face.

"You have not touched your fish," Angelique said. "Does it not meet your exacting Scottish standards?"

The stranger laughed, his teeth showing white against his tan face. His dark blue eyes sparkled with mischief, and he leaned in close, his voice pitched low so that only she could hear. "I ate enough fish in my years at sea to last me a lifetime."

It was Angelique's turn to laugh, and once more she did not keep her voice pitched in its usual seductive tones, but indulged in open, genuine mirth. She still had not asked his name. She waited, wondering if he might offer it, but he simply smiled at her as if he could see behind the mask of social grace she wore, as if he knew who she was already.

That, of course, was utter nonsense. A fanciful notion at best, a foolhardy one at worst. Only a handful of people had ever seen behind her mask, and only two of them still lived. Anthony Carrington, Earl of Ravensbrook, who even now sat across the table from her with his lovely young wife, ignoring Angelique's very existence. The other, Arabella Hawthorne, never came out in public, so was not at the ball. No matter how warm his smiles or his touch, the man beside her did not truly know her. She would do well to remember it.

Never before had any man blotted out Anthony Carrington's existence for her, especially when her old lover was in the room. Not just in the room, but across the dining table from her. But for the entire dinner, Angelique found that she had little interest in the man who had abandoned her, nor in his wife.

On any other evening, Anthony's presence at his wife's side would have rankled, getting under her skin like an itch she could not scratch. But tonight, Anthony sat less than six feet away, and Angelique felt nothing but fascination for the man beside her. Whatever his name might be, whoever he was, friend or foe, she owed him for that.

The elaborate meal ended, and the company adjourned once more to the ballroom, where they would dance into the morning. Angelique meant to leave then; she even placed a guiding hand on the sea captain's arm to steer him gently toward the front hall, but he took hold of her. It was he who guided her through the ballroom, past the dancers, and out onto the balcony beyond.

"You are presumptuous," she said as he took her in his arms.

"Are you complaining?" he asked, drawing her close as the strains of the second waltz of the evening filtered in from the open windows.

"Simply observing a fact."

She did not speak again, for his hands were on her, and the warmth of his body surrounded her with the scent of cedar. In that moment she did not feel like a woman of nine and twenty, but like a girl having her first dance in the arms of a man she wanted.

How long had it been since she had felt this way?

Perhaps with Anthony, long ago, though with him she had always been guarded, always careful, for she had known during all the years of their liaison that she loved him and that he did not return that love. She had known it, though she had lived in hope. Hope that he would value her, hope that someday he would see her as she was and love her for herself. Anthony had seen her, he had known her, but still, he had never loved her. Perhaps that was why it was so difficult to let him go.

But that night, as she danced with a stranger on the terrace of Claremore House, Anthony Carrington might as well have vanished from the earth. All she felt were the strong arms of the man who held her, the scent of his body, leather, and sea salt closing in around her, cocooning her in an illusion of warmth and serenity.

The music ended, but still they moved across the terrace beneath the shadows of the linden trees as the rising moon shed its light on them like a blessing. The sea captain drew her into the shadows along the edge of the terrace.

The warm candlelight of the house glowed from the windows and doorways they left behind. The sound of laughter followed them, and as Angelique listened, she heard a new set of dances beginning.

She turned away from all that, away from her life as she knew it among the London *ton*. He drew her deep into the shadows, and she let him. She raised her head to the man who stood beside her, offering herself to him, seeking a few moments' respite from the life that she knew, the life she was growing tired of. He did not disappoint her.

Five

THE SEA CAPTAIN'S LIPS WERE SOFT, SHEATHING HIS strength in silken pleasure. They moved over hers in lazy contemplation, not as if he would devour her, but as if he had all the time in the world to savor the taste of her, to feel her body warm beneath his hands.

A breeze blew in from the garden, chilling her under the thin linen of her shift, beneath the soft silk of her gown. When she shivered, he drew her closer still, opening his mouth over hers, drawing her mouth open beneath him so that he could feast on her even as he kept her warm.

Angelique felt herself drawn into him bit by bit, little by little, as if he were a conjurer who offered all she had ever desired. She followed where he led as he brought her deeper into the shadows, off the terrace altogether, into the darkness of the garden beyond. Between the flowering bushes and hedgerows, not even the moonlight could reach them.

He kissed her in earnest then, his hunger coming to the fore, driving her to answer him. She felt her desire rise as a wave might swamp a ship, but she did not go under. She floated along the surface of that wave and shivered as it carried her higher, bringing her deeper and deeper into the realm of pleasure.

She gasped beneath his hands as his coarse, calloused fingers dove beneath the scalloped bodice of her gown. This was no gentleman who wore gloves when on a hunt. This was a man who worked the rigging of his ship himself, a man who carried his own load and who burdened no one. The touch of his calloused palms on the softness of her breasts made her lose her breath.

He moved to stand behind her, and she leaned her head back against his shoulder, letting him touch her as he would, savoring this man she did not know as his hands caressed her body beneath its casing of silk. His hands ran over her curves again and again, one hand on the top of her gown, the other beneath her bodice. He did not untie her laces or even loosen them, but grasped what he could, for her ample bosom was pushed high by her corset, raised high for a man's contemplation or for his touch.

His lips played along the edge of her jaw as his hands cupped her breasts. She gave herself over to the feeling of his hands on her body, knowing that she would never see him again. This moment was a stolen one, and she was bound to savor it.

It was he who drew back, who righted her gown before turning her to face him.

"I would not take you here in the duke's garden."

She laughed, and this time the sultry sound was not calculated to appeal, nor was it feigned. Angelique leaned back in his arms, raising her hands behind his neck to toy with the ribbon that bound his hair. She could almost see that long hair falling around her as he leaned over her on the soft sheets of her bed.

She sighed then, for she knew that she would not bring this man into her home, that night or ever.

"You will not take me anywhere," she said.

Still, her deft fingers slipped the ribbon out of his hair. His hair was bound also by a leather band, so the silk of the navy blue ribbon caressed her fingers, almost as soft as the waves of auburn it held in place. She lowered her arms and slipped the ribbon inside her bodice, a trophy of war.

"This has been a pleasant interlude," she said. "And now, I must depart."

His chuckle was like molten lava on her skin. Her own desire rose to meet it, like a flower turning toward the heat of the sun. She had to force herself to lower her hand and to take a step back from him.

"'Wouldst thou leave me so unsatisfied?'"

It was her turn to laugh at his clumsy attempt to quote Shakespeare. *Romeo and Juliet*, while filled with lovely poetry, had never been one of her favorites.

She pressed one more kiss along his jaw, trailing her lips to his mouth. She thought him in control of himself until his mouth opened over hers, devouring her again as if she were a sweet that he had a powerful craving for. She trembled once before she reminded herself of where she was. Angelique drew back.

"I must go," she said.

"Must you? Then let me come with you."

His hands smoothed over the tops of her breasts again, and she trembled for one moment beneath an onslaught of pure, unadulterated fire.

"Believe me when I tell you that I would let you come with me," he said.

His voice was thick with desire, as heavy as the gown she wore. The double entendre hung in the air between them. Her stays had cut off her air long since, and she fought now to bring her breath back to steadiness. For the first time since Anthony, she fought for self-control.

She could not remember the last time she had wanted a man so badly. But she could not have him, she would not have him, and she knew it.

"I have an etching or two at home," she said. "No doubt you would benefit from surveying them."

"I have benefited already." He reached for her again, but she knew that if he touched her, she might give in to her own lust. She danced backward, out of his grasp.

"Or I could show you the art my husband collected. He had quite a taste for paintings of horses and dogs."

The stranger laughed, his voice still thick with desire for her. She could not see his face, but she could feel the warmth of his smile from where she stood.

"I did not know that you had a husband, Angelique."

She shivered at the sound of her name on his tongue. "He is dead," she said. "His art outlasted him."

"As even bad art will," he quipped.

She laughed a little at his jibe and took another step back.

"I would like to see this art," he said, following her, pacing slowly, like a panther that would devour her if she took one false step. "Perhaps we might enjoy making fun of it."

"No doubt we would," Angelique said, backing down the path, straightening her gown as she went. Her long hair, falling in curls across her shoulders, was a lost cause, and she knew it. "But alas," she said, "I must leave alone."

He moved close to kiss her again, but she drew back, and this time he let her go.

"I hope we meet again," he said.

Angelique walked away from him for the second time in one day. She tried to stop herself from looking back, but this time, she failed.

"I do not think we will. But thank you for the ribbon."

She drew the length of silk from her deep décolletage as she stepped into the light of the terrace. She could hear the sound of music, but it was distant, almost drowned out by the beating of her heart.

She raised her arms and tied her long hair back with the ribbon she had stolen.

She did not ask his name. She held her tongue and turned away, sliding through the shadows into the safety of the house. She moved quickly to the front door, where the duchess had her carriage waiting for her.

Angelique did not hesitate but climbed inside and rapped on the roof, that her driver might pull away quickly. But she need not have bothered. The stranger with the hot, calloused hands had not followed her. He had taken her at her word. He had let her go.

Six

SHE LEFT HIM FLAT.

James Montgomery could not remember the last time a woman had done that. He thought back over the indiscretions of his youth and realized that a woman never had. Nellie Graham had left him with a cock stand when they were both twelve years old. After frolicking in the stables of his father's country house, the lass had run away, afraid of what had come up under her hand.

He had finished himself off that day, but not before his balls turned blue with wanting. They were practically blue now.

James stood in the shadows of a duke's house, trying to bring his body back under control and failing. He did not swear under his breath, but laughed a little, a low caress on the air. His hands flexed into fists and back out again, as if he could still feel her body between his palms.

He had been a fool to let her go.

She talked too much. That was one of her faults. And he had let her. He usually didn't give a tinker's damn what a woman said, in bed or out of it. But that night, beneath those linden trees, he had fenced with her, sparring with her as he might have done with any man.

He corrected himself. Few of the men he knew were intelligent enough to fence with him like that, verbally or otherwise. He wondered if Angelique Beauchamp played chess.

He wondered what she was like with a blade.

That thought simply made him harder, so he banished it. Of course, like the best and worst of thoughts, it lingered without his say; it stayed in his mind without his permission. For once, he wished he was a man of the Orient, given over to meditation to maintain his self-control. He wondered what the Lord Buddha might have said about a woman like Angelique.

He doubted that the Siddhartha had ever met a woman like her.

James went back inside alone. The orchestra was still playing, this time some mincing French dance he had never bothered to learn. He caught the eye of several young ladies, each of whom giggled when he looked at them. He smiled and bowed slightly, but quickly moved on. Each of those girls reminded him of his sisters, if his sisters had ever wasted their time learning to simper.

As he made his way through the crowded ballroom, he caught the eye of more than one matron. It seemed the women of this rarified part of London rarely got to see a real man, for they were all intent on drinking him in. He stopped by a column and let them, waiting long enough for his hostess to come and greet him. He did not have long to wait.

Maybe he could quench his desire in her.

"Captain Montgomery, the duke is ill abovestairs and cannot receive you."

"I am sorry he is under the weather. I hope he mends quickly."

The Duchess of Claremore smiled, her own auburn hair catching the light of the chandelier overhead as she lowered her gaze. "When a man is five and seventy, illness is to be expected. Or so his doctor tells me."

She raised her eyes to his then, and he was caught for a moment in hazel flecked with green. James leaned closer to her, taking in the hint of lavender water on her skin. He breathed deep, waiting for his body to respond, but it did nothing. If anything, what was left of his arousal from the garden deserted him completely.

"Please give His Grace my regards," James said, bowing to her.

The duchess looked displeased at the fact that he would not follow her into a dark corner or come upstairs with her once the rest of her guests had gone. Still, in spite of her displeasure, or perhaps because of it, she took great pains to bid him farewell, nodding to him, ever the gracious hostess, as bloodless in the end as all those other fops seemed to be.

All save Angelique.

James walked out of the ballroom with the stride that, on the sea, ate up the deck beneath his feet. He took his bicorn hat from a waiting footman in the hallway and discovered the Earl of Ravensbrook watching him as he waited for his carriage. The pretty blonde who had been with the earl at dinner was nowhere in sight.

"So you found her," Ravensbrook said.

"So I did," James answered. He shifted on his feet, wishing he had worn a weapon. As it was, he had only his boot knife on him. He swallowed hard, and it was as if he could hear his mother's voice shrill in his ear. He could not skewer an earl at a dinner dance. It would be unseemly.

It had been so long since he had cared for niceties that he almost laughed at himself out loud. As it was, he kept his eye on Ravensbrook and his back to the door.

"And you leave alone," Ravensbrook said.

"So it would seem." James wondered for a moment if he was going to make it out of that entrance hall alive. But then the blonde appeared and wrapped her arm around the earl's waist. She smiled quizzically at James, but did not speak, as they had not been introduced. It took James a moment to realize that this tiny woman was the earl's wife.

"Good night, Captain," Ravensbrook said, as if that ended the matter.

James sketched his third foolish bow in an hour, turning toward the door. "My lord."

It took all his nerve to turn his back on that man, but he did it without hesitation. He had seen only a few men look at him with murder in their eyes. He had been forced to kill most of them. James knew he could not kill the Earl of Ravensbrook in public with the knife in his boot.

He wondered for a moment if Pembroke had been right, if the earl would murder him in the street somewhere, or if he'd pay some flunky to do it.

If James had any sense, he would be back on the sea by dawn. But he had no sense. He only wanted to see Angelique again. Things were not finished between them.

Not by a long shot.

It was good that nerve was one thing James Montgomery had in abundance.

Seven

ANGELIQUE WOKE LATE WITH THE SUN SHINING IN HER eyes. She had not drawn the curtains closed over her windows the night before, and now she lay in a shaft of sun, blinking against the onslaught of the light. She rolled over, burying her face between the feather pillow and bolster. She sighed and stretched, reaching for the man who had made love to her in her dreams. She opened her eyes and found that her ship captain was not there.

She sighed and sat up, pushing her long midnight curls back behind one shoulder. Angelique accepted her morning cup of chocolate from Lisette, sipping from the delicate china. She felt the touch of the man on her body still. She felt the delicious ache of unsatisfied desire in places that she had almost forgotten about.

"Will you bathe, Madame la Comtesse, before you see Monsieur Smythe?"

"Indeed," Angelique answered. "Has he been waiting long?"

"Only an hour, Madame. He is in the library."

Angelique set her hot chocolate down on a tray. "I had better not keep him waiting much longer, or he'll be peevish. There is little that is more annoying than a peevish man."

Lisette smirked at that remark as two girls from the kitchen brought up Angelique's silver hip bath half full of hot water. Two more girls followed, bringing silver urns of hot and cold water with them. Silver did not hold warmth or cold worth a damn, but Angelique liked the look of it. As a widow, attached to no one, she was her own master, and she could please herself. The thought was not as much comfort in the light of this particular morning as it usually was.

She rose naked from her bed and slipped into the tub. Angelique sighed at the feel of the hot water on her skin as Lisette bathed her back. Before she came out of the tub to dry off, her bed was already in order, its sheets removed and new ones put in their place, its duvet of satin arranged as she liked it, as if the man whose name she did not know had never touched her in her dreams at all.

Dressed in a morning gown of dark blue silk, Angelique sat behind the gilt-edged desk in her library across from her man of affairs. George Smythe was a decent sort, intelligent enough to carry out her orders to the letter, but not so intelligent that he might try to think independently or try to make decisions for her.

She had spent five years sifting through clerks and lawyers before she had found a man who would serve her without question. Smythe liked things in order and did not mind taking those orders from a woman. As far as she knew, he was unique in this. She paid him double what anyone else would have and sent his wife a stuffed goose every Christmas Eve. Those small gestures seemed to keep him happy, and he served her better than the men on her ship had once served her father, long ago.

"My lady, there is trouble in the country," Smythe said, peering at her above his eyeglasses rimmed in gold, the spectacles that she had paid for.

"Indeed," Angelique said. She poured herself a cup of black tea and sipped at it, taking no cream and no sugar. Take things as they are, her father always said, even small things. She had learned to drink her tea black and her champagne cold, though she still had not managed to stomach coffee. "And which country is troubled, Smythe?"

"Your own, my lady. There is trouble in Shropshire."

Angelique froze for one long moment before setting her teacup and saucer down. She had only one property left from the wreckage of her marriage, a small estate in Shropshire called Aeronwynn's Gate.

She had loved the place from the first moment she saw it. Once she was won and bedded, Geoffrey had left her there during the first year of their marriage, while he had gone off to chase after whores. He had died of a pox he had acquired from one of them and had never come home, and she had been left a widow at the age of eighteen.

Most of the estate was entailed, and she managed to salvage all of it, leaving it mostly intact for Geoffrey's heir, his little cousin living in Yorkshire who would not come into his majority for another five years. Once she had paid all Geoffrey's creditors and salvaged what was left of her married name, Aeronwynn's Gate was all that remained to her. It was a small seat close to the Severn river where the people raised barley and oats along with their cattle.

She visited once a year as a reward to herself for another year of prosperity, for all her money and her position in the *ton* had come from her own work and abilities. Though she loved the sea, she loved that patch of land in Shropshire too, with its rolling hills and deep green fields. The life she had built for herself was and always would be in London, but a part of her longed for that quiet, green country with its fields of white flowers and even whiter sheep.

"Has there been a death?" Angelique asked, drawing her mind back to the here and now.

"No, my lady, nothing so dire. But it seems your husband left a legacy behind him."

"A legacy other than debt and destruction? Enlighten me, Smythe. What legacy has my dead husband left us now?"

"He fathered a child, my lady."

Angelique pressed her hands together in her lap. She felt the blood run out of her face, along with all her usual color. The Aubusson carpet Anthony had given her on their second anniversary swam before her downcast eyes, and the floor beneath it seemed to move like the waves of the ocean. She closed her eyes and took a breath.

When she opened them again, the room was still, the carpet steady beneath her feet. She thought of her own dead child. Even after all these years, her husband still had the power to wound her.

"My God," she said. "The child must be at least twelve years old by now."

"Thirteen, my lady."

"Is it a son?"

"No, my lady, a daughter."

Smythe sat in silence, allowing this information to percolate in his mistress's mind. When Geoffrey had died, with both her parents dead as well, Angelique had been left alone. She had been cut off from the world she had known, adrift in an uncharted sea. She could only imagine what such a fate must feel like at the age of thirteen.

"The girl lived with her mother, a barmaid in a tavern, until this winter, when her mother caught a fever and died. Since then the girl has lived on the charity of the parish, until the curate let me know of her existence."

"How long have you known, Smythe?"

"I was told of the girl only last week, my lady. I brought the knowledge to you as soon as I was sure it was true."

"Is she safe?" Angelique asked.

Smythe understood at once what she meant. "The tavern keeper and his wife have taken the girl in. The parish sends them support, but the curate thought you should know."

"Yes. Thank you, Smythe. I will go to Shropshire at once."

"Tomorrow?"

"Today."

"Please, allow me to make the arrangements. There is still the matter of the captain of the *Diane* to settle, as well as some other business matters to look to…"

"I appreciate that, Smythe, as well as your diligence, but it will all have to wait. I leave for Shropshire as soon as I can pack and have the horses brought up from the stable."

"My lady, please. There is the matter of the Prince Regent's card party this evening."

Angelique rose to her feet, swearing under her breath. Prinny was a close friend of Anthony's and, as such, a constant burr under her skin. But he was also the ruler of the Empire. She was bound to him through years of court intrigue and nonsense that she no longer wanted to remember. An invitation to a private gathering at Carlton House could not be overlooked, not even by her.

"Tomorrow, then," she said. "I will leave for Shropshire at first light."

"Lady Devonshire, there is still the matter of the commander of the *Diane* to be settled. I have three candidates for you to interview over the next few days."

"Cancel those interviews, Smythe. I need to see that girl. My husband may have abandoned her to her fate, but I will not."

"But, my lady, the crew cannot wait idly in port without pay. We will lose them all."

"Pay them, then. But dole it out each week. I don't know how long I'll be gone. If they ship out with other concerns, we'll replace them." She met her secretary's gaze, turning the full force of her will on him for the first time in years. Mr. Smythe blinked behind the flimsy protection of his gold-rimmed glasses. His brown eyes seemed caught by hers, captured in a vise tightened by her hand. He stared at her as a snake would its charmer, and Angelique was reminded once again that for all his virtues, Smythe was still a man.

"The *Diane* will be in port too long, my lady," he managed to protest, however feebly, under the force of her gaze. "We will lose money and time on the sea," he said.

Angelique smiled and unbent long enough to press one hand against his arm as if to support him, as she might a comrade in arms. Her touch had a different effect, and she drew back at once, watching the color rise in Smythe's pale cheeks. She could not afford to lose this man to lust. It would take too long to find another like him. She would have to be more careful in the future.

She crossed to the door, and a footman opened it. She turned back and faced Smythe, who seemed relieved to have the distance of an entire room between them. "Make the arrangements as I have ordered, Mr. Smythe." His mouth opened and closed like a grounded fish, but he stayed silent. Angelique nodded to him before she withdrew. "The girl is more important. We have money enough."

Eight

ANGELIQUE COULD NOT THINK OF HER SEARCH FOR A captain for her ship, nor could she bring herself to pack for the journey on the morrow. She left her portmanteau to Lisette and the *Diane* for another day. The idea of her husband's daughter, set adrift in Shropshire with nothing and no one, pressed upon her.

Whenever she was this far out of sorts, Angelique knew there was only one cure for it. She called for her carriage, and after donning a dark blue pelisse to match her day gown, she drove to the home of Arabella, Duchess of Hawthorne.

Arabella's husband had been dead only two days, but he had been a pompous old fool whom few would mourn. He had never loved or respected his wife, which Angelique had found unconscionable. There was no woman kinder, or more lovable, than Arabella Hawthorne.

Angelique had always held her tongue on the subject. Even if she had ever tried to fill the duke's ears with her opinions, he would no doubt fall asleep in the middle of her tirade.

Though Arabella heard all of the scandalous rumors attached to Angelique's name, she never judged her for it. And Angelique knew better than to take Arabella's quiet calm at face value. There was a love for life hidden beneath her drab gowns and pale countenance, if only Arabella would consent to show it.

Hawthorne House loomed above the street as Angelique's carriage drew up before it. Her footman opened the lacquered door of her carriage and handed her out just as the butler of the mansion opened the high front door. Angelique ascended the staircase, offering her card to the butler whose frown of disapproval never wavered. The duke had never forbidden her the house, but as Angelique was well known in the *ton* as a woman who did as she pleased, she was never truly welcome. Of course, she did not mind the duke's displeasure, or his butler's, so long as Arabella did not.

She was not called on to wait in the drawing room but was led immediately to Arabella's private sitting room, which had a view of the back garden. Arabella's prize-winning roses were just beginning to return to life, their leaves unfurling with the first flush of spring. In another month or two they would be blooming, and Angelique and Arabella might take tea among them, cut off from the rest of the world.

Arabella, though one of the few duchesses in the land, lived cut off from the world almost all the time. She preferred to stay at home, and her husband had rarely allowed her out into society. The old duke had always spent a good deal of time at his club and with his mistress, and Arabella had spent most of the evenings of her marriage at home alone, making lace or embroidering a new pair of gloves. Even that morning, as Angelique stepped into her friend's sitting room, Arabella, wearing widow's black, worked at a bit of embroidery which she set aside as soon as Angelique entered.

"Good morning," Arabella said, her thin, pale face lighting with pleasure. The death of her husband did not weigh on her, but had freed some part of her soul that had been in chains. Like a flower blooming, her life had just begun to open.

Her cornflower-blue eyes shone and her fair hair escaped its pins beneath her black cap of lace. Angelique took her friend's hand in hers, pressing it between her palms.

"Thank you for receiving me," Angelique said.

"You are always welcome here," Arabella said, drawing Angelique with her to sit before the fire. The grate held a small coal fire, but the flames chased off the chill of the house. Sunlight poured in from the south-facing windows overlooking the garden. One of the windows was open to allow fresh air into the room, and Angelique could hear birdsong.

"You have created a haven for yourself in this place," Angelique said.

"We must take our refuge where we can find it," Arabella answered. "What has happened?"

"You know I am not making a purely social call."

"I can see it in your face. There is news about your husband, isn't there?"

Angelique was not certain how Arabella did it, but her friend always saw in her eyes, or in the set of her mouth perhaps, when she had discovered yet one more unsavory bit of knowledge about her late husband and his habits. He had an uncanny ability to hurt her, even now, when he had been dead over ten years. Loving him had cost her a great deal, and she found that she was still paying.

"Geoffrey left a bastard behind him."

"More than one, I imagine." Arabella closed her mouth as soon as she saw the look of pain on Angelique's face. She reached out and took her hand. "I am so sorry, Angelique. I do not mean to be glib."

Angelique drew herself up straight, locking the pain that had sprung into her chest like a boulder back into her heart.

During their whirlwind courtship, when Geoffrey had pursued her almost relentlessly, he had behaved as if the sun rose and set in her eyes. As soon as their vows were spoken, the chase was over, and he had lost interest. Her husband had been unfaithful to her even on her wedding night, leaving the company of what he called a callow virgin for the heady delights of his mistress, an opera dancer named Cecile.

He had been cruel, striking her when it suited his fancy, ignoring her almost completely when it did not. Her money had been welcome, as had her father's shipping interests, but her low birth on her father's side had always spoken against her.

Geoffrey Beauchamp, Earl of Devonshire, had never fully accepted his wife, not even in his bed. Only once or twice had he bothered to have her before turning back to his whores. In spite of all this, she had loved him, perhaps not the man he truly was, but the man she thought he was, the man she had fallen in love with when she was seventeen.

Arabella rang for tea, allowing Angelique a moment to compose herself. The duchess poured a cup for Angelique before taking a cup herself. Arabella watched in silence, waiting for her to speak.

"Geoffrey left a daughter behind in the village of Wythe."

"But that is where your home is," Arabella said. "You have been there countless times. How is it that you are only now learning of this?"

"Her mother kept it a secret," Angelique said. "I suppose the village knew all the time and simply did not see fit to tell me."

"Perhaps they thought you would be angry," Arabella said.

"In that, they are right," Angelique said. "But I am not angry at the child."

"Why reveal her presence now?"

"Her mother just died."

Arabella set her teacup down, reaching for Angelique's hand. "The poor girl. Alone and friendless in the world."

She knew well how Angelique felt about women left alone to fend for themselves.

"She has me," Angelique said. "I will go to her tomorrow, as soon as the duke's funeral is over."

"So soon?"

"Not soon enough. The girl's mother has been dead a week. I only just learned of her."

"I am sure someone in the village has been caring for her."

"Someone has: the innkeeper and his wife. But

she is Geoffrey's child. I cannot leave her to rot in a country inn. I will not."

Angelique heard the tears in her own voice, startled to feel her emotions rising so close to the surface. She thought of the lost years of her marriage, of the emptiness of her childless houses.

Geoffrey's daughter would not be left in the world alone. Angelique would take her in and educate her. Perhaps the girl had a love of art or of music, as yet untapped and unrealized. Perhaps Angelique could make a difference in her life as she had once longed to make a difference for her own daughter.

She thought of the tiny body, wrapped not in a shroud but in her mother's best silk shawl. She had buried her in winter, near the summerhouse at Aeronwynn's Gate. She visited her grave every summer, though she never needed to bring her flowers. Queen Anne's lace and bluebells grew there, all the way down to the river.

"Bring the girl to London," Arabella said. "The Duchess of Hawthorne will come and visit her."

Only Arabella would make such an offer, to come and greet a bastard from the country as if she were a lady, gently born and bred. Only Arabella could know what such an offer meant. Her friend knew of her own origins, of her life as a sea captain's daughter, and she had never cared. She had always valued Angelique for herself.

Angelique could not speak, for her throat had closed as tight as a drum. One tear slid down the curve of her cheek. Arabella leaned close and, with the handkerchief she had been embroidering with black thread, wiped the tear away.

Nine

IT TOOK VERY LITTLE TROUBLE FOR JAMES MONTGOMERY to discover where the Countess of Devonshire would spend her evening. All he needed to do was visit the closest newsstand. All the broadsheets wrote of her, of the gowns she wore, of the gowns she might wear, of the lovers she had taken, of the lovers she might allow next into her bed. He could not believe that such things were written about a lady with no sign of censure.

Clearly, he had been too long at sea.

There was a sort of breathy quality to the papers' speculation on the countess's life and her pursuits, which seemed to be confined to the drawing rooms and ballrooms of the *ton*'s elite. She crossed the thresholds only of dukes and princes, always a step ahead of the men who pursued her, leaving the light of a cool smile and a whiff of orchid perfume behind her.

James remembered the softness of her flesh pressed against him in the Duchess of Claremore's garden. Angelique had walked away from him, out of that garden, and out of his life. But he was not done with her yet.

She had not slipped his nets; for the moment, he was caught in hers.

He had not slept, which was unheard of. He had lived too long, and too well, to have his sleep broken by any woman. And yet when dawn came, he lay awake, still unsatisfied.

He had been at sea off and on since the age of twelve; he had made love to women in every port from London to the West Indies and beyond. He had fought at Trafalgar with Admiral Lord Nelson, and he had fought in the islands to keep the French from poaching British shipping lanes. Now that the war was over, he would put his prize money into a ship of his own. He was a man of action who knew his own mind. Why he had thought, even for a day, that he might live on land was beyond him.

But for the moment, James found that he could not think of ships or of his future, for every time he closed his eyes, he saw Angelique with her head thrown back against his shoulder, taking his caresses as if they were her due. He remembered the taste of her, the spice of cinnamon and cardamom that seemed to seep from her pores into his own skin. When he had found her the night before, when he had seen her across the press of the duchess's ballroom, he knew that he would have her.

And now he stood outside Carlton House, a stolen invitation from the Prince Regent in his hand, waiting to enter the fortress, to brave the guards and the prince himself. He'd been on more frightening sieges, but rarely. He would have felt better waging this battle on deck, with his gunners behind him.

"Captain Montgomery, well met." Pembroke stepped forward to shake his hand. "Still in town, I see."

"Indeed. I'll be here for the next week at least."

"So long? I didn't think you could be away from sea for seven days running."

"When there's a good enough reason."

Pembroke was fairly sober for so late in the evening, much to James's surprise. His friend's blue eyes met his frankly, with no screen of alcohol between them.

"You're not still chasing Angelique."

"I'm not certain that she's actually running away."

Pembroke groaned, but the door to Carlton House opened then, and he gave no more dire warnings about the folly of pursuing the wrong woman.

James had no doubt that it was folly to pursue the right one.

The guards said nothing, nor did Prinny's major-domo ask to see his pilfered invitation, as the gentlemen stepped inside. Together they walked into the huge entrance hall, its vast expanse leading to the grand staircase of gilded wood and marble.

James had never entered the hallowed halls of Carlton House before. He had been away from London for years and had spent little time in the capital since the war had ended. He preferred the open sea to any city, but now, as he strode up the grand staircase at Pembroke's side, he saw why so many curried the Prince Regent's favor.

The opulence that surrounded them was elegant if not understated. The walls were papered with brocade, and the high ceilings stretched above them, held in place by gilded columns. With so much wealth on offer, no doubt those courtiers worked day and night to procure some of the prince's favor for themselves.

James checked the knife tucked into the leather sheath in his sleeve as he entered the Golden Drawing Room behind Pembroke. He had never trusted men who lived in too much luxury.

The elaborate furnishings were covered in deep-red velvet, porphyry vases standing at intervals as tall as a man. The room was large enough to overwhelm any gathering, and that night only a handful of the Prince Regent's closest acquaintances had been invited to play at cards.

The prince himself stood in the center of the room, away from the gaming tables. A gaggle of hangers-on surrounded him, each trying to catch his eye, the ladies with their beauty, the men with their wit. James could not care less about any of it, for he sought only one woman. He found her almost at once, standing at the Prince Regent's elbow.

"Come, man, I'll introduce you to His Highness. Unless you've met already."

"Once, after the Trafalgar action, a few of us were honored in Nelson's place," James answered.

"He might remember you then. Stick close, and let us roll the dice."

Prinny's eye fell on James Montgomery. The fop standing beside the prince, holding forth about the allure of his newest racehorse, fell silent as Pembroke and James approached. Both men bowed before the Prince Regent, James a bit lower, as he was not titled. He could feel the heat of Angelique's gaze on him.

Though he greeted the most powerful man in the

realm, James had trouble focusing on the prince. All he could think of was how Angelique had tasted and the way her breasts had filled the palms of his hands. He caught the scent of her orchid perfume.

"Your Royal Highness, may I present Captain James Montgomery, formerly of your Royal Navy."

James bowed again, and Prinny raised his quizzing glass to take him in. Everyone knew that the prince had no need of the assistance of a quizzing glass, but that occasionally he enjoyed the affectation.

"Good evening, Captain. I seem to recall your face. Did you serve with Nelson?"

"Yes, Your Royal Highness. It is good of you to remember."

Prinny nodded, his eyes still assessing him. Though the Prince Regent was well known for his debauchery and his misplaced politics, he was a shrewd man with a clear grasp of the people who surrounded him. James felt himself weighed, judged, and evaluated within the space of a breath. Prinny smiled in the next moment, and there was a trace of genuine warmth behind his light blue eyes.

"You are welcome here, Captain Jack Montgomery. We are a small party this evening, just a gathering of a few friends. It was good of Pembroke to bring you along. One of the gentlemen could not attend, called away to a closed session of Parliament. So you can stand in for him."

James flinched at the mistake the prince made with his name but held back from correcting him. If that was the worst thing he was called all evening, it would be a good night. Better than most.

"It would be my honor, sir."

"Yes, well, Pembroke will see to your comfort."

Prinny nodded his dismissal before leading his coterie of sycophants toward the cold supper that had been laid by to tempt the royal palate. James would have to join the Prince, but he had a few moments to speak to Angelique first.

She stared at him, her blue eyes darkened with displeasure. The tilt of her full mouth still curved in a slight smile. "Captain Montgomery," she said. "I had no idea you were an intimate of the Prince Regent."

"We are so intimate that His Royal Highness has trouble remembering my name."

Her lips quirked in what might almost have been the beginning of a laugh, had she not squelched it. "No doubt you are a loyal subject, whatever the prince calls you."

"Indeed, my lady. It is my honor to be called the wrong name by one so illustrious."

She must have understood his mockery of the sycophants around them, because she did smile then. "I understand he has the same trouble with his mistresses."

"Too many to remember?" James asked.

"I imagine that he is gratified to inspire loyalty wherever he may find it, among his paramours and among the officers of his navy."

James laughed out loud at that. Never before had he been put on a par with whores. But by the same token, most men who met him remembered his name. He could not fault her logic, even if her tact was questionable. But then, he had not come to her looking for tact.

"I am in his navy no longer. I have sold my commission."

"Indeed?" One of her sculpted brows rose. "Is that why I found you on my ship?"

James paused for a moment, surprised that she would bring up her ties to trade among those people. No one else seemed to be listening to them. Pembroke had stepped away to greet a friend, and as the crowd had moved away with the prince, James and Angelique stood alone.

"I never gave you my name," he said.

"No need. I heard Pembroke offer it."

"Let it be my gift to you then."

"Free of charge?"

He smiled. "Nothing in this world comes free, lady."

She laughed then, and he said, "Captain James Montgomery, at your service."

"Are you really?"

James moved closer to her so that he could take in the heat of her skin along with the smell of her perfume. "In every way."

They stood staring at each other in silence.

She wore dark blue again as she had the night before, and the silk of her gown wrapped itself around her figure, revealing every curve. The low neck of her bodice showed a sapphire gleaming between her breasts on a string of pearls.

Sapphires flashed at her ears, but no jewel could detract from the light in her eyes. He had sailed the seven seas from the age of twelve, and he had never before seen a woman like her.

He had better be careful, or he might be dismissed from the royal presence for drooling like an ass.

The rest of the company moved to sit around Prinny in an informal clump. James offered her his arm, and she took it, barely touching him. He almost could not feel her fingertips where they rested on his sleeve. She walked with him, a picture of serenity, as he led her to the buffet. She took up a plate without looking at him and raised a few pieces of fruit and cheese onto its golden rim.

He watched her, the swell of her breasts rising beneath the dark silk of her gown. He stood close enough to see the generous curves disappear into the folds of her dress, close enough that the heat of her body radiated against his arm. He leaned even closer as if to take up a strawberry from its bed of cream, though all he wanted was to brush his arm against her breast.

Angelique anticipated his move and countered smoothly, taking one step back from the table. She did not reprimand him, and she did not walk away. He smiled then, sure he had won, and bit the strawberry off at the stem.

"Very sweet," he said. He dropped the remnant of the fruit and leaned over again, coming close to her. This time, she did not retreat.

The front of his coat brushed against the swell of her breast as he picked up another strawberry. He leaned forward, offering her the bit of fruit, wondering if she would take it into her mouth.

She looked at him for a long moment before she ran her tongue across her bottom lip. She raised a berry of her own and sucked the cream off it, before eating it all in one bite.

She chewed and swallowed, and he watched, his own fruit almost forgotten in his hand. Cream began to drip into his palm from his fingertips. He could not take his eyes away from her, and from the sight of her consuming that red berry.

Her lips were rosy in the soft candlelight, and James suddenly wished the rest of the company to perdition, the Prince Regent and Pembroke included. He must see her alone, or his cock stand would kill him.

"You think to toy with me, Captain. I warn you, I am no man's plaything."

James could not find his tongue. His glib, smiling talk, the lines he used to smooth his way with every woman he had ever known seemed to dry up on his tongue, unspoken. He simply stared at her, the heat of his lust in his eyes for all to see like some green boy who had never had a woman.

Angelique did not look away from his naked desire, and for a moment he thought that perhaps she shared it.

She began to move away from him, but it seemed she could not step away without speaking again. She quoted Shakespeare, of all things, almost as a warning to him, her midnight curls falling around her shoulders from the diamond clasps at the crown of her head. "'I know you of old,'" she said.

"Beatrice from *Much Ado About Nothing*!" Prinny said, as if they were playing a game of charades and he had just won, the triumphant tones of his voice breaking their intimacy. James stood staring at Angelique, his eyes unable to leave the contours of her face. But Angelique had been a courtier for many years, for she smiled easily, shifting her attention to the prince without missing a breath.

"Indeed, sir, you are right, as always. We must

prevail upon Titania to produce the play again. You must use your influence with her as a favor to me."

She stepped toward Prinny, no doubt thinking to dazzle him into forgetting James altogether, but the prince had seen them standing close and speaking low. Something in the intimacy of their voices must have alerted him. He smiled on them both, his eyes gleaming, a golden plate still in his hand, half-filled with cold chicken and asparagus.

The prince's gaze lingered first on her, then on James, before flickering to the tall, dark man who stood beside him. It seemed the Earl of Ravensbrook was there too, watching. "Do you know Captain Jack of old, Lady Devonshire?" the prince asked.

Angelique smiled, ignoring everyone but the prince while still seeming to include the company in the indifferent warmth of her smile.

She must have noticed that the prince had called him by the wrong name, but she did not comment on it. James wondered for a moment if she had bothered to remember his name at all. If he could get her alone for even five minutes, he would make her remember him.

"I know his type, sir."

Prinny laughed, and for a moment James thought that he might let the matter rest. But he did not yet know the royal wit. It was his first time at Carlton House, and James knew with unwavering certainty that it would be his last.

"The heroic type, you mean, Lady Devonshire?" Prinny glanced once more at Ravensbrook, as if to gage his reaction.

"No doubt you are right, sir, as always," Angelique said.

James thought he saw a flash of malice behind Prinny's lazy smile. "I have a prediction then, Lady Devonshire, that you and our Captain Jack of Trafalgar fame will one day become better acquainted. More than friends, shall we say. I believe I will open a wager on it. All here may bet, of course, though it is never politic to bet against your prince. Especially since, as you say, I am always right."

Angelique did not speak but curtsied to the Prince Regent. Ravensbrook frowned like thunder but remained silent. The rest of the company laughed uproariously, as if they were all privy to a great joke. Only the Prince, Ravensbrook, and Angelique did not smile. James stepped forward as if to protect her, to put himself between her and the laughter of her friends that suddenly sounded like mockery. It was one thing for him to poke and prod her, but he would be damned if he let these popinjays do it.

"Who would not be enchanted to spend even one moment at this lady's side?" James asked.

Angelique raised one eyebrow, as if he had surprised her. He had shocked himself with his sudden poetic turn of phrase. If he had ever read a poem, he had long since forgotten it.

The Prince Regent laughed, his eyes gleaming with mischief. "Indeed, Captain Jack. Well spoken. In the interests of furthering my bet, I excuse you both from play this evening. I give you access to the Blue Velvet Room where you might…enjoy each other's company at your leisure. You may take your ease there, and no one will disturb you."

James stared at the prince, certain that he had misunderstood him. But this time, it was no joke. No one else laughed.

He reached for the sword that was not there. He had not worn his dress uniform tonight, but plain brown wool and a silk waistcoat covered by a brown superfine jacket. He was well dressed by Aberdeen standards, though not compared with the men around him. Of course, none of these so-called men had done a day of work in their lives, save for perhaps Ravensbrook and Pembroke.

Pembroke was at his side then, his hand on his sword arm. James forced himself to relax, to remember that he was not on deck being besieged by the French, but that he had just been insulted by the ruler of the realm. Had the prince been any other man, he would have called him out. As it was, he stood silent and let Pembroke remind him of where he was, and with whom.

Angelique did not look surprised or horrified to be whored out by the man whose home she had been invited into. She did not look to her friends but nodded to the prince, curtsying again with grace. She set her plate down and moved to James's side. Pembroke gave way before her, and she took James's arm.

"You are gracious as always, sir," Angelique said. "We will retire to the Blue Velvet Room and revel in your generosity."

James bit back a curse, almost shaking her hand off his arm. He looked at her face then and saw how pale she was. Her lips, no longer rosy, were as gray as ash. He was not sure, but he thought he felt her hand tremble where it rested on his arm.

He wished to God he could strike the prince down

where he stood for hurting her like that. His sudden rage, the rage he had learned to tame so that it would not be his death, loomed large now, as it had not in many years. Rage like that got men killed on the open sea. If he had not learned self-control, it would have been he and not his enemies who fed the fish of the deep.

He placed his hand over hers, fighting the urge to push her behind him, the need to shield her from their sight. Instead, he let her lead him out, like a lamb to the slaughter, like a hound on a leash.

Ravensbrook caught her eye as they passed him, but did not speak. Something seemed to move between them, some memory of pain, a wound that had just now been reopened.

James wanted to stop and call him out, too, just for being her ex-lover, just for knowing her when James did not. He wanted to run him through for throwing her away, as if she were nothing.

He did not examine the vehemence of that last thought, for Angelique was taking him out of the Golden Drawing Room. They followed a footman into the corridor beyond. James did not take his leave of the prince or even look at Pembroke. It was all he could do to fight back the wall of red that clouded his vision and his judgment.

Behind them, the party picked up their conversations where they had left off, each vying for the prince's attention, trying to dazzle him. James looked back in spite of himself and saw that all present had completely lost interest in Angelique and in him, moving on to more profitable waters. Only Ravensbrook stared after them, his dark eyes unreadable.

Ten

"RAVENSBROOK WANTS YOU BACK," JAMES
Montgomery said, following her into the Blue Velvet
Room.

Angelique did not answer him, but moved past the
footmen on either side of the doorway. A fire was lit
in the large hearth, and Angelique stepped close to
it, as if it might warm her heart. She was shaking and
nauseous. It had been a long time, almost a decade in
fact, since the prince had attacked her. She had forgotten how vulnerable it made her.

She knew every time that she went out in Society
that she chose to swim with sharks. Though she had
received shots across the bow from more than a few
women during her time in the *ton*, it had been years
since Prinny had turned his venom on her.

She surveyed the room, taking in the wine punch
set on a side table with fruit and cheese. She caught
the eye of the footmen standing by, waiting for her
command. She gave one nod, and they both bowed
before withdrawing from her presence, closing the
door behind them.

When asked, they would report that all was well. As he decreed, Angelique was ensconced in a hideaway with the man the prince thought she should take as her next lover. No doubt Prinny had already heard that she had disappeared with Montgomery into the Duchess of Claremore's garden the night before.

She stared into the fire, extending her kid-gloved hands toward the warmth that could not seem to make its way into the marrow of her bones, where she needed it. Perhaps Prinny thought to stab at her as a gift to Anthony. Or perhaps the Prince Regent toyed with her in front of the Carlton House set for no other reason than that it amused him. The prince always wanted to be amused.

"Your old lover, the married one, wants you back." James Montgomery said this as if it were fact, as if by saying it out loud, he might make it true.

"He does not want me. Trust me when I tell you this."

"You're wrong."

"No doubt I am, about many things. But not about this."

Angelique turned to the sideboard and poured herself a glass of punch. She knew she should offer the first glass to Montgomery, as he now ostensibly had become her guest. He clearly had no more knowledge of the Prince Regent or his cohorts than she had when she had first come to London eleven years before. When she had been a new widow, alone in the city, Anthony had taken her under his wing and into his bed. She had never regretted that alliance, until now.

She sipped at the punch and found it too sweet, so

she set it by. She turned to James to ask if he would fancy a drink himself, but he waved her off. He stood staring at her, as if she had somehow deceived him.

A deep color of puce rose from the high points of his collar and his well-tied cravat to suffuse his face. If Angelique had not known better, she would have sworn the man was jealous.

"I've never had a rival for a woman before, but I know one when I see him."

Angelique smiled then, enjoying the fact that James Montgomery took nothing else away from their time under the prince's knife than some imagined obsession between her and Anthony.

"I was unaware that you were vying to come to my bed, but I am sure you cannot want a catalogue of my lovers. It would be tedious for both of us and would overtax my memory."

Angelique moved toward the door. Though Prinny himself had sent them into that room, she was done with this farce. She had her fill of the Carlton House set and the Prince Regent's whims.

She needed to be up in only three hours to pack for her journey to Shropshire, for she would leave for Aeronwynn's Gate after the Duke of Hawthorne's funeral. Angelique would not endure another moment as the Prince Regent's pawn.

She thought for a moment that James would simply allow her to leave without another word. But his silence did not signal his indifference. Before she had taken another step, his hand was on her arm, drawing her close until the buttons of his coat were pressed hard into the soft silk of her indigo gown.

Angelique could not remember the last time a man had made a habit of handling her so casually, without her permission. She felt her anger begin to rise, her temper flaring like a fire when coals are cast onto it. Angelique found this anger directed not at the man who held her but at herself, for she hungered for him as much as she had ever hungered for Anthony.

The edge of her hard-won control began to slip as she took in a deep breath of the perfume of his skin. He wore no scent, but smelled only of the salt of the sea and of the cedar his clothes had been pressed in. His warm breath on her cheek took her mind from where she was, and who she was. She fought hard to bring her good sense back again.

Angelique tried to step away, but his grip on her tightened, and his other arm rose around her, pinning her against him as in a vise. She felt the last of her breath escape between her teeth, and her hunger for his body rose even as she fought it down. She had come too far, and lived too long as her own master, to be bested by a man like him.

"You should not taunt me with your other lovers," James Montgomery said. "It is not wise."

"Go to the Devil," she said. "And take Prinny with you."

James laughed then, but there was a hard edge to his laughter. He kept her close, running his hands over her body almost as if to mock her. She trembled as he slid one hand down to cup her backside, drawing her flush against him so that she could feel for herself how much he still wanted her. His other hand rose into the softness of her hair.

As always, she had left it uncovered, and her midnight black curls fell in an artful disarray from the diamond combs at the crown of her head. He drew those combs out, one by one, tossing them onto a side table as if they were made of paste. Angelique struggled to get away from him; she had paid good money for those combs only a month before. But then his lips came down on hers, and she forgot her combs completely.

Until he touched her, she did not realize how much she needed to forget.

His lips were gentle, though his hands were not. His tongue coaxed hers out to play even as his hands ran over her body, from her scalp down her throat, then over her breasts to caress her thighs beneath the silk of her gown. All the while, his hands moved over her restlessly, as if they would devour her, and his mouth tasted her, teased her, drawing her in deeper and deeper until thoughts of all else melted away and she could taste and feel nothing but him.

Angelique never allowed herself the luxury of forgetting.

He must have felt her surrender, for his hands began to gentle as they moved over her body, drawing her down onto the sofa before the fire. The tall back of the sofa hid them from view had anyone else stepped into the room from the corridor beyond.

Angelique knew, however, in the small portion of her thinking mind that was still working, that Carlton House, and the Blue Velvet Room itself, had many hidden doors. She would have no way of knowing from which direction someone might come upon them, or how quietly.

Though she had made it her life's work to always

be in control, to use caution anytime she dealt with the palace or anyone in the *ton*, she lay back on soft cushions while the man she had met only the day before knelt over her, caressing her thighs as he raised the skirt of her gown.

Before she gave herself up to pleasure, Angelique made a vow: after this night, she would never let James Montgomery touch her again. She could not afford to develop the habit of losing control. But she was here, and so was he. What harm could one indulgence do?

Her vow made, she relaxed beneath him, savoring the feel of his hands and lips on her body. He seemed to sense the change in her, for he raised his lips from hers to search her face.

"Angelique."

He spoke her name almost as a question, as if only now it occurred to him to ask her permission to touch her.

She drew him down to her, her hand on the back of his head. His auburn hair came loose from the brown ribbon that bound it, falling around them both like a curtain that shut out the rest of the world. She had never known a man to keep his hair so long. It was against the fashion. No man of her acquaintance, not even Anthony, would ever do such a thing. But this man did not seem to care about fashion or anything else but his own pleasure. That thought made her desire flare higher, and she ran her hand down his chest to the waistband of his trousers, seeking another part of him that might give her pleasure.

James Montgomery laughed a little under his breath as he drew back from her lips and caught her hand in his. His palm was so large that her hand disappeared into it.

Angelique savored the warmth of his touch even there, though she wanted to direct his attention elsewhere.

"No," he said. "Not here."

Angelique felt another rise in her temper, blotting out her pleasure. How dare he think to dictate the terms of their encounter? Did this man have no idea who she was? Before she could form this thought into a coherent sentence, before she could push him away and rise from the blue velvet sofa unencumbered, he kissed her again.

His mouth wrought havoc with her senses, and she debated with herself whether to hold on to her ire. It had been months since she had taken a lover, an oversight this man was offering to amend.

She felt her anger slide away as on an outgoing tide, even as a wave of pleasure began to rise in its place. His insistent hands moved down to her thighs, drawing her gown up past her garters, sliding beyond the slippery silk to find the core of heat beneath. His fingers played her as if she were a stringed instrument, one tightly tuned to the nuance of every move he made.

She felt herself rising toward fulfillment so quickly that she lost her bearings. She clutched the silk-edged pillow beneath her head, and the grain of the cloth gave her succor, grounding her in the here and now. Then she was over the edge, spiraling higher and higher until she lost her breath altogether. When she finally gathered enough air to gasp, she found herself saying his name.

He smiled at her, as smug as a cat in the cream. At the sight of that gloating smile, her pleasure left her, fading away as quickly as it had come.

"Get off me."

"No," he answered.

It took all of her control not to hit him.

"Let me up, now."

He smiled down at her, running one thumb over her bottom lip. He licked the fingers that had just been inside her, lapping at them as a cat might.

"Why would I do that?"

She kicked him.

Her control was good, so she missed his groin and struck at his inner thigh instead. Still, her aim was just as good, for he doubled over, instinctively covering himself to protect his most valued assets from her. When he did that, she wriggled out from beneath him and stood.

"Save your smugness for your whores," she said. "If you forget all else about me, Captain, remember this. As I told you before, I am no man's plaything."

Angelique straightened her skirt, knowing that her gown was wrinkled beyond repair. Even Lisette with her damp cloths and heated iron would have difficulty getting such wrinkles out. As she collected her hair combs from the side table's lacquered top, she knew that she would never wear it again.

She had no mirror close by with which to rearrange her hair, so she simply tossed her dark curls over one shoulder, slipping her combs into her reticule. She straightened her gloves and moved to the door. The prince's staff would have her cloak waiting below, along with her coach. It was past time for her to leave.

James Montgomery was on his feet.

Angelique tensed, ready to run, ready to cry out if he moved toward her. But he did not. He straightened slowly, rearranging his wounded loins, wincing as he did so.

"I need you to teach my sisters how to do that," he said. His dark brown coat was askew, as was his cravat. His hair still fell around his shoulders in auburn waves, his ribbon lost between the sofa cushions on which he had possessed her.

No doubt he had others.

"You're leaving me," he said.

He sounded almost as if he wanted her to stay.

She had never kneed a man in the groin before, and as effective as it had been, she hoped to never do it again. Her anger was gone, and she felt tired, spun out.

"I am leaving Carlton House. There is not enough between us to leave anything behind."

She left the house then, walking slowly down the grand staircase to the entrance hall below.

Above her, she could hear the raucous laughter of Prinny's guests. She wondered if James Montgomery would rejoin the party once he had straightened his clothes. Though she listened for his feet on the marble stairs, he did not follow her.

She pushed him out of her mind as she stepped into the cool air on the prince's doorstep. This early in the morning, even in London, the air was almost clean.

She felt a moment's pang that James Montgomery had turned out to be a smug bastard. She was not sure why she had expected any different.

The sun would rise in an hour, and she needed to get some sleep. She had no time for errant sea captains or for men who thought they could take her at her own game. She had built her life carefully and walled it round for good reason.

There was no room in her world for a man like him.

Eleven

JAMES MONTGOMERY DID NOT FOLLOW ANGELIQUE out of the Blue Velvet Room. His cock was so hard that he could barely move, much less walk. He simply stood and looked at the empty doorway where moments before Angelique Beauchamp had stopped to mock him.

He shifted, rubbing the place where she had kneed his thigh. No doubt he would have a bruise in the morning, if not before.

The spoils of war.

James did not know why he had not taken her. He might have, there on the corrupt prince's velvet chaise. But he had not. Something about that place put him on edge. As much as he wanted her, as certain as he was that he would have her, and soon, it would not be there.

Two silent footmen came to flank the door in her wake. Neither looked at him, and James remembered what his brief moments among the *ton* had always felt like when he was in Town after Trafalgar: a cold winter that never saw sunlight.

He would rather face a crew of Spanish pirates on a stolen schooner than a ballroom full of the London elite. Strange company she kept. Perhaps he could persuade her to improve it.

He left Carlton House without a word to anyone. He had taken a hackney coach to the prince's doorstep, but as the sun began to rise beyond the trees of St. James Park, he did not call for another. He moved toward his hotel, nestled only a mile from Regent's Square.

He strode the sidewalks of London, his high brown boots striking the concrete, making a sharp sound in the early morning quiet. James searched for his anger as he walked in the cool morning air, but he could not find it. He went over the events of the last two evenings in his mind to see if that might refresh his ire.

He had drawn her out of the Duchess of Claremore's ballroom and had caressed her in the garden, only to be left flat. And tonight he had hunted her down, braving even the Prince Regent's lair to get to her, defying her powerful ex-lover to take her in hand. He had pleasured her, and instead of gratitude, she had tried for his groin.

He laughed then. His sisters needed to learn her finesse at defending herself. He had not felt Angelique move until her knee was buried in his thigh. If she had wanted to, she could have hurt him badly.

James would have to assume then that she wished him well.

He had never pursued a woman who had given him so much trouble. Sweet and willing in his arms, she just as soon changed into an adder, sliding away from him or burying her fangs in his flesh when she no longer wanted him.

It was intoxicating.

He knew he was arrogant. His mother had always said that no one would ever guess he was a younger son. His years on the sea had not tempered his self-regard, but had increased it.

There was nothing like knowing that left on a desert island with only a blade, he could save himself and whoever might be marooned with him. Life on the sea taught a man to face what was, both in himself and in others.

He had been forced, time and again, to test himself against his opponents and the elements both, even against the men under his command. He had lived to the ripe age of thirty and risen to the rank of captain on his own merits. He did not hesitate to do whatever needed to be done. He knew he would not hesitate now.

He would go to Angelique and talk to her, without games, without pretensions. He might even apologize for whatever it was she thought he had done.

She had melted beneath him that night, just as she had melted against him in the garden the night before. He had thought to take her back to her home, to make love to her again in her bed.

But she had done what no other woman had ever done. She had walked away from him for a third time.

He ached for her, and not just because of the bruise on his thigh. Very few men had the nerve to stand and face him as an equal, to defy him without hesitation. Coming from her, he found that he liked it.

If he had any sense, he would go to a whore to take the edge off his desire. But the thought of a brothel bored him. Soft and willing those women might be, but none of them had flashing sapphire eyes and adder's teeth. He wanted to bury himself in Angelique's sweet body and worry about the fangs in his flesh after.

Angelique was the most beautiful woman he had ever seen, and he had made love with women in ports all over the world. It was not just her beauty that drew him in, nor her beauty that held him. There was an inner fire that lived in her soul, a flame that shone out of her eyes.

James was certain she had made it her life's work to hide that glimpse of who she truly was. He wondered if her other lovers had seen that inner fire. If they had, how had they let her go?

He climbed the stairs to his room and realized that she must have been offended by something he had said, or by something he had failed to say. He would just have to bring her flowers, and apologize, and play each move after that as it came. With Angelique Beauchamp, he had a feeling that anything could happen. Just one more reason she intrigued him.

James went into his rented room and bathed his face in the tepid water the hotel had left for him. He did not call the room's valet to help him undress. The day he needed a man to tend him was the day he put a bullet in his brain.

Once he had taken off his coat, waistcoat, and cravat, James lay down on the softness of the hotel's feather bed. He leaned back against the bolster, trying to forget the contours of Angelique's face. He measured his breathing, waiting until the sight of the sapphire blue of her eyes might fade from his mind. Though he lay there for an hour, Angelique's image stayed with him, a woman who would not be conquered, a woman who would not let him sleep.

With a sigh, he rose once more from his rented bed and rang for hot water. He would face the new day with no sleep at all, and over a woman. It would be comical if it weren't so annoying.

Once he was dressed in fresh linen, shaved, and pumiced, James retraced his steps to Angelique's house on Regent's Square, the address Ravensbrook had given him. He would speak to her if she would receive him. And if she would not, he would push past her household staff and make her listen to him.

He stopped along the way and bought roses from a flower shop that had just opened its doors. Without his captain's uniform on, the shopkeeper looked down his nose at him, but James didn't care. He just needed the flowers to smooth his way with the woman he wanted more than any other.

He watched as the flower seller stripped the leaves and thorns from the chosen bouquet, wrapping them in paper three times to keep the stems damp as James traveled to Regent Square.

When he reached her doorstep, her butler stared down at him as if he were a bit of refuse that an ill wind had blown in. The scuttlebutt he had paid good money for said that her butler was Greek, a man she'd rescued from the Turks.

He had heard from the same source that her lady's

maid was a woman she had rescued from Paris. It seemed that Angelique was quite the humanitarian, at least where her servants were concerned.

James was not sure he believed the information he'd paid for, but the man in front of him dressed in immaculate dark clothes might have been Greek. He might have been Zeus himself.

"I am sorry, sir. Her ladyship is not at home." The man wrinkled his nose, as if James smelled of day-old fish.

"I'll wait," James said.

The butler drawled his next words lengthening them until James wondered if he was not a full-blown English butler after all. "I am sorry, sir. You may not."

James weighed the man's words, as well as his disdain. Something in his opponent's eyes told him that he was not lying. Angelique was not lounging abovestairs in her dressing gown. For the moment at least, she was gone.

"When will she be back?"

"She does not keep me informed, sir." He began to close the door in James's face.

James drew a golden guinea from his pocket and offered it, along with the roses. "Perhaps you might leave these for her."

The deepening contempt on butler's face forced James to pocket the guinea. A Scot, no matter how grand, would have taken the money, and gladly. But James had to remind himself that in the south, among the English, things were different.

The man did accept the offering of flowers, taking them between two fingers as if they were pox ridden and might infect his person.

"I will see that she gets them, sir. Good day."

James stood staring at the closed door. He turned to look out over the shaded square which had just begun to stir with nurses taking children out in their prams. He watched one woman walk by with her charge, a footman at their heels, until he shook himself awake. He would come back that afternoon and camp out on her doorstep, if need be. He was on the scent, and he would have her. He would not let her slip away.

And once he caught her, he would keep her under him until his hunger was sated.

Twelve

THE DUKE OF HAWTHORNE'S FUNERAL WAS ONE OF
the longest hours of Angelique Beauchamp's life.

She had always thought that her own husband's
funeral was the longest, but at least she had loved him,
and during his funeral, she had been in shock. Now,
from the third pew, she could do nothing but watch
her friend Arabella suffer.

Hawthorne, the new duke, sat beside her friend, a
hulking gray shadow that no amount of candle or sun
could shed light on. He was dressed in immaculate
dove gray, with an appropriate black armband. He
watched over Arabella as a hawk might, hovering over
her before his claws struck home.

Angelique knew that she had to help her friend get
out of London and away from him.

At the Claremores' ball two nights before, she had
thought she and Lady Westwood had managed to
squelch all rumors of Arabella's supposed infidelity.
But now she sat in the middle of St. Paul's, surrounded
on all sides by people speaking of little else.

One lady murmured how ill the widow looked and

speculated how such a plain and sallow-faced woman could find a lover at all. Her seatmate said that perhaps Arabella had paid her lovers to look the other way as they serviced her.

Neither woman looked in her direction, but they both spoke loudly enough for her to hear.

Angelique had never thought of herself as a violent woman, but as she listened to that twattle while watching Hawthorne usher Arabella out of the church without letting her speak to anyone, she felt the first desire to kill that she had experienced in over a decade.

Before this, only her dead husband had brought out such ire in her. She needed to discover the source of the rumors that were ruining Arabella's life, and put a stop to them.

She tried to attract Anthony Carrington's attention, but he shook his head once and escorted his elderly aunt up the aisle. His blonde young wife had not come.

It was Lady Westwood who caught her gaze and held it. Anthony's aunt placed one imperious arm on his, coming to a full stop, heedless of the well-dressed traffic behind her, all of whom wanted to get out of that gloomy cathedral and out into the sunlight.

Lady Westwood simply didn't care. Angelique smiled at her and took her hand.

"My lady, the rumors are still flying."

"So I understand." The old lady was in a foul humor, and Angelique wished once again that she knew who was spreading the vile lies, because when Lady Westwood turned her eye on prey, she never missed her mark. Their attempt at damage control had failed. They would need to go to the source of the lie and shut it off.

"I am heartily displeased," Lady Westwood said. She glared at the younger members of the *ton* as they passed, as if each one of them was responsible for her displeasure. Angelique would have laughed out loud at any other time to see the wealthiest and most influential members of the elite shrink under that old woman's gaze, but Arabella's reputation in tatters was not a laughing matter.

"We will regroup," Lady Westwood said. "Come to tea at my home tomorrow, and we will discuss strategy."

Angelique thought of her husband's illegitimate daughter waiting for her in Shropshire, but she did not hesitate. "I'll be there. Will five o'clock suit?"

Before Lady Westwood could answer, Anthony said, "No, it will not."

His aunt turned the full brunt of her glare on him.

He did not wait for her to rebuke him. "Aunt, if you receive her, the entire *ton* will assume that Angelique and I are once more bound together."

"Let them think what they please on that subject, Tony. As long as you and I know differently, on that matter, they can sort themselves out."

"Caroline won't like it," Anthony said. He did not have the grace to look at Angelique but stared over her head, as if wishing himself anywhere but there.

"Your domestic matters are your own concern, nephew. My household and whom I receive within it are mine." She turned back to Angelique. "Tomorrow at five o'clock will do."

Angelique felt a heated blush burn her cheeks, but

she kept her eyes fixed on the dowager countess's face. Lady Westwood had been her friend for over a decade. Unlike the rest of the *ton*, she had not looked down on Angelique when Anthony turned her away. Even now, she stared Anthony down until he stopped glowering in Angelique's direction.

"Thank you for your help, my lady. I hope to discover the source of the rumors before then, so that we might know whom we are fighting."

Arabella had nothing but her husband's good name to protect her. She had come from nothing and would return to nothing if the *ton* listened to the rumors of her infidelity and decided to cast her out. Men might do as they pleased, but ladies were not so fortunate. Unlike Angelique, Arabella had no powerful friends like the Prince Regent to protect her.

Lady Westwood seemed just as determined to keep Arabella safe. Protecting lone women was one of the older lady's pet projects. It was clear she did not intend to stand idly by and let the jackals consume Arabella without a fight.

"Agreed," Lady Westwood said. "I will canvass my own acquaintance as well. Until tomorrow."

She bowed and Angelique bowed back. Anthony's dark eyes met her for a fleeting moment before his aunt took his arm and led him away.

"Good riddance," Titania said.

Angelique jumped at the voice of Pembroke's light o'love. The actress owned a successful theater in Drury Lane and was patronized by the Prince of Wales himself. She had done very well, almost as well as Angelique had done in the cotton trade. Angelique was a silent producer in her theater and a longtime friend. The profits that came in from Titania's versions of Shakespeare's plays were always quite handsome.

Angelique nodded to her, one self-made woman to another. "Indeed," she said. "I am always glad to see the back of him."

"And a fine backside it is," Titania mused, her gaze following the Earl of Ravensbrook down the long aisle.

Angelique laughed out loud at that bit of irreverence and said, "Shall we walk out together then, and contemplate his finer attributes from a safe distance?"

Titania smiled. "Indeed, my lady. We fallen women need to stick together."

❧

Angelique tried to get Titania to come to her town house for a glass of brandy, but the actress claimed she had a performance that night and could not take any alcohol until after.

Angelique did not press her but left her to her own conveyance as she climbed into her lacquered coach outside of St. Paul's. The afternoon was still sunny, but it seemed to Angelique that all the warmth had gone out of the day.

She had missed her chance to leave for Shropshire at dawn. The trip, and her new ward, would have to wait. She would spend the rest of the day figuring out how best to deal with Arabella's unseen and unknown enemies.

She did not go home at once, but ordered her carriage to take a turn around Regent's Park. She did her best thinking behind the reins of a carriage. In the city, it was considered unwomanly to drive herself, so she forced herself to be content with the motion of the carriage. She stared up into the branches of the trees overhead, pondering which of her acquaintance to go to first to suss out the culprit, the man or woman who had begun the rumors about Arabella. She had no idea where to start.

An hour later, when she arrived on her own doorstep, her butler, Anton, stood glowering from his perch on the landing. The red roses that had mysteriously appeared that morning still sat in their vase on the entrance hall table behind him. He waited until she was out of her carriage and climbing the front steps before he delivered the bad news.

"My lady, the Duke of Hawthorne waits for you in the drawing room."

Angelique swallowed hard, suppressing a groan. Of all the men she would rather not see, the new Duke of Hawthorne was at the top of the list.

"I am not currently receiving, Anton."

"I told His Grace as much. He was very insistent."

Angelique stepped into the entrance hall and was greeted by the chill of the Duke of Hawthorne's voice.

"And I will become more insistent still, Angelique, if you refuse to see me now," he said.

The interloper was not tucked away in the softness of the drawing room but stood in the middle of the black- and white-tiled floor of the hall. His dove gray coat was as immaculate and unwrinkled as it had been at the funeral, and the silver knob on the end of his walking stick gleamed in the candlelight. The sun had begun to set, so the candles had already been lit.

"Of course I will receive you, Your Grace," Angelique said, her breath even, her tone smooth.

She led him into her formal drawing room. Hawthorne did not wait to be offered refreshment but crossed to the sideboard where she kept brandy for gentlemen callers. He poured himself two fingers of it, took one sniff, then left her expensive brandy on the sideboard like rejected refuse.

He moved in a leisurely manner to the fireplace, surveying the room as he went as if she and all that were in it were on sale at auction. He placed one well-polished boot on the grate as if staking his claim to her home.

"You are kind to call on me, uninvited," Angelique said. She did her best to keep the ire from her voice but was not certain she succeeded.

"A peer of the realm may always call on another peer in times of need," the duke answered, his voice cold as an Arctic blast. She could almost feel the icicles forming along her skin.

The duke stood relaxed against her mantelpiece, straightening the cuffs of his coat, flicking away a nonexistent bit of dirt from his glove.

"What could you possibly need from me?" Angelique asked.

Hawthorne turned his gray eyes on her. She felt as if the blood in her veins had begun to freeze.

It was rumored that he had some power over the Prince Regent, some information that even Prinny, as debauched as he was, did not want aired. If she had somehow inexplicably made an enemy of this man, she could rely neither on Anthony nor on royal favor for refuge. She was on her own.

Hawthorne smiled then, and Angelique's stomach clenched. His smile was one of the most unpleasant things she had ever seen, as if a curtain had been drawn back from a darkness that no one wanted to acknowledge even existed. "I have need of you, indeed, my lady. I need you to cease your ill-advised support of the Duchess of Hawthorne. I mean to keep her away from your influence."

"And why should I acknowledge your opinion on the matter, Your Grace? As you no doubt have heard, I am a woman who looks only to her own best interests. I gain nothing by abandoning Arabella. She is my friend."

The shadow of the duke's smile faded, and Angelique released her breath. She had been unaware that she had been holding it, waiting for that look to leave his face. "What kind of friend have you been to her? What have you done but expose her to censure and degradation by association with you?"

Angelique was tall for a woman, and she used her height now to meet the Duke of Hawthorne's eyes and stare him down. He might be used to bullying women, but he would not conquer her.

"I am Arabella's friend. I will stand by her and help her in any way I can."

Hawthorne crossed the room to her in three strides, his long legs eating up the distance between them in a blink. He moved so fast, almost like a tiger that had simply been toying with her and now was willing to pounce. She felt the hard clench of his fingers on her upper arms as he drew her toward him. She thought he would shake her like a rag doll, but instead, his left arm drew back in a clenched fist.

She stood her ground, wishing she could remember the knife lessons her father had given her onboard ship as a child, wishing that she still carried a blade as Anthony's young wife was said to do. As it was, she stood vulnerable and alone, facing the Duke of Hawthorne's wrath. But she did not back down.

She watched the shadows of his face, taking in the cold gray of his eyes, a wintry gray that matched the color of his coat. He stared down at her but did not strike. Instead, he leaned closer and breathed deep, his lips close to her temple. He smelled her as a dog might, searching for weakness. He did not find it.

"Leave Lady Arabella to me," he said.

Angelique heard the front door slam and the sound of Anton's feet tapping on the black-and-white marble of the hallway. The Duke of Hawthorne stepped back from her then, leaving her shaking. He walked away without looking back.

Thirteen

"WHO THE HELL WAS THAT?"

James Montgomery stepped into the drawing room as a tall man in gray left. The man must have been some kind of lord, because he did not glance at James or acknowledge his presence as he passed, certain of his own worth and equally certain of James's worthlessness.

For the first time that day, James's sword hand started itching to take up the blade that was not there. But he was in civilian clothes, entering a civilized drawing room. In Angelique Beauchamp's world, one did not settle matters at the point of a blade. From all he had seen, the point of a blade might improve the *ton* immensely.

"What are you doing here?" Angelique asked, turning away from him.

"I came to see you. Did you like my roses?"

"So that's where those came from."

He watched her walk across the room to pick up a glass of brandy from the sideboard. At first, he thought she meant to offer the drink to him, but she poured the remnants into the fire, casting the glass in after it.

"Not a fan of brandy then?" he asked.

She smiled a little, and he saw a shadow chase across the indigo of her eyes. Something had upset her. He wondered if he had walked in on a lovers' quarrel.

"It was contaminated," she answered.

She sat down heavily on a settee close to the small fire. Though he had not been asked, James crossed the room and sat down with her. He had not slept a wink since he'd seen her last, but she looked as fresh as a daisy in her simple silk gown.

More like an iris, he thought. A dark blue flower with velvet petals, color and softness meant to draw him in. But she was not trying to draw him in now. Her face was shuttered, troubled. He felt a stab of ire in his belly, just below his spleen. He had never felt such a thing before. It took him a moment to realize that the odd feeling was jealousy.

"So who was that man?" he asked again.

"No one of consequence."

He was about to ask again when the door burst open and Ravensbrook strode into the room.

"Damn it, Angelique, stay away from my family."

James was on his feet, placing himself between her and Ravensbrook without thinking. The earl stopped as soon as he saw him, sizing him up as he would a rival. James wished for his sword for the second time in ten minutes.

Then he felt her hand on his arm, a gentle touch, almost like a caress. He stood down, because without speaking, she asked him to. But he kept his eye on Ravensbrook.

"Anthony, I have no designs on your family,"

Angelique said. She sounded weary, worn out. Her fight
with the man in gray must have taken a lot out of her.

"I will thank you not to speak to my aunt in
public," Ravensbrook said, sounding like a prig. "I
must also ask you to stay away from her home."

Angelique rounded on him, her weariness falling
away like a cloak she had cast off. James watched her
eyes take fire and felt his admiration for her flare to
life as well. He had experienced the edge of her wrath
himself, and now he was going to see her tear into
her ex-lover. James relaxed for the first time since
Ravensbrook had entered the room and settled back
on his heels to enjoy the show.

"I will speak to whomever I wish, whenever I
wish, Anthony. You no longer have any rights where
I am concerned."

"I have the right to keep my family above gossip."

"Do you indeed? And with your wife throwing
knives at everyone in sight, how is that going?"

Anthony Carrington took a deep breath as if trying
to rein in his temper. James almost laughed to see
him do it. He had not known Angelique long, but
he knew that he had never met a more provoking
woman. Ravensbrook was going to lose this battle,
and James was going to savor his defeat.

"Leave Caroline out of this," Anthony said.

"Get out," Angelique countered.

"I will leave, and gladly, as soon as you tell me that
you will not take tea with my aunt."

"Then we are at an impasse, because I will take tea
with whom I wish."

Ravensbrook forced his breath out between his teeth,

his right hand flexing. James kept a sharper eye on him after that, for he knew the look of a man wishing for a weapon. But the earl did not reach into his coat or into his boot, but turned from her to pour himself a glass of brandy instead.

"One of your glasses is missing," he said.

"I had to break it. Hawthorne touched it," she answered.

Ravensbrook turned back to her, his brandy forgotten. "Hawthorne was here?"

"He left just before you arrived."

James smiled as he waited for the jealousy he felt to flood the face of her old lover. He was well rewarded. At the sound of Hawthorne's name, Ravensbrook seemed to pale beneath his tan.

"Hawthorne is dangerous," Ravensbrook said.

"I gather that," she answered.

"He is the source of the gossip that you and my aunt are trying to squelch. I tell you again, Angelique, leave this alone."

"Hawthorne started the false rumors about Arabella?" Angelique asked.

"Who the hell is Arabella, and why should I care?" James asked the room at large.

Angelique and Ravensbrook both turned to him, as if they had forgotten he was there. The earl's eyes narrowed, but it was Angelique who spoke.

"Arabella is the Duchess of Hawthorne. She is also my best friend. Someone has started a rumor that she was an unfaithful wife…"

"And now her reputation is ruined," James finished her sentence for her.

"Yes."

James thought of his own sisters, the eldest, Margaret, and the other four girls whom the men of his family would die to protect. He had not seen the girls since he had gotten leave last Christmas while he was in port at Aberdeen. But they wrote him letters perfumed with scent, written on expensive parchment so that the ink would not run if the pages got wet.

He had a trunk with his personal belongings stowed in it, and tucked away into the leather lining, his sisters' letters were hidden from the prying eyes of the world. He took them out and read them from time to time, to remind himself of home.

He spoke without thinking of anything but keeping his sisters safe. He knew what he would do if some man, duke or no, had threatened them.

"He deserves to be shot," James said.

"Jack, isn't it?" Ravensbrook sneered. "Captain Jack, a man does not simply murder a peer of the realm."

James was almost certain that Ravensbrook remembered his real name and simply meant to taunt him with the false one. His anger, usually banked, caught flame behind its wall of steel.

He kept his rage tempered, unused, except as fuel in a fight. He knew he would not strike Ravensbrook in Angelique's drawing room, no matter how much he might enjoy it.

"A man should ne'er get away with threatening a defenseless woman." James couldn't help the accent that rose to his lips whenever he got angry.

"Keep your plaid and your war paint in their trunk,

Jack. In London, amongst your betters, you'll find that
we deal with things differently."

Angelique stepped between them before James
could show Ravensbrook exactly who had the better
left hook.

James's hands flexed at his sides. There was little he
loved more than a street brawl.

Ravensbrook did not take his eyes from James's
face. "I am leaving now before I violate the sanctity
of your home. But I warn you, Angelique, leave
Hawthorne be."

James felt the need to smash the earl's smug, good-
looking face. He clenched one fist and breathed.

"Consider me warned," Angelique said. "Good
evening, Anthony."

The earl did not speak again. He did not look at
her or touch her, but still there was some awareness
between them, some old flame that had not yet died.
James saw it even as Ravensbrook left the room. It
lingered in the air after he had gone, like the remnant
of heat lightning.

"That bastard threw you over for the blonde at the
ball?" James asked at last. "He's a damned fool."

Angelique laughed then, and James felt the tension
run out of her. She rang for her servant, and when a
footman came in, she asked for red wine from Burgundy.

"Will you take a glass with me?" she asked him
once the servant had left.

"Of course," he said. "Though I've always been a
whisky man myself."

"I fear I have none," she said.

"Not to worry," he answered. "Compared to the

rotgut on board my first ship, your Burgundy will be ambrosia."

She laughed again, as he had meant her to. She sat down on her settee, and he settled himself comfortably beside her, careful to leave enough room between them so that she would not feel trapped, so that she would not feel his net closing until it was too late.

He leaned back, his boots toward the fire, watching the flames dance over the bits of broken glass in the grate. They sat in silence as the wine came and stayed silent as the footman poured it. James toasted her silently, and she bowed her head in acknowledgment. They both drank, companions in arms, as if they had come through a battle together unscathed.

"So, there's Hawthorne and Ravensbrook," James said. "How many more rivals do I have?"

Fourteen

ANGELIQUE LAUGHED OUT LOUD FOR THE THIRD TIME in ten minutes. She felt her laughter rising from her belly. It came on her almost like a sneezing fit, and once it started, she was afraid she would not be able to stop.

"As charming as your laughter is, you haven't answered my question."

She caught her breath, wiping the tears from her eyes with one finger. She would not let herself be drawn into verbal sparring over Anthony and Hawthorne. Both men were gone, and she was glad to see the back of them. The fact that James Montgomery would ask about them so openly made her like him more.

Angelique drank deep, finishing off her glass of wine. The carafe sat where her butler had left it, but instead of ringing for a footman as one of her more rarefied acquaintances might have done, she refilled her own glass, leaning over to top off Montgomery's as well.

"This wine is not bad," James said.

"I should hope not. I paid the smugglers enough for it."

It was Montgomery's turn to laugh at her. "Why, countess, I would never have taken you for the smuggling type."

She smiled at him. "I must admit, I did not do the run to shore myself."

His blue eyes rested on her face. She could feel their touch almost as if they were fingertips. There was a warmth in his gaze that seemed to have nothing to do with lust or their usual game of wits. For once, she thought she actually saw affection in a man's face. Though it might just have been the glow left by the wine.

"The war is over now," she said. "I no longer need to patronize the smugglers of Brittany."

James smiled. "I imagine the smugglers' prices are lower in peacetime."

"No doubt. But I am a patriot."

"I could tell that about you as soon as we met."

Angelique shifted on her uncomfortable sofa. Despite the brocade pillow behind her back, she could feel the wood digging into her spine from the frame of the settee. The longer he looked at her, the tighter her gown felt. Her stays dug into her sides, reminding her of propriety, of the fact that she did not want to let her guard down with this man, or anyone.

James leaned close enough that she could take in the scent of cedar on his clothes. His fingers touched hers, but barely, as he lifted her wineglass away. Her tongue had thickened with drink and rising desire, but she managed to speak anyway.

"I'm not done with that."

"I may give it back, once you've answered my question."

He set the wine down on the table beside him, then turned toward her. He slid close to her on the narrowing settee. That sofa had seemed so much roomier when she had first bought it in Paris. Now, it felt as tight and enclosed as the gown she wore.

She tried to rally her wits. "What question is that?"

"How many rivals do I have?"

"I lost count," she said.

His breath was warm on her skin. Though he had not touched her, he leaned close, the heat of his body like a furnace beside her, or a small sun. She wanted to come even closer to it, and to him, and lose herself. She knew that she should not, but his nearness was so tempting, she was having trouble remembering why she had sent him away in the first place.

"Maybe I can make you forget them all," James said, his hand coming to rest on her cheek. He took her lips with his kiss, very gently, as if he had all the time in the world to partake of her, as if she had offered herself to him on a plate.

Angelique knew she should push him away. She knew that she had no time to take a lover, even an amusing one. Arabella needed her, as did her husband's bastard daughter. She needed to find a new captain for her ship. She needed to counter Hawthorne's attack on Arabella's future.

The laundry list of things she owed to others paraded through her mind like sentinels. She acknowledged them all, even as James's other arm came around her shoulders and slowly drew her toward him.

His lips were soft, but there was heat behind them. The heat was banked for the moment, but Angelique knew that if she gave him the least encouragement, those embers would catch fire.

His wool coat was rough against her palm as she raised her hand to his arm. She moved her hand across his chest to push him away. Instead, she found herself sliding her palm past his waistcoat, to the softness of the linen shirt beneath it. His heart beat steadily under her hand, and she opened her mouth beneath his.

James Montgomery did not need more of an invitation than that. His mouth slanted over hers as if he would devour her, as if he had fasted for days, and she was meat and bread together. The strength of his ardor swept her thoughts away. Like twigs on an incoming tide, she watched her worries splinter apart, just as the warm heat of his hands suffused her with desire.

Angelique pressed herself against him, her hands going up into his hair. She found the leather thong that tied it back, and she loosened it, so that his hair surrounded them like an auburn curtain.

He drew her down onto her purgatorial settee, but she did not care that its short arm was pressing into the base of her skull. Her body came alive under his hands in a way it had not in many months. Victor had been a decent lover, but nothing like this man.

She forgot Victor, too, in the next moment, as James's calloused hands slid over her bodice, cupping first one breast, and then the other, as if he would sample both of them at once. His lips moved down her throat, but they did not stay there.

His hands smoothed over the skin along the scalloped neckline of her gown, then drew her bodice down. Both her breasts rose from the lace cups that held them until James pushed that lace down, too. Angelique arched her back in invitation, and then his mouth was on her, drawing one nipple between his teeth. He suckled, then bit down gently, so that she moaned beneath him, and writhed, reaching for the waistband of his trousers.

"Where is your bed?"

James Montgomery's brogue was in full throttle, and the sound of it made her shiver. She pressed herself to him, trying to assuage some of the ache at her core against his hard body. He pressed back, so that she felt the hard heat of him nestle in the cleft of her thighs. She writhed against him, hoping he would reach down and draw her skirts up. He kissed her again, hard, but instead of loosening his trousers or raising her gown, he spoke again.

"I don't know if I can hold on much longer, *mo ghaoil*. Where is your bedroom?"

Angelique heard the word *bed* and almost didn't understand it any better than the Gaelic endearment he had murmured against her skin. She did not want to think, she did not want to move. She only wanted to have him enter her there, on that purgatorial sofa.

"No," she said. "Here. Now."

He laughed a little, his breath hot on her breast. He blew gently on her nipple, and it puckered for him. He laved it with his tongue then did the same to the other. She began to realize that he was more in control of himself than she was. His next words were like a wash of cold seawater at Brighton.

"You deserve a bed, Angelique. Where is it?"

She felt sanity returning. She sighed, her body still aching, her breasts still heavy with need, still rosy pink from his touch. She reached for her self-control, and found it, and pulled it on, the way she pulled on her stays every morning. She was not a fan of stays just as, at the moment, she was not a fan of calm reason. But both served to keep her from making a fool of herself.

No man had entered her bedroom since Anthony, and no man ever would. Anthony was the last man she would allow past her defenses. She had almost not recovered from letting him inside. Her bedroom was her sanctuary. She never brought men into it anymore. She slept with them in theirs.

But she knew that she would not take herself off to whatever place James Montgomery laid his head. The lust had come upon her like a fever, but it was passing, even as she caught her breath. Indeed, her skin was still fevered with desire. But she knew herself. She would not be making love to him that night. She could not afford the luxury of making love to him, ever.

As amusing as he was, James Montgomery seemed very good at enticing her to forget herself, where she was, and who she was. Walking any further down the path of seduction with him was just not worth the risk.

"I don't take men into my bedroom," she said.

"You'll take me."

His brogue was just as strong, but now she could tell that it was anger, not lust that drove it. She pushed him away and sat up, raising the bodice of her gown. The silk was wrinkled but repairable. Lisette would be annoyed, but would understand that when lustful Scots came to tea, these things happened.

"This is the third time you've left me unsatisfied."

She laughed but stopped when she saw the muscle leap in his jaw. "You're counting, are you?"

He rose to his feet, looming over her. For a moment, she almost relented. She almost drew him down to her again and set about persuading him to forget about her bedroom there on her hearthrug. But his anger was real. She had insulted him, though she had not meant to. It seemed they were destined to offend each other. It was best that he was leaving.

"It won't happen again," he said.

"That, we can agree on."

His dark auburn hair fell around his shoulders like an old Highland warrior. She knew he was from Aberdeen, and that the Scots had been relatively civilized for decades. Still, the thrill she felt as she stood to face him was real.

His brogue was gone now, replaced with the clipped accent that the British Navy no doubt had beaten into him. "This isn't over," James said.

"This conversation is."

She thought he would storm out then, and that she would not see him again. She did not know a lot about James Montgomery, but she knew men. She had insulted him too badly, passing through the realm of challenging into offensive. He would not be back.

He did not storm out.

Instead, he stepped toward her and took her in

his arms. He did not ask for permission, and he did not hesitate, but kissed her once, hard, as if to seal a bargain between them.

"I'll be back," he said.

"I'll be gone."

He smiled, as if he thought she was simply toying with him, and picked up the leather thong that had held his hair in place before she freed it. He did not bother to tie his hair back but slipped the thong in his coat pocket and walked out of the room without looking back.

James Montgomery left, just as Hawthorne had, as Anthony had. The front door closed behind him. She stood in silence for a moment, the quiet of her house for the first time sounding like emptiness.

She always had valued her privacy, and she always had cherished her time alone. But that evening, with James gone, the room seemed too still, the corridors and rooms above her head too quiet.

She drank the last of her wine, but her favorite Burgundy tasted like bitter dregs on her tongue. She set her wineglass down and rang for Anton.

She would call for her carriage. Angelique desperately needed the distraction. Though she was leaving for Shropshire in the morning, though she had not finished choosing which gowns she would take, she knew she could not stay in that house with only Lisette for company.

She would go to see Arabella, locked away at Hawthorne House. She needed to warn her about the duke and his rumormongering. She told herself that this was the real reason she donned her light cloak and left the silence of her sitting room behind.

Fifteen

IT TOOK JAMES UNTIL MIDNIGHT TO CALM HIS IRE.

He was a man of the world and had known many women. He had women friends, widows and brothel keepers, all over the world. He had taken his ease with these women and had a friendly cup of wine after. He had even been known to sleep with a bored, married heiress or two when he was deep in the West Indies on shore leave.

Never, not once in all his years, had he ever taken the abuse he had taken from Angelique Beauchamp.

After he left her town house, James hired a hackney coach. He was not in any state to walk ten feet, much less all the way to Drury Lane to see a play, or farther still, to his favorite whorehouse in the West End. Instead, he rode to his father's club and walked past the officious butler to the gentlemen's smoking room on the first floor. He did not smoke, but he thought he might start.

"Why, if it isn't Captain Jack," one man said as James took a seat in one of White's very comfortable overstuffed leather chairs. "Still in London, are you?"

James stared at the man in front of him, wondering if the clod was asking for a fight. His erstwhile erection had finally dissipated, but a fight might be just the thing to improve his mood. James looked around at the staid old men and wealthy aristocrats. If they had ever seen a fight, it had been at Gentleman Jackson's. If he went a round or two with this imbecile, it might do them all some good.

"Have we met?" James asked. He did not rise to his feet when the man crossed the room to stand in front of him.

"Not officially. Allow me to introduce myself. Victor Winthrop, Viscount Carlyle, at your service."

James did not stand even then, but nodded to him. "Captain James Montgomery."

"And yet the Prince calls you Jack."

Carlyle sat down across from him and waved one hand. A whisky was poured and set down next to him. James nodded, and the footman poured him one as well.

"And if the Prince says the moon is made of silver mercury, then that must be true as well?" James asked.

Carlyle caught his eye, and James saw a gleam of respect there. "I see you share my opinion of the good prince."

"I have no opinion," James said, sipping his whisky.

White's kept the best single-malt Scotch outside of Aberdeen. Or so his father had always said.

"'Only civilized place in London,'" James mused, quoting his father again.

"Where's that?" Carlyle asked.

"White's."

Carlyle laughed. "No wonder I seldom visit."

There was a moment of silence, while both men paid homage to their drinks.

"I understand we have similar taste in women," Carlyle said.

"I would be surprised."

"I believe you know Angelique Beauchamp."

James felt his stomach clench. He looked at the man in front of him and set his whisky down. "If I was a fool, I'd say that you put a bit too much emphasis on the word 'know' in that last statement."

"Did I? I wasn't aware of it."

James did not answer this time but stared him down.

Carlyle stopped smiling and set his own drink down. His hands went up in a semblance of surrender. James was not sure whether he was mocking him, but better a stranger mock him than throw Angelique's name into the mud.

"She is a lover of mine," Carlyle said. "She was. She left me."

James saw nothing but red. He could see nothing else for a long time, so he listened closely to see if Carlyle might say anything else.

"It's been four months since I saw her last, save for the Claremores' ball. You met her there, I believe. Or so the gossips tell me."

James swallowed hard, trying to control his fury at this insolent bastard.

"She's a good woman," Carlyle said. "Whatever else you may hear about her. She was always good to me."

"Stop talking about her."

Carlyle eyed him over the rim of his glass. He sipped at the whisky, then downed it, as if it was not expensive liquor but medicine, and he was in need of healing.

"I've offended you. I'm sorry. Angelique's a law unto herself. I was never good enough for her."

"I'm glad you know it."

Carlyle smiled. "Worse luck, she knew it, too, but she put up with me anyway."

"Stay away from her."

Carlyle kept talking. "She'll be gone to the country in the morning. She's up in arms because people are speaking ill all over town about her little mousy friend, the Duchess of Hawthorne. As if anyone of conse- quence actually gave a damn about who that woman might have slept with."

"You will shut your mouth, or I will shut it for you."

James was on his feet then, and he had taken Carlyle with him. He gripped the other man by the collar, his elaborate cravat crushed in the palm of James's hand. James twisted the cloth, and Carlyle gasped for air. The man's face was turning puce, and James knew he did not have long before his prey passed out.

"Never speak of Angelique Beauchamp again. Not here, not in company, not to your mother."

James dropped the man back into his chair, and Carlyle gasped for breath, clutching at his throat. James waited for an army of footmen to descend on him and drag him down to the cellar, or wherever these posh Englishmen stashed violent Scots. But no one approached him. The two footmen in the room looked the other way, as did the rest of the titled gentlemen.

"You've got no friends here, it seems," James said.

Yet Carlyle was not to be deterred. "I hear she's leaving for Shropshire in the morning," Carlyle said.

James turned and started for the door, walking through the room of lords and gentlemen as if they were not there. A few stared at him before hiding behind their papers. James could not fathom how such milksops had ever conquered the Highlands.

"Where are you going?" Carlyle asked, almost plaintively. "I thought we might have another drink."

"It looks like I'm going to Shropshire."

ACT II

"O god of love! I know he doth deserve
As much as may be yielded to a man.
But nature never framed a woman's heart
Of prouder stuff than that of Beatrice."

Much Ado About Nothing
Act 3, Scene 1

Sixteen

Village of Wythe, Shropshire

AFTER HER VISIT TO ARABELLA'S HOUSE, ANGELIQUE slept badly, but she did manage to sleep. As soon as the sun was up, she sent her footman back to her friend with a message entreating Arabella to leave the city or to come to her.

William returned late, for when he did not find Arabella at home, he went to the Earl of Pembroke's town house, as Angelique had instructed. Arabella had thrown him over years ago, but Angelique knew that her friend was still in love with him. If Arabella ran pell-mell out into the night, fleeing her house before dawn, she would go straight to Pembroke.

Her second footman brought the news that the duchess had indeed gone to Pembroke House. Arabella had left from there on the North Road to Derbyshire disguised as a Cyprian, smuggled out of London posing as the Earl of Pembroke's mistress.

Angelique did not know whether to laugh at that bit of nonsense or be vexed at Pembroke for maligning her friend's honor even further. Of course, Arabella's reputation was already in shreds.

Angelique sent word to Lady Westwood, saying only that she would not be able to come to tea that day. Now that she knew who her enemy was, she did not want her old friend involved any more than she already was. As Anthony had said, Hawthorne was a dangerous man.

Angelique felt a chill all that morning in spite of the warmth of the day. It was as if she could feel the oppressive weight of Hawthorne's gaze on her, even though she knew he was unlikely to come back. She had known him for years in a peripheral way, as they both attended on the Prince Regent. She did not want to know him any better.

She finished her preparations to leave for Shropshire by midmorning and added a layer to Pembroke's deception by wrapping Lisette in one of her own fine cloaks. In front of her town house, in full view of anyone passing on the street, William helped the hooded Lisette climb into the traveling chaise. He took her hand as he would a lady's, while Angelique called her by Arabella's name.

After their interview the day before, the Duke of Hawthorne was almost certainly having her house watched. She meant for his spy to carry the news that Arabella had gone into the country with her. With a second trail to follow, it might take longer for the duke to discover where Arabella was actually hiding.

Lisette enjoyed the deception, smoothing the fine cloak over her own gown and smiling sideways at her mistress. Angelique laughed as the carriage drove away.

"Lisette, keep the cloak. You wear it better than I ever could."

"And where would I wear it, madame? I am not often asked to fine balls or to the opera."

"One never knows, Lisette."

"*Bien sur*, madame. One never does."

Angelique's well-sprung traveling coach took her and her lady's maid to her house in Shropshire. Her husband's bastard was waiting for her at the inn in the village of Wythe. After her last meeting with James Montgomery, she was grateful to have good reason to leave London behind.

Lisette had seen James as he left the night before. She had hidden on the staircase, waiting to see if Angelique would bring him upstairs. When her mistress had not, Lisette had watched the tall Scotsman leave, whistling low as he passed. Angelique had found her waiting with her cloak in the hallway.

Lisette had said, "You should not let that one get away."

"He already has, Lisette. I sent him away."

Her maid had shrugged one shoulder as she adjusted the fall of her mistress's cloak. "That one will be back, madame."

Angelique had left without answering, for it did no good to discuss anything with her maid. Lisette had never changed her mind about her own opinions.

Angelique's maid, while a hard, pragmatic woman, was in raptures that Angelique was going to rescue her husband's daughter from poverty and oblivion. Lisette called it as romantic as an old troubadour tale that the countess would take her husband's bastard into her household. Angelique did not think herself romantic, but she could not leave Geoffrey's daughter to suffer alone.

The girl was the last remnant of her husband. Faithless he had been, and cruel, but she had loved him once. She would honor that love, even if her husband had not. She would find this girl and take her home.

The rolling hills close by the river Severn gave way to fields of barley and wheat. Cattle dotted the land, and on the village commons, sheep grazed just out of range of the highway. The road itself was dusty from a lack of recent rain, but in spite of the dirt on her traveling cloak, Angelique was grateful that the roads were dry.

The Four Horses Inn and Tavern stood at the center of the village. Men coming in from the fields stopped there for a pint of ale or cider before heading home to their dinners. It was not midsummer yet, and the men often stayed late in the fields.

That day was a holiday of sorts, and they were coming in before five o'clock, calling to each other. When the men of the village saw her coach, her coat of arms on the door, they doffed their caps to her and waved. Angelique waved back, her gloved hand rising from the open window, feeling the last of the tension in her neck begin to fade.

She was always on guard in London, for there everyone tried to interfere with her life and her freedom. Only here in the country and on board her ship was she free of the backstabbing that went on in Prinny's presence and among the *ton*. In Shropshire, people greeted her warmly because they valued her, not for the title she bore but for the things she had done.

She had saved Aeronwynn's Gate after her husband's death and the village of Wythe along with it. She had used the money she made from shipping and selling cotton to pay off her husband's mountain of debts and to repair both the village commons and the green. The roses she had planted along the edge of the greenway renewed themselves each spring and would bloom again in June.

As she stepped into the Four Horses Inn, the proprietress, Mrs. Withers, came to the door to greet her, taking her traveling cloak.

"Well met, my lady. You are welcome here."

"I hope Mr. Smythe sent word of my coming."

"He did indeed, though the courier only arrived an hour ahead of you."

Angelique took the seat Mrs. Withers offered by the fire in the public room, sitting on the settle while Lisette plumped a cushion to place behind her back. Normally Angelique would not have allowed such pampering, but she was tired from their two-day journey. The scent of beef stew greeted her like an old friend, and she asked for a bowl, along with a hunk of fresh bread. Mrs. Withers beamed at the request and went to fetch the food while Mr. Withers set a newly drawn pint of cider at Angelique's elbow.

"It is always a happy day when you come to the village, Your Ladyship. I know you are here on business, but we are glad you've come."

Angelique smiled at him, the look on her face soft and welcoming. Here was one place where she need not hide behind a mask of stone. No one here wished her harm. Any man in this village would stand up for her, to defend her from an interloper, should one ever wander this far. Angelique leaned against the high back of the settle, sipping cider. The warm, sweet taste of the fermented apples exploded on her tongue and she sighed, allowing herself a moment of peace.

"You are the picture of a woman contented."

Angelique set down her pint. Lisette, who had come to take a seat herself, stayed on her feet. She raised one brow, turning with her mistress to stare into the face of James Montgomery.

"What are you doing here?" Angelique asked.

Lisette heard the warning note in her voice and took herself away to look for their dinner. James smiled as he leaned back against the far wall of the tavern, his long legs spread out before him toward the fire. Angelique could feel the eyes of the village on her, curiosity making their conversations fall silent so that they might better hear hers.

"Well, my lady, I brought word of your coming. Your illustrious Mr. Smythe sent me."

"My man of affairs does not know you from Adam. He would never have entrusted a stranger with such an office."

"No indeed," James said affably, lifting his tankard of ale. He crossed one fine booted ankle over the other. Angelique took in the tight buckskins he wore with his dusty linen and coat. A riding cape lay close by, also covered in dust. He must have ridden like a hound of hell to reach Wythe before she did.

"Mr. Smythe and I had words about the captaincy

of your ship, the *Diane*. My horse is a fast one, and since I was coming to Shropshire anyway, it served us both for me to bring his message myself."

Angelique raised one imperious brow. "You just happened to be coming to the wilds of Shropshire? What business could you possibly have here?"

"Why, I came to see you, of course. We have unfinished business between us."

His voice was mild, his face still set in the lines of an easy smile. But behind his eyes, Angelique saw the heat that had melted her bones more than once during their time together in London.

Angelique reminded herself of her vow, but her resolve seemed as far away as Prinny himself as she felt the warmth of her own body rise under the heat of James Montgomery's gaze. His eyes ran over her as if he might undress her, drawing off her pelisse and gown, her shift and stays until she sat before him naked. As she reached for her pint to cool her tongue, her hand trembled, spilling cider on the wooden table beside her.

He was beside her then, sitting on the settle with her, his long legs stretched before her so that she could take in an even better view of his hard thighs in their buckskin breeches. James leaned close and offered her the cider she had dropped. His hand did not falter or shake as he raised the cup to her lips, shielding her from the prying eyes of the villagers by the bar.

Angelique savored the way the heat of his gaze felt on her skin. All her thoughts of caution, all her common sense and self-preservation, seemed to have fled. All she could see was his face, smiling at her as if he knew her well. All she could taste was his skin beneath her lips and on her tongue. She took a sip of the cider he offered in an effort to obliterate the memory, but the taste of him lingered, mingling now with the sweet warmth of the drink in his hand.

Before she could draw another breath, James set the cider down and leaned back, giving her space and room to breathe. Neither of them spoke for a long moment while she fought to regain control of herself. She thought him unaffected by her nearness, but when he ran a hand through the auburn fall of his hair, she saw that hand tremble.

James did not press his advantage but let her sit in silence and gather her strength. He simply took another drink of his ale, leaving his eyes to rest on the fire beside them instead of on her. Slowly, Angelique's breathing evened out, just as Lisette returned with bowls of beef stew.

"Forgive me, my lady. I did not mean to intrude on your meal," James said, as if the moment before had never been.

Angelique could not find her voice, and Lisette answered for her, her black eyes drinking in the sight of his thighs in their buckskin breeches. Lisette smiled at her mistress and winked, for she liked what she saw. "No intrusion, my lord. Take this bowl of stew. I will find myself another."

James stood at once to accept the wooden bowl, a protest on his lips, but Lisette waved it away, her eyes flashing with pleasure, her French accent thicker at the sight of him. "Sit. Converse with my lady. I will return."

She went away, still smiling, and James sat once more beside Angelique, closer this time, so that his heavy thigh pressed against hers where no one else could see.

He did not remark on their proximity, though. He simply handed Angelique her stew and hunk of bread and began to eat his own. Angelique's appetite for food had fled when he first sat down beside her, but as she took in the aroma of the rich beef, her mouth watered for more than just his touch.

His thigh still pressed hot against hers, Angelique put aside her scruples and indulged herself in a perfect moment of sensation with his body close, the scent of the road still on his skin. The scent of him mingled with the creamy taste of the stew, the beef so well-cooked and succulent that it melted on her tongue. She ate the entire bowl in silence, leaving her bread untouched.

When she set her bowl down, James saw that she would not eat her buttered slice of rye so he took it himself and devoured it in three bites. She laughed, her eyes gleaming.

Perhaps here in the country she could allow herself the luxury of an affair with him. Away from London and all its influence, she wondered if she might enjoy this man and the heat of his touch without compromising the rest of her life. No one here would judge her for knowing him, for she could do no wrong in Wythe. In a week's time, she could return to London, her charge here settled, and her lust for this man behind her.

She knew that she was lying to herself somehow, but she also knew that she did not care.

James wiped the last of the rye crumbs from his lips with his handkerchief. She watched his hands as he folded the cloth and slipped it back into his coat pocket. The brown wool clung to his broad shoulders like a second skin. Angelique wanted to see those shoulders looming over her that night in her bed.

"For all your faults, Captain Montgomery, I am glad you're here."

He smiled at her then, and she felt as if the sun had come out after months of rain. He took her hand in his, and her small hand disappeared into the warmth of his palm. She did not feel lust in his touch this time, just joy in being alive. When had she last met a man who brought her joy?

"You are a hard woman to run to ground. Before I met with Smythe, I almost lost hope."

Angelique felt the walls of her defenses thinning, and she wondered why, even as she gave him her habitual, seductive smile.

"All men should live in hope," Angelique said.

"And so I do."

As she stared into the blue of his eyes, she found it difficult to look away. The rest of the room had resumed their conversations, though Angelique could still feel the village watching them.

No doubt they knew he was her latest paramour, for the people here knew she was a woman who chose to live as freely as a man. In spite of their country ways, they did not judge her for it. She supposed because she was their chatelaine, the woman who lived in the old manor house, the woman who settled their debts and saw to it that no one went hungry when the crops failed or the winter was overly harsh.

Angelique felt free in Shropshire as she did nowhere else, and she savored that freedom and James's touch in front of the public house fire.

It was Lisette who broke into her reverie, reminding her of why she had come to Shropshire in the first place.

"My lady, the girl is here. Mademoiselle Sara Burr." Lisette leaned close to Angelique's ear. "Your husband's daughter."

Angelique felt as if a sluice of cold water had been thrown over her. She drew her hand from James's grasp and rose to her feet.

She knew her duty, both to herself and to the dead. How she had managed to forget it, to wile away an hour in front of that fire with her lover when her husband's daughter waited for her, she did not understand. James Montgomery seemed to take over her wits as well as her senses whenever he came near.

"Thank you, Lisette. I would speak with Sara. Where is she?"

A voice spoke from behind the crowd, and a girl stepped forward, her blonde hair hidden beneath a fine white cap, a clean apron covering her simple brown dress. "Here, my lady. I am Sara."

Seventeen

THE GIRL HAD GEOFFREY'S EYES. IT WAS THE FIRST thing Angelique thought as she took in the sight of his daughter standing before her. She forgot James Montgomery in all his masculine glory, his heated looks and her own desire for him. All that fell away as she stood abruptly, moving without thought toward her husband's daughter.

The girl saw her move and took a step back as if to get away, checked by Mrs. Withers's hand on her arm. The innkeeper's wife stayed close by Sara as if to protect her, even from Angelique.

The girl also had Geoffrey's hair, thin wisps of gold that escaped the braids that fell down her back. Her light blue eyes seemed to catch and hold the summer sky within their depths. Looking into those eyes, Angelique was taken back to the first time she had ever seen Geoffrey, one night at some debutante ball.

Her father had finagled the invitation out of a business contact. Angelique and her mother were sadly out of place, French nobility disowned by their family, the wife and daughter of a mere sea captain. The entire press of people at that ball had made it clear they did not belong there. Only Geoffrey had approached them, bowing low, asking her to dance.

Geoffrey's daughter did not look thirteen, her fine-boned face too young and thin, her body as slight as a child's. The girl stared at Angelique half in fear, half in defiance, as if she expected Angelique to eat her alive, or to cast her into the pit of hell. Mr. Withers came out from behind the bar and stood a little apart, watching Angelique and Sara anxiously.

Angelique swallowed hard, searching hard to find her voice. She had never been struck speechless before, but her old grief rose to engulf her even as she stood there and looked into her dead husband's eyes. She took a deep breath and forced herself to speak.

"Good evening, Sara," Angelique said. "I am Angelique Beauchamp. I live in the house up on the hill."

"I know, my lady. You are the Countess of Devonshire. My mam used to cook for you when you had a big party. Sometimes I would come, and eat a scrap of pastry she made me."

The girl's voice broke the connection with her father in Angelique's mind. Geoffrey had been a nobleman with the nasal cadence of a man about Town. This girl's soft country speech would have to be trained out of her, Angelique thought. Already she knew that she would not just give the girl a governess and forget her. She would not leave this child in the country alone. This girl would be a member of her household, for better or for worse.

Angelique hoped desperately for better, but she

knew how hard it would be for the girl to take on a
new role in the world. Even if she wanted it, learning
to be a lady in only five years' time would be no small
feat. Angelique would have to begin instructing her
almost immediately. There had been no one to teach
her those hard lessons. Once she was married, she had
worked hard to lose the last of her Marseilles accent,
the last of her childish ignorance. Nothing she had
done had been enough, however. Geoffrey did not
love her anyway.

Sara's face had become a mask of misery at the
mention of her dead mother. Angelique saw not an
echo of Geoffrey, but a girl who was cut off from the
only thing she had ever known, a girl whose life would
never be the same again. That was someone Angelique
recognized. Once, that lost girl had been herself.

"Not that my mam stole from you, my lady. She
only gave me ruined scraps, bits that would have gone
to the dogs."

"I am sure your mother was an excellent woman."

Sara's blue eyes took on a sheen of tears. "My mam
was the best woman in the world."

Angelique suddenly became aware of everyone
looking to her expectantly, as if she might have some
magical method to assuage this child's pain, as if she
might heal the breach between this girl's life now and
what it had been. Angelique had helped with many
things in the last decade in the village of Wythe, but
faced now with the misery of one little girl, she was
not as sure of her success. She could educate her,
make a lady of her, settle money on her, and arrange
a decent marriage for her, but those were trifles

compared to what the girl had already lost. Her world had ended. There was nothing Angelique might do that would bring her mother back.

In that moment, three of the Withers boys came running through the public room. The oldest looked to be about five years old, chasing the three-year-old twins. Mrs. Withers was obliged to corral them all, leaving Sara in the center of the room facing Angelique alone.

Sara was thin, but Angelique assumed that she simply was naturally slim. The abundance of food at the Four Horses Inn spoke for itself, the scent of delicious beef and mutton still hanging in the air. She could keep feeding her, at least. Maybe under Angelique's care the girl could gain enough weight to look healthy.

Angelique's old longing for a child welled up within her, a many-headed Hydra, its tendrils reaching for her heart, threatening to drag her down. Seeing this orphan girl alone and bereft before her made her think of her own daughter, buried beneath Queen Anne's lace beside the river Severn.

James's hand was on her arm then, a heavy weight that brought her back to the here and now. He had come to stand beside her, and his touch seemed to offer support and strength. That this man she barely knew had seen enough of her pain to offer the comfort of touch made her burn with shame.

Her back straightened, and she blinked her tears away. If he, a virtual stranger, could see her pain, no doubt the rest of the public house could as well. She drew herself back once more behind her wall of stone, the brittle façade she had perfected during her years as part of the Prince Regent's set. But when she turned to look at Sara, she found that wall had a crack in it.

"Sara, I know Mrs. Withers told you of my arrival today. Did she also tell you that you will come to live with me in the manor house on the hill?"

Sara turned pale, her blond braids standing out like yellow gold against the pallor of her face. "No, my lady. I am to live here. I can work. I can earn my own keep. I am almost a woman grown."

Angelique took in the thin shoulders of the girl before her, her long arms ending in narrow wrists and small hands. Sara looked as if she would blow away with the first strong wind, until you looked into her eyes. There Angelique saw the beginnings of a stubborn strength that reminded her of herself.

"I am sure you can, Sara. You are no doubt a hard worker and a great asset to Mrs. Withers."

"Yes, Your Ladyship, she is at that," Mrs. Wither piped up, desperately trying to hold on to two wriggling three-year-olds at once. Sara stepped toward her and placed one of the boys on her hip, where he stopped moving and leaned quiet against her shoulder.

Angelique could see that the people around her expected that she would leave the girl here, among the people she had known all her life. She would be within her rights to leave her husband's bastard to rot in the village of her birth. If she felt any obligation, she could offer the Witherses a bit of money to help with the expense of an extra mouth to feed. The girl could work in this public house until the keen edge of the intelligence reflected in her eyes was blunted by the years of endless labor, eventually suffering indignities under the straying hands of traveling men, until she too gave birth out of wedlock like her mother before her.

She looked into the child's bright blue eyes set beneath feathery brows. Geoffrey's daughter would not be left to that fate. Angelique would offer her another.

"Sara, as much help as you are to Mrs. Withers, I would offer you another path. Come with me tonight, and we will speak of it."

Sara's mouth opened and closed, but no sound came out. Mrs. Withers stepped forward to speak for her, one unruly boy still caught between her hands. "My lady, I ask that you let Sara spend this night with us. Send someone to fetch her in the morning. She will be happy to come to the great house then."

Sara's look of misery did not fade, but Angelique steeled her heart against it. She would not leave this bright, beautiful child behind, one day to become the plaything of some man passing through on his way to Wales. She would take her in and make a lady of her. This girl would become the daughter she did not have, the daughter she would never have. After a few months or a year, the girl would see the new world opening before her, and she would be grateful for the opportunity Angelique had given her.

But as Angelique looked at the fear on Sara's face, she knew that she would grant the girl one more night in the familiar inn where she had lived all of her life. It was a small thing to give.

"Very well," she conceded. "I will send someone for her in the morning. Please see that her things are packed, Mrs. Withers."

The innkeeper curtsied, still clutching her son by the shoulder. The boy thought it a game and bowed as well, laughing. Only Sara stood frozen as if she could not see or hear. The boy she held still had his head on her shoulder, for by this time he had fallen asleep.

Angelique felt the eyes of the village on her. When she had arrived, she had been one of them. Now she was separated by the gulf of money, of power, the gulf that had truly always been there. She was the lady of the manor, and she would take this child out of the village and into a new life. As she looked at the village men around her, she saw that they did not approve of her choice.

Lisette caught her eye and brought her traveling cloak. Wrapped in the folds of soft wool, she steeled herself to hold to her decision. Whether they approved or not, she would make Geoffrey's daughter's life better. Angelique forced herself to smile.

"Thank you again for your hospitality, Mrs. Withers. My man will return tomorrow for Miss Burr, sometime around ten o'clock. Will that be convenient?"

Mrs. Withers blinked, for a moment not understanding who "Miss Burr" was. When she realized that Angelique referred to Sara, she bobbed another curtsy. "Of course, Your Ladyship. I will have her things ready by then. She doesn't have much."

Angelique nodded to Sara but did not offer her hand. The girl had retreated behind her own wall of stone, her eyes downcast, misery clear on her face.

Mrs. Withers still held her errant son in one hand but reached out to shake Sara with the other. "Her

Ladyship is leaving, Sara. Make your curtsy as your mother taught you."

Sara curtsied then, and Angelique observed her inherent grace. Now, as she rose from her curtsy to frown like thunder, Angelique saw the stamp of her husband's willful stubbornness on the girl's face.

Angelique smiled in the face of Sara's frown. The girl, surprised, allowed her frown to soften. "I like your courage, Sara. We will get along well together."

She left the public room then, raising a hand to acknowledge the farewells called out to her by all who stood at the bar and sat along the benches of the inn. She stepped out onto the porch, taking in the sweet scent of the spring evening. The sun was still setting over the hills to the west, and the sky was lit with the softening colors of orange and mauve. Angelique took in the sight of it as Lisette came forward with James at her heels.

"You would leave me without a word then?" James asked.

"Are you still here, Captain? I am headed for home and for my bed."

He let the incendiary mention of her bed pass. "We still have unfinished business."

"Must we discuss this business tonight?"

"Tonight, tomorrow, whenever you choose. But we will talk, Angelique. I came to Shropshire only for you."

She met his eyes and saw he spoke only the truth. He had set aside a bit of his arrogance; he had left something behind in London, just as she had. For the first time, she felt as if she were speaking to him without his mask. If a journey to the country improved him this much, she wondered what he must be like on his own ship, out on the open sea.

Still, she did not bend.

"A bit out of your way, is it not, Captain? Far from the sea, and from the ship you hope to procure. Very well, we will talk, but tomorrow. I am tired. Call on me in the morning."

James did not accept her casual dismissal but stepped close to her until his broad shoulders blocked out the rest of the world. "I do not know the men you have dealt with in the past. They may all be milksops, knaves, and fools. But I am not one of them."

Something electric stirred in the air between them, lightning crackling before thunder struck. Angelique found herself caught once more by the blue of his eyes and by the heat behind them. She did not know what it was about this man that kept drawing her in, but as tired as she was from her journey, as emotionally exhausted as she was from meeting her husband's daughter, she wanted to find out. He intrigued her as well as maddened her. Perhaps that was reason enough to do as he asked.

"What do you want of me?"

He spoke low, so that no one else might hear him. "Angelique, you know what I want."

The cadence of his voice made her shiver. The burr of his accent from Aberdeen ran over her skin like hands, making her long to be alone with him. She thought of how much she had wanted him inside her as she lay on the purgatorial sofa in her sitting room. She remembered how he had pleasured her in the Prince Regent's Blue Velvet Room, laid out on the damask divan.

She wanted what he wanted. Why not let them both have it?

"I'll see you at my house, then, Captain. Anyone in the village can give you the direction."

James said nothing but bowed to her. His frown was as electric as his smiles had been. She felt light-headed, almost giddy, more like the woman she had been ten years before. She could not remember the last time she had played with fire. All men she had spoken with since Anthony had left her were so predictable as to be somnolent.

Perhaps that was why she kept letting him return to her after she had already dismissed him. James Montgomery was not a man who would allow himself to be dismissed.

Angelique allowed her footman to hand her into her carriage. With the black lacquered door shut firmly behind her, she laid one gloved hand in the open window, savoring the feel of the evening breeze as it came up from the river. She did not offer to bring him home with her, but raised one hand in farewell as her horses began to draw her up the hill to her husband's house. Even she was not brazen enough to take a man up to her house in her own carriage in full view of the village.

He stood looking after her. He did not turn and walk back into the inn or even call for his horse. He stayed where he was until her carriage turned the corner onto the main road leading to her home, and she lost sight of him completely. He was a man of strength, but she could not allow his strength to overwhelm her own.

Whatever he was, whatever he became to her over the next few hours, James Montgomery would not be dull.

Eighteen

Aeronwynn's Gate

LISETTE HAD NEVER BEEN FOND OF THE COUNTRY, BUT she settled into Angelique's rooms without grumbling in French even once, overseeing the unpacking and calling for bathwater for her mistress after the long journey. Angelique herself did nothing but sit by the fire in her tall, wing-backed chair, leaning against her cushions as her household put her affairs in order.

She would take her time in her rooms and prepare herself for her meeting with Captain Montgomery. She pushed all thoughts of Sara aside, to be dealt with on the morrow. Though the girl's piquant face was not far from her thoughts, she needed to deal with the question of whether she would take James Montgomery into her bed. Sara would have to wait.

She had never known a man to follow her two days into the countryside. She had left the naval captain wanting her and might have seen him again in London, if he had not gone back to the sea. The fact that he had followed her here was a little intimidating. Aeronwynn's Gate was sacrosanct, her citadel, the one place on Earth where she could be fully herself. She was not sure how James Montgomery, as intriguing as he was, as infuriating as he could be, fit into that world, if at all.

Though the evening breeze carried a slight chill, the windows to her bedroom suite were open to allow the fresh air into her rooms. Her maid set up a screen between the window and the hip bath and made certain that the tub was drawn close to the fire. Lisette did grumble then about ladies who had no more sense than a feather, bathing themselves too often in the chill of the evening, but since she grumbled in English, Angelique pretended not to hear.

Her husband's house had been a ramshackle mausoleum before Angelique inherited it. The carpets had rotted on the floors and the roof had leaked into the attics so that the damp had seeped into the rest of the house. Smythe had told her to abandon the property and to build anew, but when Angelique toured the place, she fell in love.

The eighteenth-century walls and elaborate molded ceilings held a beauty and an elegance that even the falling plaster could not hide. She had spent three fortunes rebuilding the old ruin, and now it was a showplace where no one but the local gentry came, and only then at the holidays the years when Angelique was at home. She had never invited a member of the *ton* under her country roof. Aeronwynn's Gate was her refuge from that world, from the life she had built for herself in London. Even Anthony had never come to that place. She had always been at his beck and call, always going to his home in London or visiting Ravensbrook House farther down the river Severn.

Angelique bathed and dressed in a filmy night rail embroidered with delicate filigrees of silver thread. Lisette's incomparable lace adorned the neck and shoulders of the gown but did not cover her deep décolletage. Angelique surveyed herself in the full-length mirror, taking in the sight of the curves barely hidden beneath her diaphanous gown.

She gave herself a practiced smile, tossing her midnight hair back over one shoulder. The curls fell almost to her waist in a silken mass as soft as the gown she wore. She laughed at herself. Beauty was as beauty did, her mother had said.

She looked around the bedroom she had so carefully decorated to suit her tastes, to be her refuge within her haven. Her beauty had helped smooth the way to obtaining the right contacts that she had used to make her fortune, but it was her mind that had built this place. Her mind had built her life from the ruins left by Geoffrey and Anthony in turn.

She drew her dressing gown of royal blue silk about her, belting it tightly so that not even a hint of flesh showed. She squared her shoulders, ready to face her newest adversary.

"Has he arrived?" Angelique asked.

Lisette made no pretense at ignorance. She knew of her mistress's affairs and never breathed a word about any of them. Her French pragmatism colored her views on the bedchamber. The countess was a widow who answered to no one.

"Yes, madame. He waits for you in your sitting room downstairs."

"The one adjacent to the flower garden?"

"Yes, madame. Shall I bring him up?"

Angelique smiled. "No, Lisette. I shall go to him."

Lisette blinked. Even she was scandalized at the thought of her mistress stepping out of her bedroom suite in dishabille. For once, she held her tongue, simply stepping aside to let her mistress pass.

"You need not wait up for me, Lisette. My guest may stay with me overnight. I will see you in the morning."

"Shall I wait for your call, madame?"

"Yes. I am not sure how late I may want to sleep."

Lisette curtsied, and Angelique saw in the stiff lines of her maid's thin back that she was displeased at the turn of events. But Angelique had lived too long on her own to worry what even her trusted people thought of her. So long as they held their tongues, their thoughts were their own.

Lisette retired to her own room and Angelique continued down the corridor. She moved down the carpeted stairs, the silk of her slippers barely making a sound as she walked. The door to the sitting room was open, a candelabrum set out on the table in the front hall. The house she had loved and worked so hard to reclaim was bathed in shadows. In the morning she would be able to see its beauty clearly, but tonight those walls were still her haven.

James Montgomery was waiting for her just as Lisette had said. He stood in the open French doors that led out into her flower garden. It was too early for the roses to bloom, but the night jasmine had come out with the moonlight, and even now the scent of it rode on the wind. Angelique savored it, and the sight of James Montgomery standing in her home. His broad shoulders filled the tight brown riding jacket he wore. He had changed his clothes before coming to see her, and his hair was neatly bound at the nape of his neck. The sight of that ribbon made her want to reach out and unravel it.

There was only one set of candles lit in the sitting room, casting shadows over his face. He turned at the sound of her slippers on the plush carpet. When he saw what she was wearing, his eyes widened, and he closed the door to the garden with an abrupt crash, as if there were villagers lurking among her flowers, good people who might be scandalized by her dishabille.

"Lady Devonshire, you are not dressed."

In spite of his care with his accent, Aberdeen still rode his vowels when he was upset. His Scottish censure made her smile. She crossed to the sideboard where her favorite wine waited in its decanter. A sweet white wine from Burgundy, a little-known and little-drunk wine that she had discovered in the early days of her marriage and had loved ever since. Since the war had ended it was easier to obtain, but the tariffs were exorbitant. Everything worth having must be paid for.

She poured one glass of the Burgundy she loved, replacing the cut-glass decanter. She crossed the room to James Montgomery, where he still glowered beside the door to the garden. She took a sip of the wine before offering the cup to him. It was an old gesture that she had learned from Anthony, one she liked but had never used with any of her other lovers. It was an old gesture that meant, "Accept my hospitality. I mean you no harm. Today, we lay down our weapons and drink from the cup of peace."

James Montgomery stared at the goblet before he took it from her. He drank as she had, handing it back to her. She raised the glass and finished the wine, setting it empty on a nearby table. Only then did she speak.

"I wear what I please and I do as I please in my own house, Captain. If this does not meet with your approval, we can say good night."

James's skin darkened with ire as the blood rose in his face. For a moment, she thought that he truly would leave her, certain that he would stride past her, take to his horse, and disappear into the night, never to be seen again. She waited for this inevitability, almost expecting it. But as they stood together in silence, his color faded. His skin, tanned from the sun and wind, was no longer dark with anger. He breathed deeply, as if searching for calm, and she did the same.

"Forgive my bluntness, Captain, but I always begin as I mean to go on. I do not allow people to question my actions in my own house. If I came onboard your ship, you would not allow me to question you. Is that not correct?"

James frowned for a moment, not as if he were angry but as if he were thinking of what she said. "True enough. But this is not a ship. We are not at sea. I am a guest in your home. Rudeness is unacceptable."

"True," Angelique said. "Rudeness was not my intention, only that we be clear with one another. This home is my refuge. You are the first man I have ever allowed beyond its walls. But I do not accept the dictates of anyone here, neither man nor woman. I have made this one place on earth where I can be free of restraint, free to do as I please. I will not change that for anyone, not even for you."

"You were free of restraint at Prinny's card party," James said.

Angelique sighed and stepped back, sitting in a delicate chair by the tilt-top tea table in the center of the room. James hesitated a moment before he sat across from her on the settee. This was the strangest negotiation she had ever undertaken with a lover. She wondered if she was a fool to try it. Most men simply would not accept her or any woman as an equal. Why should she expect this man to be any different?

"You were quite free of restraint as well, Captain, if I recall."

James Montgomery smiled for the first time since she had entered the room, a rueful smile that seemed to take her in not just as a woman he wanted to bed, but as a person whose company he enjoyed. He leaned back, stretching his long legs before him as he had at the inn in the village. He surveyed her from head to toe, taking in the folds of her silk dressing gown and the soft fall of her hair.

"'Thou and I are too wise to woo peaceably.'"

Angelique laughed, the sound rising between them like a bond, a sinuous connection that was as beautiful as it was fragile. "You quote Shakespeare to me, Captain? Not poetry? One would think you came not to woo but to conquer."

"You are a woman to muddle a man's mind. But you are a woman who can't be conquered. If you were some lightskirt I met in a tavern, I wouldn't be here."

"I'm the woman you met on the deck of a ship you can't have."

James's smile broadened, as did his accent. "That remains to be seen. Your Mr. Smythe seemed interested in opening a dialogue with me."

"I'd like to do more than that with you," she said.

His blue eyes were hot with desire, but this time he did not reach for her. He stayed where he was, his long legs stretched out in front of him, and let her look her fill.

Angelique leaned forward just enough to catch the scent of his skin. He too had bathed, for the dust of the road was gone from him. His clothes were well worn but serviceable.

He would never be known as a Corinthian, dressed as he was in clothes that would serve as well on a ship as they would on a hunt. His cravat was tied with flair, but she knew for a certainty that he did not keep a man, that he had tied it himself. Something about that simplicity refreshed her, the same way the Shropshire air did, bringing her back to herself in a way no other man ever had.

She dismissed that thought at once before she could examine it too closely.

Angelique thought of his huge calloused hands, his talented mouth, and of what they could do to her in the dark. She sighed as heat rose in her belly, spreading deliciously through her limbs. She felt languid with desire as she looked at him, but she forced herself to think. He was a beautiful man, there was no disputing that. But they needed to finish negotiating a truce before she let him touch her again.

Though her mind agreed to this, her traitorous body did not. Her lust for him continued to rise. Even the gleam of his well-buffed boots made her catch her breath.

"Let us be quite frank with one another, Captain. If we enter into an arrangement tonight, we must both concede that our time in Shropshire is a stolen season, one that we must leave behind without regret when it is over. You will return to the sea, I, to my life among the London *ton*. We must not pretend, either to ourselves or to each other, that there is anything more between us."

James Montgomery met her eyes without flinching. "I concede nothing. I will not end this before it even begins."

They stared at each other for a long moment, and her usually comfortable sitting room seemed suddenly tight and warm.

"The end of all things is inherent in their beginning," she said. She fought her lust down even as she took in another breath of his clean skin.

"That may be, but this will not end tonight."

Angelique could spend no more time stating the obvious. Whether he admitted it openly or not, their liaison would end, as all such liaisons did. It was inevitable, the way of the world. Happy endings resided only in fairy stories.

She rose to her feet with a languid grace that belied the need she felt simmering beneath her skin.

James stood when she did, his eyes on hers as if he could read her desire in their depths. He stepped around her tea table, and when she moved to meet him, he extended his hand to her as if she were a man, as any tradesman from the North might, offering to seal their alliance.

She took the hand he offered, thinking that he meant to shake her hand as he might a man's in a matter of business. Instead, his great calloused fist closed over hers, engulfing her fingers in warmth. He drew her close, slowly, so that she had ample time to stop him or to pull away. When she did neither, he lifted her into his arms, one arm behind her knees, the other cradling her back.

"Where is your room?" he asked, striding for the door.

"On the second floor. The third door on the right."

Nineteen

THE INFURIATING WOMAN LAUGHED IN HIS ARMS AS
James carried her up not one but two flights of stairs.

He knew that he was being ridiculous, or at the very
least, ridiculously romantic, but after their long, almost
one-sided conversation over how their relationship
was going to develop, and for what short duration, he
found that he had to assert himself as a man or leave
his ballocks in a jar at her bedside.

Her laughter did little to help matters as he carried
her to her bedroom. The halls of her house were
dark. He had no free hand to lift a taper to light their
way. His years onboard ship had made him sure-
footed, so he did not lose a step as he carried her up
into the shadows.

Angelique Beauchamp was the most maddening
woman he had ever met. James could not remember
ever wanting a woman the way he wanted her. He
knew he was a fool. He had never gone so far from
the sea and his chosen future in pursuit of a woman.

He might have blamed his madness on having been
too long at sea fighting the French, but the war was

long over and his fortune made in the West Indies a year ago. He had no excuse for his behavior, none that held water. All he knew was that the sapphire blue of her eyes turned from cold to hot on a whim, and he wanted to watch that change as she lay beneath him.

There was something in her that he wanted to possess, something beyond her beauty or her arrogance. He had known beautiful, arrogant women before, but none had held him as this one did, not even in his youth. There was something in Angelique Beauchamp that would not give him peace. Perhaps if he stayed by her side for a week or more, perhaps if he buried himself here in the country with her for days on end, and buried himself in her body over and over again during the course of those days, he might be able to free himself.

James set her on her feet within the confines of her bedroom suite and closed the door behind them. As he faced her once more in the firelight, he understood why she drew him to her. There was more behind her eyes than arrogance. A fascinating woman lived in the depths of that blue, a woman he hungered to know better.

She was still laughing as he set her down. "You are a man of many talents, Captain. The pointless, romantic gesture, I see, is one of them."

He smiled ruefully, drawing the ribbon from his long auburn hair. "Enjoy your laughter, Angelique. You won't be laughing long."

She stopped laughing then and stepped toward him, placing one small hand over his heart. She did not lay her palm against his chest over his coat, but slid her hand beneath his waistcoat so that only the thin linen of his shirt was between them.

"Brave words, Captain. I hope you'll make good on them."

He drew her to him and kissed her, thinking to wipe the laughter and the mockery from her lips, to banish it from her eyes until she could think of nothing but him. Her lips yielded beneath his, opening to welcome his tongue as her body pressed against him as a sign of submission.

He knew that she had not truly surrendered. She did not give herself over to him, but simply sought her own pleasure, as if he were any other man she might have welcomed to her bed, as if he and all men were one and the same.

James moved his lips away from hers, trailing kisses over the curve of her throat where her head was thrown back in the beginnings of abandon. But he knew that Angelique never truly abandoned herself to him, or to anyone.

That was going to change. This night, there would be no one in that room with her but him.

❧

Angelique was surprised when James pulled away from her. She thought that after carrying her up the stairs in such a wonderfully masterful manner that he would toss her onto the bed and have her without even drawing off her dressing gown. She could feel the hunger in his touch, though his kiss was restrained and controlled.

He stepped away from her, his dark auburn hair falling across his face. The firelight caught the red in it, and it glinted like bronze.

He tossed his ribbon onto the table by the fire and stood with one hand on the mantel, bracing himself with his polished boot on the grate. A log of apple wood fell, and its scent filled the room as the fire rose.

"I will not fight you, Angelique," he said. "I do not want to conquer you. I do not want to be conquered."

She blinked at the defeat in his voice. At first, she was certain that he had simply changed the rules of the game, that he sought to manipulate her emotions, to draw her into some web of deceit in which he would hold the upper hand. She took a step forward so that she could see his face better in the firelight.

He did not look at her but stared down into the flames. She waited for a long moment, but he did not move or speak again. She watched him, looking for some sign of a lie in his countenance. She was an expert at reading people, both liars and knaves. If this man was lying, she could not see it.

"What do you want?" she asked.

He turned to face her then, and his eyes were cast in shadow. He stepped toward her but did not move to take her in his arms. She could not remember when, if ever, she had spent so much time speaking with a man who would be her lover. In her experience, men preferred carnality to discussion.

She was beginning to see that this man might be different from the rest.

"I want us to be honest with each other."

"I am honest with you," she said. "I have told you nothing but the truth."

"You fight me every step of the way. Even when

you're in my arms, you're fighting me. For one night, I ask that you lay your weapons down."

Angelique stood perfectly still and listened as another log fell into the grate, sending up a shower of sparks. She stared into his eyes. He did not flinch or turn away, but let her look her fill.

The deep blue of his eyes was clear. They made her think of the open sea, where lies cost men their lives. The sea was as honest as it was cruel, which was why she loved it. The sea forced every man to meet it on its own terms.

James Montgomery had thrived in that place, as her father once had done. There was a strength in him that came not from his time on the oceans of the world but from within. That inner strength was the thing that let him sail the seas and return home richer than when he left. This was a man who accepted what was. If he could accept the oceans of the world, if he could respect their power, perhaps he could also respect hers.

She closed the distance between them, a distance that seemed more of a chasm than a few feet of carpet. He did not take her into his arms even when she stood close to him.

She did not touch him either, but raised her head to meet his eyes. She forced herself to drop her mask of indifference, her mask of mockery, her pretense at superiority. This man was her equal, and she would treat him as such, until he proved her wrong.

"No weapons," she said.

"No lies," he answered.

"So be it."

It was he who kissed her, drawing her close very

carefully, as if she might break into shards between his hands. His touch on her was feather light, as if he did not want to startle her or break the solemnity of the moment. His lips caressed hers, making her hunger for more even as he pulled away.

James extended his hand to her, and she took it, her small palm disappearing into his. He did not kiss her fingertips or her palm, nor did he perform any other empty gallantry. He did not sweep her into his arms in an effort to whisk her away from herself, to overcome her reason and her sense with her own desires. He simply led her one step at a time toward her bed set in its alcove, its midnight blue coverlet already turned down, its white silken sheets embroidered with her crest in dark blue thread.

He ran his fingers over the bird and flames. "The phoenix rising."

No man had ever commented on her crest or on its meaning, not even Anthony. A lump rose in her throat and she swallowed hard to dislodge it.

"Yes," she said. "She rises from the ash, a new creation."

"The flames destroy her again and again," James countered. "What creates her as she rises from them?"

Angelique stood transfixed, for she had never thought of this notion as he put it to her, much less shared it with another living soul. She stood quiet, thinking that she might simply ignore the question. But she saw in his eyes that if she tried to make love to him without answering, he would leave her.

"She creates herself," Angelique said.

James smiled, and she felt as if the sun had risen in the room, driving out all shadows. He drew her close until her body was pressed against his, but he did not run his hands over her curves or feast on her flesh. He laid his lips on her hair, taking in the scent of her orchid perfume, which enclosed them both like a cloak, shutting out the rest of the world.

"No woman who has not suffered and been reborn could ever be as strong or as beautiful as you are."

Angelique felt tears rise in her eyes unbidden, and she blinked them away. She found that she had lost her voice. She, who was never without a witty remark or the best defensive jab, stood silent in the arms of this man who was almost a stranger.

He leaned down and kissed her gently, his lips as soft as a blessing. She leaned into his strength, letting it surround her as his arms did, her weight resting against him. She would work at letting her defenses drop. She had promised that she would, and she always kept her word.

Angelique drew off her dressing gown, letting the silk fall to the floor at her feet in a pool of sapphire blue. James did not look at Anthony's gift but only at her body revealed beneath the thin silk of her negligee. He raised one hand and cupped her breast in his palm, hefting the weight of it, running his thumb over the mound and nipple in a soft caress.

A moan rose in her throat, and she moved toward him, but he held her back so that he could continue to look at her body. James raised his hand to cup her other breast, caressing it in the same way he had the first, before bringing his eyes to hers. "You are beautiful," he said. "I want you under me while you're wearing this gown."

Angelique lay down on the bed as if she always allowed men to command her. But he had not issued an order as Anthony might once have done; he had simply stated a desire.

She pushed Anthony from her mind, for part of the honesty of that night included having no ghosts of other lovers standing between them.

James stripped away his coat and waistcoat, his shirt, breeches, and boots until he stood naked before her. His body was well muscled from his years at sea. He was not one to sit idly by while the crew worked, but worked the ship himself. His limbs were tan from the sun and wind, and his blue eyes seemed even bluer as he lay down and smiled at her. She raised her hand to touch his cheek. His stubble prodded her fingertips and scratched the softness of her palm.

"I should have shaved before I came," he said.

"You can shave after you come, if you wish," she said, grinning at him, a wicked gleam in her eye.

This time he laughed with her, rolling until he was on top of her, drawing her nightgown up to her waist. His hands explored her legs as he drew the silk along her flesh. The warmth of his touch made her shiver, and when his fingers disappeared between her thighs, she shuddered with the first hint of promised bliss.

He toyed with her for a moment, testing her warmth and wetness, but he did not linger there. He raised himself over her, watching as her breasts rose with her breath. He pressed himself between the tight contours of her thighs and entered her in one long thrust. Her whole body shook with his motion, and she said his name.

James began to move inside her, but he did not take his eyes from her breasts as he moved. They swayed with his thrusts and he drank in the sight of them. She watched his desire for her rise, and her own desire grew with it. His body moved in hers and over hers, driving her closer and closer to the edge of reason. She lifted her legs to give him better access, but he pushed them down again until she was splayed beneath him, a willing prisoner.

He pressed himself deep into her, picking up speed as he moved. She cried out as her pleasure built, but when she tried to touch him, he took her hands in his and raised them over her head.

James thrust into her, varying his rhythm so that she almost could not catch her breath. He kept his eyes on hers, his naked longing laid out before her. He held nothing back, and she found that she could not. She came in a spiral of ecstasy with her eyes on his, his name drawn from her lips a second time, her body quaking beneath him. He joined her then, emptying his body into hers, speaking her name as if it were a prayer.

When they both were sated, he lay on top of her like a great boulder, or a tree that had been felled. Angelique did not move except to wrap her arms around him so that he would not leave her. He raised his head to look into her eyes.

"That was the best sex of my life," he said.

She smiled. "So far."

For once, he did not banter with her. For once, he did not smile back.

"It's better with no lies between us," he said.

She did not answer but drew him close. He seemed to understand her unspoken request, for all that night, he did not pull away. They lay together, spooned between her silk sheets, the music of their breathing lulling them both to sleep.

Twenty

ANGELIQUE WOKE IN THE MORNING TO ANOTHER WORLD. For the first time in over a year, her lover lay beside her, still sleeping. James Montgomery had spent the night in her bed, and now she wondered if he would choose to stay a little longer. She surprised herself when she discovered that she did not wish to be rid of him.

She wanted him to linger with her, to eat with her in the sunny breakfast room downstairs, to sip coffee across the table from her as Anthony Carrington once had done at her house in town. She wondered at herself, that she favored this man so much. There was something bewitching about him, something that drew her into the web of his honesty and guilelessness. He was different from any man she had met. For all his seeming openness, she began to think that it would take her longer to know him, if she ever truly did.

She did not know many people well, nor did many people know her. Arabella Hawthorne, run off to Derbyshire with her old flame, Pembroke. Lisette, her maid. There the list ended. She had once thought that

Anthony Carrington knew her, but he had defected to his young wife's side, never to return. That was for the best, for Angelique had lived too long and loved her own life too much to take another woman's leavings.

So that morning she was alone in the country with this Scottish captain, a virtual stranger. She stared at him, watching him breathe deeply in the confines of her bed, the silk coverlet gathered loose at his hips, revealing the contours of his muscled chest with its light dusting of reddish hair. The tone of his breathing and the sight of his face relaxed in sleep told her nothing of who he truly was. Only that he was beautiful, and for the moment, he was hers.

He seemed to feel her watching him for he woke, his blue eyes opening beneath his gold-tipped lashes. He did not startle or seem to wonder where he was or with whom. He simply gave her a warm, inviting smile as he reached for her.

"Good morning, my lady." James brought her close but did not roll her beneath him. Instead, he buried his face in the softness of her hair, breathing in the perfume of orchids.

Angelique took in the scent of him, a bit of salt and warm flannel, almost like the scent of the sea. He carried the sea with him even this far inland. Angelique missed the ocean, so she indulged herself, reveling in the fragrance of his skin, forgetting herself completely.

He nudged her, and she returned to herself, to where she was and with whom. She felt her heart lighten for the first time since Anthony had left her. She and James barely knew each other, but she liked him. She would enjoy this stolen season for as long as it lasted.

"Good morning, Captain," she said, stretching her naked body against his. He did not accept her invitation, though his blue eyes heated with longing. Instead, he raised his lips to hers and kissed her gently, sweetly, as if they had all the time in the world, as if he never planned to leave.

"So formal, Countess," he said. "You might call me James."

She smiled, savoring the lingering taste of his lips on hers and the warmth of his body so close beneath her sheets. "I might," she said.

Angelique knew that she was in danger of staying in bed with him all morning, but something nagged at the edges of her mind, some reason why she could not abandon herself to pleasure.

The girl. Sara. Her husband's daughter was being brought up to the house today. And she still was not sure how she would make her welcome, how she would begin to bridge the gap between them.

Angelique felt a chill run along her spine, though she was tucked in bed with a large and good-looking man. James seemed to sense her sudden distraction, for he pulled away from her and sat up. "Your daughter is coming."

"My husband's daughter," Angelique corrected him automatically.

"You just remembered her."

Angelique sighed and sat up with him, drawing the sheet up to cover her nakedness. "You have an excellent memory."

"I saw the girl just last night. I pity her."

She could not allow him behind her wall on this subject. Her longing for a child was too personal, her grief for her dead husband still a living wound, one she never showed another, not even Arabella. She could not afford to let this man discover this weakness, not if she meant to see him again. And she wanted to see him again.

She used her most casual tone, the one she used in drawing rooms among women who hated her. "Orphans are often pitiful. But I will care for her. She has no need of your pity."

"Your High and Mighty Highness is back on her high horse, I see," James said.

Angelique's eyes flashed as she looked at him, but when she saw no mockery in his face, her shoulders relaxed.

"I fall back on my old ways when I feel threatened," she said, invoking their agreement to be honest with one another.

James did not use her honesty against her, as he said he would not. He nodded. "Don't we all? I tend to reach for my sword before using my tongue."

Angelique laughed at that and slid against him, running her hand down his chest. "You use both to good effect, Captain."

"I meant in disputes with other men," James said, but now he was laughing. He caught her hand in his. "Call me James."

"James it is then."

She kissed him fleetingly. She thought he might draw her down with him and pull her beneath him, but when she moved away, he did neither.

Angelique rose, tossing the covers aside. She drew her dressing gown up from the floor and put it on, crossing the room to ring for Lisette.

James did not follow her but watched her as she walked, his eyes caressing her body, though his voice stayed calm and dispassionate. "Would you like me to stay and greet the girl with you?"

"There is no need," Angelique said.

Lisette opened the door from her dressing room and stepped in. The fire had been built up while they slept, but Lisette, who was thin and easily chilled, added another log before coming to her mistress.

"Some warm water, Lisette," Angelique said. "And the blue day gown and matching shawl."

"Yes, madame."

Lisette eyed James for a moment, admiring his torso where it emerged from the bedclothes. James did not spare her a glance but kept his eyes on Angelique.

"You can't face her alone," he said, as if they had never been interrupted. "You need someone with you."

Angelique opened her mouth to lie, catching herself even as she began to dismiss him. She saw in his eyes that he had already guessed something of her hidden pain, though he was too polite to ask of it. He had offered her trust, in return for her own. She had trusted only two men in her life, both to her peril. But she had given her word. They were in their stolen season. She owed him honesty still.

"I do not wish to face her alone," Angelique said, laying her usual defenses down. "Please stay."

James smiled but did not gloat over his victory. He nodded as if he had asked an easy thing, as if she had granted some small request and not laid herself open to pain.

He rose from the bed to draw on his breeches, which

had been laid by on a chair. He dressed quickly, and
Lisette turned her back at once, but when Angelique
saw her maid smile, she knew that the Frenchwoman
had taken a peek at her lover. Angelique thought to
reprimand her but winked at her instead, pushing aside
her fear of the girl she was taking into her life, her fear
that she might fail her.

She took pleasure instead in James, and in the fact
that he was with her. He was a well-wrought man,
and for the moment, he was hers. Let Lisette enjoy a
glance if she was fortunate enough to catch one.

Angelique dressed while James looked on. She
had never done such a thing before, and it seemed
to deepen the air of intimacy between them. Lisette
did not speak at all that morning, her usual tirade in
French silenced by James Montgomery's presence.
James sat sprawled in her armchair beside the fireplace
in his breeches and shirt, his long legs stretched before
him, one Hessian boot crossed over the other.

Angelique caught sight of him in her mirror as
Lisette dressed her hair, and she felt her desire for
him rise again as if they had not just spent the night
together between the soft sheets of her bed. With an
effort at discipline, she schooled her face to blankness.

Lisette seemed to notice nothing, but James caught
Angelique's eye in the looking glass and smiled as if
he knew exactly what she was thinking. Angelique
blushed like the schoolgirl she had never been and
swallowed the desire to laugh. Giggling was simply out
of the question, no matter how giddy she felt.

Lisette left them with a curtsy and one sly glance
toward James Montgomery. After drawing on his

waistcoat and coat, tying his cravat with an easy, thoughtless style, he rose and took Angelique's hand in his. She felt as clean as if she were seventeen again, as if they were childhood sweethearts and he was leading her out to walk in the garden beneath flowering trees and not down to her own breakfast room after a night of lovemaking.

Angelique followed him docilely into the corridor, thinking how fine he looked in his brown coat and breeches. His eyes gleamed as he smiled down at her. "Forgive me, my lady, but I do not know the way."

She did not relinquish his hand but drew him toward the staircase. They walked hand in hand to the breakfast room on the first floor. Angelique did not let go of him until they were seated together, the silver coffee service between them, a pot of tea at her elbow as well as brioche and jam.

She had never felt so easy with a lover in her life. All her days with Geoffrey were painful, as she had tried desperately to be what he wanted and had failed. All her nights with Anthony had been filled with fire but also with pain, for she had always known that though he was fascinated by her, he did not love her.

But here, with this stranger, she felt finally as if she had found an equal, perhaps even a friend. She had never had a man for a friend before. It was almost disconcerting.

They ate in companionable silence and had almost finished their meal when her butler, Jerrod, stepped into the breakfast room.

"My lady, the young lady from the village is come to see you."

Twenty-one

ANGELIQUE SWALLOWED HARD, HER NERVES SUDDENLY fluttering like birds. "Thank you, Jerrod. Please bring her in."

Looking only slightly scandalized, the older man moved to obey. If her Greek butler Anton had an opposite, it was this man. Staid and set in his ways, Jerrod was a holdover from her husband's days as Earl of Devonshire.

In spite of his very strict ideas about a lady's place in the world, the elderly butler had been won over by Angelique's charm early in her disastrous marriage to his lord, and his affections had been assured by the assiduous care she had taken of the house. Aeronwynn's Gate had not looked so well in a hundred years, and as he was close friends with her estate steward, Billings, Jerrod knew exactly how much money Angelique had lavished on the place to reclaim it from ruin. So Jerrod said not a word of censure, nor did he even lift an eyebrow as he left to escort his lord's bastard daughter into his lady's presence.

Angelique stood and smoothed her gown. James

caught her hand and squeezed it. "She will love it here," he said. "She will come to love you."

For once in her life, she did not try to hide her old losses. She knew their shadow must be visible in her face, along with her hope. "I hope so," she answered.

Sara Burr entered the room behind the butler, her blue eyes wide with fright. Angelique saw pride in the tilt of the girl's chin, but she also saw the pale, drawn look around her eyes. The child had not slept last night. Angelique remembered her own youth, how she had been left alone with her ailing mother, a sailing ship, and her beauty her only dowry when she was seventeen. Angelique had been forced to become a woman, and quickly. She would see to it that this girl got to be a child for a little while longer.

Angelique pushed aside her own memories and crossed the room to the girl, extending her hand. "Welcome, Sara. Come and have some breakfast."

Sara did not take the offered hand. She curtsied prettily but did not meet Angelique's eyes.

"I ate at the inn, my lady. I thank you."

The girl stared around the well-appointed room as if it were a den of lions and she expected to be torn apart. Angelique withdrew the hand she held out and gestured to a chair.

"Well, if you're not hungry, please join us for a cup of tea. Or would you prefer a cup of chocolate?"

Sara's blue eyes flitted about the room like a bird that did not mean to roost, finally coming to settle on Angelique's face. "Yes, my lady. I mean, no, my lady. I have never had chocolate."

Angelique smiled in an effort to bolster the child's

spirits as well as her own. "Today you shall try it then. We will all have a cup."

Jerrod nodded to one of the footmen, who stepped out to take the order to the kitchen. A second footman stepped forward and drew out a chair. Angelique sat and finally, Sara followed suit, her small bag still clutched in her hands.

"Jerrod will take that, Sara. Please see that Miss Burr is put in the blue room."

"Yes, my lady."

Jerrod took the child's case in hand. She clearly did not want to relinquish it, but when the tall older man loomed over her like a specter in a fairy story, her grip loosened and Jerrod whisked the bag away.

The footman returned with a silver pot of chocolate and tiny demitasse cups. James looked bemused but accepted his cup without question. Angelique filled his cup first, adding a touch of milk to it, before filling her own and Sara's.

Angelique nodded to William, and he withdrew. It was not usual for her to sit and eat her breakfast unattended, but she wanted time alone with the girl she had taken into her home.

Sara stared at the thick chocolate in the bottom of her tiny cup. She watched Angelique as she stirred the chocolate and the milk together, then lifted her own and took a sip. Sara imitated her every movement, down to the graceful tilt of her wrist.

Angelique felt a strange moment of pride. This girl was a quick learner. She would be a credit to her in a few years' time. Perhaps, if the girl wanted it, she might even arrange for Sara to have a season in London. The *ton* might not accept her, but Angelique's business acquaintances would.

By now the whole city must have heard where she had gone and why. Her people were discreet, but the London elite was not. She knew Victor alone would work assiduously to spread the rumor that she had taken in her husband's bastard daughter. The story was simply too delicious for the gossipmongers to ignore.

"Your room has a lovely view of the park," Angelique said. "I am sorry that I am not better prepared for your arrival. When we return to London, I will find a suitable governess to teach you, but until then, I am afraid you will be on your own a good deal here."

"I am happy to go back to the inn, my lady. I do not want to cause any trouble." Sara's voice was soft but firm. Angelique was not certain if it was her fancy, but she thought she heard her own tones echoed in the girl's voice. She smiled at the strength that lay beneath Sara's supposed diffidence. Angelique wondered how one encouraged a girl to obey without curbing that strength in the process.

"Your home is here now, Sara. It should have been here since your birth. You must forgive me. I only learned of your existence last week, or I would have come sooner."

"Your ladyship need not trouble yourself over me. I am happy where I am." Sara's chin rose again, and Angelique heard the distinct note of stubbornness in the her voice. Stubbornness was an asset every woman needed.

"I am grateful you are here, Sara. It is a lonely old house and it needs young laughter in it. I spend as much time here as I can. I hope we can come to know each other better."

For the first time, the girl's eyes began to show a hint of hope. Angelique watched Sara battle with herself, uncertainty beginning to war with her desire to return to the inn.

She wanted to reach out and take the girl's hand, but she knew that Sara would shy away. Angelique held herself very still the way she would with a horse that had not yet been broken to harness.

"I thank you, my lady, but I do not belong here." Sara rose to her feet as she said that, her chocolate left with only one sip taken from it.

Angelique stood also, facing the girl across the length of the breakfast table. She forced herself to keep her voice even and calm. She could not remember the last time one of her dependents had challenged her.

"Sara, you are my charge now and my responsibility. You will live with me, and I will care for you."

The girl did not flinch but squared her thin shoulders. "I'm old enough to take care of myself."

Angelique felt her temper rise. It slipped from her grasp before she could catch it and rein it in. "I will not leave you to make your way in the world alone. Not as long as I draw breath."

Sara's temper matched hers, and her voice rose with it. Though the girl did not shout, she spoke very firmly, her voice never wavering. "Respecting Your Worship, I do not want to be here."

James laughed out loud at that. Angelique turned on him and glared.

"She has you dead to rights, Angelique."

He stood then and offered the girl his hands. "Her Ladyship hasn't seen fit to introduce us, but I'm James Montgomery, formerly of the Royal Navy, at your service, ma'am."

Sara did not know whether to accept his hand or curtsy to him. When she hesitated, he bowed and smiled.

"It's an odd world you're coming into, Miss Burr. But I can vouch for our lady here. She'll do you no harm and a lot of good. It seems to me you both need each other. You're both alone in the world."

Angelique felt tears rise in her throat, and she swallowed hard. Sara was blinking hard too.

"I have a sister about your age," he said. "Her name is Sarah, too. Perhaps one day, you will meet her."

Sara spoke then, her voice quiet. "I would like that. Your sister, does she still play with dolls?"

"She sleeps with one. But only in secret."

Sara smiled at him. Angelique knew that she could not rely on James Montgomery to intervene for her. She and the girl must come to an understanding of one another, and the sooner, the better. But she made sure her tone was gentle when she spoke again.

"Sara, there are many things in life we do not want, but which we must face. I did not want to lose my parents, but they died. You did not want to lose yours, but here we are."

"I never had a father," Sara said, her eyes shining with unshed tears. Angelique did not back down at the sight of them.

"Your father is best not spoken of. He was a worthless wastrel and a ne'er-do-well. But your mother was a good woman."

Sara's tears overflowed then, and Angelique ignored them. She remembered herself at that age and the humiliation she would have felt to weep in front of strangers. Angelique held herself back and stayed where she was.

"My mother was the best woman who ever lived," Sara said.

Angelique felt her own throat thicken. She swallowed hard to clear it. "Well. Then we will educate you for her sake. She would want what is best for you. And I can give you the best."

"I want my mother back."

The girl's voice was so soft that Angelique almost did not hear it break. Sara's thin shoulders rounded beneath the worsted gown she wore. A strand of hair fell from her braids and into her eyes. Angelique tried to hold herself very still, but she could not leave the child to cry alone. She stepped around the table and took the girl into her arms.

Sara flinched as if Angelique had struck her, her body rigid in a stranger's embrace. But perhaps the embrace of a strange woman was better than none, for the girl relaxed in her arms. The girl's moment of trust was like a dagger in her heart, and her longing for her own daughter rose in her, an old ghost that would never be completely vanquished.

Angelique stroked the errant lock of hair back from Sara's eyes. "If I could give her back to you, I would. But that is beyond my power."

She stepped away from the girl, offering her the handkerchief from her sleeve, the soft linen square beautifully edged with Lisette's lace. Sara wiped her nose with the back of her hand, both her tears and her anger fading. "Oh, no, my lady. That is too fine. I cannot use that."

"Indeed you can, and indeed you will. In my household, the finer things will be at your disposal. You will live according to your father's birth, and you will learn to be a better person than he was."

Sara blew her nose loudly into the cloth, wiping her eyes and tucking it away in her own sleeve with almost the same gesture Angelique had used to draw it out. "I am a better person than my father already," Sara said.

"You are indeed," Angelique said. "We will be two orphans together. Perhaps we can make the best of it."

Angelique smiled and offered the girl her hand. This time, Sara took it.

"We will see you at dinner. Please go with Mrs. Bellows, and she will help you get settled in your room. Come down to the drawing room at five sharp. Dinner will be at five thirty. We keep country hours at Aeronwynn's Gate."

"I will join you for dinner?" Sara asked, her voice almost a squeak.

"Of course. You are a lady and this is your home. You will take your meals with us."

Sara's face lit up, and Angelique felt her heart clench.

Sara turned and bolted into the hallway without a backward glance, gone before Angelique could call her housekeeper. The girl's coltish beauty, which had not yet fully flowered, gave Angelique pause. She wondered what might have happened to the girl, left in a public inn.

"You've rescued her then," James Montgomery said. "Does that good deed leave any time in this day for yourself?"

Twenty-two

"THAT WENT WELL," JAMES SAID.

He watched as Angelique tried to collect herself, as she struggled to put together the pieces of her broken composure. The girl had unsettled her.

"I hope so. I am a bit out of my depth with children."

"She is not a child anymore," James said. "I would advise you not to call her that when she's in the room. I've made that mistake with my own sisters a time or two. It didn't end well."

"I should have introduced you sooner. I'm sorry about that."

"It's awkward. There's no precedence for introducing your husband's bastard to your current lover."

She laughed then, as he had intended, and her face lightened a little. James stepped toward her and took her hand, drawing her close. He took in the scent of her hair, the soft smell of orchids in the fall of dark curls. His body hardened at her nearness, and he wished he could drag her back upstairs. No doubt, like at a fine hotel, the bed they'd left behind had been made already.

All the more reason to muss it again.

She was talking, so he tried to listen.

"Thank you for hanging back for so long while I spoke with Sara," she said. "You hold your tongue when I need you to. Not one man in six hundred would do that."

"Not one man in six hundred could, my lady. But I have five sisters, all of whom know their own minds. I know to hold my tongue when a woman has the bit between her teeth."

He moved even closer so that he could feel the rise of her rounded breasts against his coat front. Still, she talked on.

"So I have your sisters to thank for those rare occasions when your good manners arise," Angelique said.

"My mother is the one to thank. You may do so when we see her."

"I don't know when that will be."

"Neither do I. But time will tell."

She had noticed his body finally, and she had started to lose her train of thought. Angelique leaned back so that she could look up into his eyes. Her blue gaze was as fathomless as any sea, as full of mystery. It could take a man all his life to unravel her. But James didn't have that long.

He leaned down, his lips hot over hers. Her mouth was soft beneath his light kiss. He caressed her gently, as with a feather, teasing her, taunting her with his desire, as he watched hers rise. Angelique opened her eyes when he pulled away, and he saw that she had truly lost her train of thought.

"Is there someplace we can go, somewhere without

a hundred servants and hangers-on, where we can be alone?"

He whispered into the hair at the nape of her neck as his lips traveled up behind her ear. He caught her earlobe between his teeth and bit down gently. He felt her body give way as she leaned against him. Still, her voice was only slightly breathless when she answered him.

"It occurs to me, Captain, that you might like to see the summerhouse."

He matched her formal tone, unable to keep the laughter from his voice as he ran his tongue over the line of her jaw. "Well, then, if you would show it to me, my lady, I would not mind escorting you there."

"How kind of you."

"I am a humanitarian."

He kissed her then, and he stopped toying with her. He dove into her lips as into a pool of cool, clear water, awash in sensation as he touched her. His hands roamed down from her waist to cup her buttocks in his palms. He kneaded them, drawing her body against his to press his erection against her softness. If he did not have her again, and soon, he would not be able to answer for himself.

James kept his voice even, but he heard that he had lost his breath when he raised his head, drawing away from the siren song of her lips to speak again.

"And the gardens, too, Angelique? I have great hope of seeing your fields of green and gold."

"My gardens are indeed in bloom this time of year. I will show you the flowers that grow there."

He pressed his lips to her throat, unable to trust

himself to kiss her again. One of his hands came to her breast, almost against his will. He cupped the round fullness of it in his palm, weighing it, smoothing one calloused thumb over it. Though encased in silk and lace, her nipple rose against his palm, and he slid his hand over to caress the other.

"Perhaps I will pick one of those flowers and bring it home," James said.

She was breathless, but she still had her wits about her. She gave as good as she got.

"Ah, but if you pick a blossom, it dies. Better to enjoy its scent, then leave it to grow where you found it."

She pressed herself against him finally, taking on a more active role. She seemed to relinquish the need to retain her self-control and rubbed her body against his, as if his erection was her plaything, something that would bring her pleasure with or without his consent.

He felt her move, and he froze, the pleasure overwhelming him so that he forgot everything else. It took him a moment to find his voice. When he did, it was hoarse with longing. If he didn't take her under him soon, he was going to die.

James did not drop her gaze. "I find I desire to take up gardening myself, my lady. Perhaps you will allow me to take a flower from your garden as a token, so that I will have that beauty with me wherever I go."

"Let us not be hasty, Captain. You have not seen the garden yet. You may not find it to your liking."

"Trust me, Angelique. Everything about you is to my liking."

He kissed her again, but this time she pushed him

away. "Come with me then," she said. "We can take a walk outside. My sitting room leads out into this mythic garden you are so fascinated by."

He let her pull away from him, adjusting his coat to cover his throbbing loins. "Lead on."

Angelique turned to the door, but before she made it out of the breakfast room, he put his hand on her well-rounded derriere, stealing one last caress before they walked into the hallway.

Twenty-three

ONCE THEY LEFT THE HOUSE, HE DID NOT DRAG HER TO the ground behind the first rosebush as she almost hoped he might. Instead, he kept his wicked, calloused hands to himself, only offering his arm as they strolled through her gardens. She wanted him with a fierceness she had never experienced before. She was in uncharted territory, and she liked it.

Angelique and James took the overgrown path that led down by the river. The flow was slow and stately there, a wide expanse beyond which were myrtle and hawthorn and oak, more of Geoffrey's lands that now were hers.

Willows grew in clumps down by the river's edge. The summerhouse was not nestled among them but sat on a bluff edged in Queen Anne's lace and buttercups. Wild roses grew there, bluebells and irises, flowers that added blue and deep red to the riverbank.

Holding James's arm, Angelique came to her favorite point of her property, the willow gate that enclosed the summerhouse. Faded with age, its paint worn away, the gate was entwined with rose vines and clementine. Angelique placed her hand on the gate and turned to look up at James before pushing it open.

"Aeronwynn's Gate takes its name from this place," she said. "In Welsh, *aeronwynn* means 'blessed river of white.'" She opened the gate, and he held it for her. As they stepped through the fence that enclosed the summerhouse, she felt as if they had stepped into another world. The Queen Anne's lace was blooming all the way to the Severn, surrounding the tiny house in a blanket of white.

She felt nothing of her daughter's presence that day. It was just a beautiful spot that one day soon would lose its flowers as time moved on, and the river with it.

"I can see how it earned its name," James said, his arm slipping around her waist. His touch was a welcome distraction from her sorrowful thoughts. "There was a Welshman on my last command named Davies," he said. "He was a fierce fighter as well as a poet."

Angelique smiled at him. "The Welsh are still renowned here for their fearlessness."

"And their madness, like as not."

"Madness can be a good thing," she answered.

"Many a Scot would agree with you."

A faint echo of Aberdeen came into his voice, sending a shiver down her spine. Angelique leaned closer to him, taking in the scent of his skin: leather and cedar. He held her close as they looked over the field of grass and flowers to the river below.

A strange feeling of intimacy seemed to rise between them, nurtured by the sunshine and the warm wind. She found herself longing to speak of her dead: her daughter, her mother. In an attempt to stop herself, she asked about his family. "You spoke of your sisters. Does your mother still live?"

"Yes," James said. "And my father. Sir James Montgomery, the king of Aberdeen."

"So your father is a lord," she said.

"A minor baronet only," James answered. "The circles you dance in London would be far too rich for his blood, as they are for mine."

"Sometimes I think they are too rich for my own." In spite of her resolution to hold her tongue, she found herself speaking of her family. "My mother was a lady from Marseilles. She ran off with my father and went to sea with him. The war drove them here, and they backed the British and their allies."

"Why?"

"My father's trade depended on the British need for cotton. After his death, and the death of my husband, I took up the cotton trade again."

"And it has treated you well."

She took in the way the sunlight hit his auburn hair, drawing out the gold hidden in it. His blue eyes looked not at her but across the river, as if to see what lay beyond the trees ahead and beyond those hills to the horizon. Even on land, his gaze was long-sighted. He looked beyond where he was to where he might be going. She pushed aside her misgivings and raised his hand to her lips.

That brought his attention back to her. His eyes heated with the same fire she had seen in the breakfast room half an hour before.

But this time, James did not move to touch her. He waited instead, to see what she might do next. He was a man used to command, but so sure of his own power that he did not feel the need to encroach upon hers. It was a heady combination.

"My daughter is buried there," she said, raising one hand toward the spot several feet beyond the wooden fence.

Her stark words rose between them, a wall she feared would stand. But James did not bolt, as she had thought he might. She saw no judgment in his face, only sorrow. He relaxed beneath her hands, drawing her even closer. His voice was soft as his arms came around her, not to offer sex, but comfort. A strength she could lean on.

"I did not know you had a daughter. I am sorry for your loss."

Angelique felt tears rising, but they came too fast for her to blink them away. Instead, she pressed her cheek against his shoulder, letting the wool of his coat absorb her sorrow.

"She was Geoffrey's. I lost her a week after he died."

"I am sorry," he said again. "No words are adequate. Those are the only words I know."

She leaned back, wiping her tears away with her fingertips. "They are the right ones."

He kissed her then, gently, without a hint of lust hidden in it. When their lips parted, she leaned against him once more, and as she matched her breathing to his, she felt his hand in her hair.

"Why is your ship called the *Diane*?" he asked.

Angelique clung to his question as to a life raft. She forced her mind away from her sorrow and focused on him.

"It was named for my mother."

"It is beautiful."

"Not one man in a thousand is worthy of her."

"The same could be said of her mistress."

James's embrace changed then, as he pressed the length of his hard body against her, inexorably, like a tide. He was offering the only comfort he knew, and she took it.

Her daughter was long dead, but she was alive. It was summer, and the sun was high above her head, shining down on her like a blessing. She would savor this day and the man who stood with her.

Her senses filled at once with the scent and taste of him. His coat of brown wool felt rough beneath her hands, for he only wore superfine to dinner and in town. On the land as on the sea, James dressed as a working man might, if that man had taken prize money in the West Indies. There was something delicious about the feel of rough wool beneath her fingertips. She ran her hands over his chest, past his jacket, across his linen shirt.

He groaned at her touch, opening his mouth over hers, changing the angle of his head to give him better access to her as if he might devour her in one bite. She shivered with the strength of his need, feeling her own desire rise to match it.

She drew back from him but could not catch her breath as she stood enthralled by the hot light of his eyes. "Come inside," she said. "There is a young girl in my house, and I am trying to be discreet."

James laughed, sweeping his hair back where it had come loose from its ribbon. Angelique could not resist slipping her fingers into his straight auburn hair, taking the brown velvet ribbon between her fingers and drawing it out. His hair fell around them both like a curtain as he leaned down to kiss her again. This time his lips did not linger, but she felt his smile against her own before she even opened her eyes.

"Discretion is wise," James said, all traces of his Scottish heritage banished from his voice, his tone dripping with false propriety. "I am never wise."

He drew her closer to him, his fingers unbuttoning her spencer so that he had access to her thin silk gown. His questing fingers dove past the lace fichu she wore in an effort to cover her breasts above the low-cut bodice. The lace fluttered to the ground at their feet, lying across the lacelike flowers in a second veil of white.

"James, the house," she murmured, her eyes closed, lost in the way his hands felt on her body as he drew her bodice down.

"I want to see you naked in the sunlight," he answered. "No one will see. And if they do, no doubt they have seen something like it before."

She laughed and drew back from him, her hands catching her gown before it could slip down to her waist. His hands caressed her hair, and her long dark curls fell from the combs that held them.

She knew not to wear diamonds when she was with him in case they might be lost, the way she seemed to lose her mind every time he touched her. With her enameled combs in one hand and her gown held closed in the other, she backed into the summerhouse, her smile teasing him.

He did not move at once, but his eyes watched every move she made. He followed her slowly, like a stalking cat, a man who knew what he wanted and how to get it.

The interior of the house was shaded, filled with a watery green light. Ivy grew along the open windows, almost blocking out the sun and the view of the river completely. The effect was somewhat like a fairy bower, and as she stepped inside, Angelique felt as if her cares had fallen away.

He stood in the doorway, casting a long shadow into the soft light of the room. He leaned one shoulder against the door frame, watching as she let her gown fall.

His blue eyes were hot on her skin as she untied the fastenings of her skirt and petticoats, letting them settle to the floor in a foam of silk and lace. She carefully stepped out of them and left them where they lay. She unlaced her stays with a few deft motions, drawing her shift over her head. She slipped off her ankle boots and stood naked except for her hose and garters.

He made no move to enter the house. James watched as she set her foot on the chaise that was the small room's only furniture.

Dust rose from the cushions but she ignored it, unrolling the silk of her stocking down until she cast it and its garter onto the foam of her skirts. She bent to draw off the second garter and stocking, but suddenly he was there, kneeling beside her, one hand caressing her instep, the other, the smooth skin of her inner thigh.

Angelique felt her core begin to heat, and she almost shook with longing. James raised his eyes to hers, his hand stroking the soft nubbin of flesh between her thighs. He caressed her, all the while watching her face as he drew the second stocking down. He was not as careful or as neat as she had been, but tossed it over his shoulder in the general direction of the rest of her clothes.

His eyes ran over her breasts as the peaks tightened in the warm, perfumed air. All the while, his hand kept up its work between her thighs. When she tried to lower her leg and draw him with her onto the chaise, James only smiled at her and held her where she was.

"You started this," he said. "And now I'll finish it."

His fingers caressed her hard one last time and she felt the spark of her desire catch fire, burning her in a firestorm of pleasure. She shook with the tremors his fingers had begun in her. She would have fallen had he not caught her in his other arm and pulled her against him.

The rough wool of his jacket and the smooth buckskin of his breeches were intoxicating against her naked body. She shuddered with her release, the feel of him against her, completely clothed, his hand still on her flesh. He sent her over the edge of pleasure again until she was quaking against him a second time, so sated that she barely remembered her own name.

James ran his hands over her naked body, caressing her breasts as he laid her down on the chaise. He did not take off his own clothes but pressed her into the softness of the feather cushions. Dust rose to cover them both, but neither noticed or cared.

He kissed her deeply, drawing her tongue into his mouth to tangle with his own as his large, calloused hands slid from her breasts to her hips, raising them as he finished unfastening his breeches.

He moved inside her in one long thrust, and she cried out beneath him as she clutched at his back. James kissed her throat and her breasts before drawing her hips up to take the onslaught of his rhythm. She moaned beneath him as he thrust relentlessly into her body, driving her closer to overwhelming pleasure until she fell over that edge again.

She shook beneath him, crying out his name as he came inside her. He answered, murmuring her name into the softness of her hair, and for a moment Angelique was so overcome that she could not tell if the dampness on her face was tears or simply perspiration.

James lay on top of her, still clothed, his breath warm in her hair. He drew away from her slowly, as if reluctant to leave her body. He adjusted himself, then lay down with her again, bringing her close against him until she lay across his chest. Neither of them spoke.

Angelique's head was nestled on his shoulder. She stretched in languorous pleasure, the aftershocks of her ecstasy still moving through her. If she had ever been this content in her life before, she could not remember it.

The silence stretched between them, and neither seemed to feel the need to break it. All Angelique could hear was the sound of birdsong and the music of the river as it flowed past them, beyond the walls of their haven.

"My lady?"

Jerrod called for her from outside the open door of the house. It seemed their brief idyll was over.

Twenty-four

"FORGIVE THE INTRUSION, MY LADY. BUT THERE IS news from London. Mr. Smythe instructed the courier that it is of the utmost importance that you read his missive at once."

James came back to earth with a thump. The bliss he had just found with Angelique was not meant to last, but he wished the moment after had lasted just a little longer.

She leaned up on one elbow and caught his eye. The absurdity of her proper English butler coming to the door of their love nest struck them both. He laughed, deep from his belly. His laughter shook her body, where her soft curves were still sprawled out over him. Her warmth trembled against him, but this time, it wasn't out of longing or fulfillment. She was laughing, too.

"One moment, Jerrod," she said. "I…"

James lips were on hers then, silencing her with his kiss. He rose from their makeshift bed, closing his breeches as he moved to the door. He stepped outside and met Jerrod's eye. The older man did not look embarrassed, and James was impressed with his coolness in the face of his mistress's lover. Then he wondered what else this man might have seen, how many other lovers Angelique might have brought there.

She said she had brought none. James reminded himself that he had no reason to doubt her.

He accepted the letter and nodded to the man, thinking Jerrod would leave then, but he should have known better. Angelique's people only took orders from her.

James stepped back into their haven to find Angelique sitting up on their divan. She had not tried to cover herself, but lay naked against the dusty pillows. James wanted to toss the paper aside and fall on her again. But he was a man in control of himself. He handed the letter to her.

Angelique frowned as she read it. "Smythe is having some trouble with our business contacts," she said. "I'll need to go into town to clear it up."

"What trouble?" James asked.

She smiled at him and stood, closing the distance between them to offer her lips. "Nothing that can't be handled by a well-placed bribe," she answered.

There was a shadow in her eyes that belied her easy words. James thought to run the truth to ground, but she pressed her body against him, and he kissed her in spite of himself. He lost himself in her for a long, lingering moment, and it took what was left of his self-possession to let her go when she pulled away.

"Is our idyll over so soon?"

"I'm sorry," Angelique said.

He stared down at her body, the curves of her

breasts, her narrow, tapered waist, and the generous curve of her hips. He wanted her again, and he had just had her. He did not know when he would be satisfied. He had the sinking feeling that by making love to Angelique Beauchamp, he had jumped off a burning ship into the drink.

Not that he regretted it.

"We'll be leaving for London in an hour," she called to Jerrod. "Please have Lisette repack my things."

"Yes, my lady. I will inform the staff."

Jerrod moved away as silently as he had come. James stood in the summerhouse door and watched the proper man walk carefully through the greenery, as if every leaf and flower hid an adder that might rise up and bite him.

"So, are you coming with me?"

James turned at the sound of her voice and watched as she made short work of putting her gown back on. She sat down and began to draw her stockings up her legs. He moved to kneel beside her then, his hands caressing her calf and inner thigh as he tied her garter.

"And spend another dozen nights in your bed? I wouldn't miss it."

He listened to her breath catch as he slid his hands up her skirt, running his calloused fingertips over the inside of her knee. He tied her second garter, and she shivered.

"You would undo me, Captain," she said, standing up.

He stood with her, drawing her close. "Gladly."

He kissed her lightly, fleetingly, and she tasted of chocolate and bread, of warmth and desire.

Angelique slid her little hands down from his waist

to cup his buttocks. She pressed the full curves of her body against him.

"I may need you for longer than twelve nights."

His mouth was on hers then, and her lips opened beneath his. He explored her with his tongue as her hands shifted over his backside. He came up for air and laughed a little. "So you like the goods then, countess?"

"Not enough to buy, but a long-term rental sounds divine."

He laughed louder and swatted her sweet, round ass as she walked away.

❧

James could not face two days in a carriage with Angelique's maid and new bastard ward, so he rode her stallion, Spartacus, all the way to London. The brute tried to live up to his name, but despite his years at sea, there was not a horse born that James couldn't ride. He did not try to persuade the mount, but simply showed him that they were both men of action, and that their lives would be smoother if they worked together.

When Spartacus realized that James could not be intimidated, he settled down, and only tried to throw him once every other hour.

Even from his horse, James could hear the women talking in a mélange of English and French over the long road to the city. When they stopped for the night, he cared for Spartacus himself, both to bond with the beast and to keep any errant stableboys from getting bitten.

He slept in Angelique's bed, while Sara and Lisette shared a room. He snuck out before dawn so that

Angelique's ward might not notice. But he saw that the ruse was pointless as soon as he sat down to breakfast with the women. The girl had been raised in an inn and was too shrewd to fool. But still, James did his best to behave with discretion, and only stole a kiss from Angelique when the girl was out of the room.

When they finally arrived in London, James entered Angelique's town house and followed the ladies into the drawing room for tea. None of them seemed interested in resting after their long journey, but all three seemed ready to run a mile after being confined in the carriage for two days. Lisette stole a tea sandwich, then went upstairs to supervise the unpacking and the arranging of her mistress's things. Sara and Angelique settled down with the tea cart between them. James was pouring a shot of whisky into his Darjeeling when Anton appeared.

"My lady, there is a gaggle of Scots at the door."

James slipped his flask back into his coat pocket. He left his teacup in its saucer on the table beside him.

His father came into the room then, and his mother and two of his sisters were not far behind.

"Jamie!" Constance cried. "We've looked for you everywhere!"

His eight-year-old sister ran across the room to him, heedless of manners or of her mother's restraining hand. James stood up just in time to catch her as she leaped into his arms. He held her close, her thin frame as delicate as a bird in his hand. "I missed you, Jamie. Where have you been?"

"I was on the sea, moppet. But I'm here now."

She snuggled down into his arms, and he breathed

in the scent of her honey hair. His oldest sister, Margaret, was on him then, hugging him close before drawing Constance out of his arms. She was seventeen and treated Constance as if she were her own. Unfortunately, Connie did not always care for having two mothers.

"No, Maggie, I want Jamie!" Connie cried.

Margaret kissed his cheek before stepping away and setting her sister down. "Behave yourself, Connie," she said. "Mother wants to greet him."

James turned to his mother then, who had curtsied to Angelique almost as an afterthought before making a beeline to him. He was six feet four and a man grown, but his mother drew him down into her arms as if he were still in short clothes. She caressed his hair, mussing the ribbon. She clutched him close convulsively for a long moment. It had been months since he had made it home to Aberdeen.

"Jamie," she said. "It is good to see you."

"And you, Mother." James kissed her, aware for the first time how soft her cheek was. Martha Montgomery looked good for a woman of five and fifty, and James saw that her love for him was part of her beauty, and always would be.

"We left Charles at home," his mother said.

"Someone had to run the shipping business, since Father's here," James answered.

"Exactly!" John Montgomery crossed the room to him and wrapped him in a bear hug. His father was as tall as he was and twice as broad. James lost his breath until his father let him go.

"I looked for you all over London and Greenwich,

Jamie. A kind gentleman at the club said you were out of town but that when you came back, you'd be here. I'm happy to see he was right."

"Father, that kind gentleman wouldn't be Victor Winthrop by any chance?"

"Yes indeed, Viscount Carlyle himself. Exalted company you keep, boy, since you came in off the sea."

James's father bowed low to Angelique as he said that, and she smiled at him. She rose from her place on the settee beside Sara, who sat frozen, staring in awe at James's boisterous kin. Angelique turned her smile on his family. "You are all welcome here. Please, sit, and take tea with us."

Martha Montgomery said, "We wouldn't want to put you to any trouble, your ladyship."

"No trouble at all."

Anton and three footmen were bringing in a second tea tray and more chairs from the sitting room. The tea things were added to the cart, and in a moment, Margaret had served Connie and her mother, pouring tea with as much grace as she would in her own house. Angelique sat back and let her, smiling all the while. Sara watched the older girl with wide-eyed wonder as she replenished the tea in her cup.

"One lump or two?" Margaret asked.

"Two please," Sara answered. James's sister obliged and smiled on the younger girl before taking a cup of hot tea to her father.

John Montgomery accepted the drink but did not look pleased until James passed him his flask. He caught his father's eye and saw that his family was not down to London on a pleasure jaunt. His father wanted something badly enough to come all the way south and to bring some of his women with him as an inducement. James wondered if his father wanted him to come into the family shipping business. They had had that argument fifty times since he had turned eighteen. He hoped they did not have to have it again.

Margaret was sitting with Angelique, talking about London fashion as if she took tea with a countess every day. Connie sat quiet by her mother as she ate her weight in cakes and scones, but James knew that as soon as she was done, she would be back at his side again.

As if she knew his thoughts, Connie interrupted her sister's talk of bonnets to shout, "Jamie, we came to London in a sloop! All the way from Aberdeen! It took three days on the water! I only got sick once!"

"Good girl," James said, toasting his little sister. His father, still clutching James's flask, put another dollop of whisky into his now-empty cup.

"We'll talk of the sloop later," his father said, downing his renewed whisky in one gulp and rising to his feet. His mother stood, as did Margaret. Connie took two scones, one for each hand, and made a curtsy to Angelique.

"Thank you for tea and scones, miss," she said.

"My lady," her mother whispered.

"My lady," Connie parroted, curtsying again.

Angelique smiled, rising to her feet. "You are very welcome. Please come again. My home is always open to any of James Montgomery's kin."

John and Martha beamed at her, and at him. James pocketed his flask, knowing that he needed to discover what his parents were up to and why they thought they needed to bring two of the girls along to assist in whatever scheme they had hatched to take over his life.

James bowed over Angelique's hand, as proper as if they were in church. "I've got to see what's going on here," he said, speaking low so that only she could hear him. "I'll come back tonight."

Angelique smiled her formal smile, but her eyes were lit with the same desire he felt. "Don't keep me waiting."

James checked over his shoulder to make sure that his mother and sisters were out of sight in the hallway before he leaned down and kissed Angelique's soft lips. He drew her closer to kiss her again, his hands starting to wander, but she pushed him back.

"Your other women are waiting," she said.

"Does that mean you're one of them?"

"Come back tonight and find out."

He laughed then, heading out to the entrance hall to follow his family back to the town house his father always rented in St. James Square.

Twenty-five

ANGELIQUE AND SARA SAT ALONE IN THE WAKE OF
James's family, the tea cart a wreck, cups abandoned
around the room. Angelique looked at her ward and
started to laugh.

"I like them," Sara said. "They remind me of home."

"I like them, too," Angelique said.

They sat together in comfortable silence for a long
moment before there was a loud knock at the outer door.

"Maybe they forgot something," Sara said.

But it was not Sir John or her butler Anton who
stepped through her drawing room door, but the
Duke of Hawthorne.

Angelique was on her feet in the next moment,
placing herself between the duke and her ward. She
was not quick enough though, for Hawthorne's cold
gaze was on Sara in an instant, skewering her. A hot
flame seemed to take light behind the ice in his gray
gaze, and Angelique swallowed hard.

"Sara, go upstairs and find Lisette."

Geoffrey's daughter knew more of the world
than Angelique had given her credit for. Sara's eyes

hardened as she took in the duke's imposing form by the door. The girl flanked her as if she would not leave her alone.

Hawthorne's eyes took on a sickening gleam. He seemed to have a taste for defenseless women, the younger, the better. The sight of his lust made Angelique want to retch, but she held on to her self-control. Her voice did not waver when she said again, "Sara, go upstairs."

Geoffrey's daughter obeyed her then, but reluctantly. The girl had enough sense to give the duke a wide berth as she slipped from the room, but there was not enough space in the house, much less in the drawing room, now that Hawthorne had seen her. Angelique felt as if she and the girl both had been covered by the slime of the duke's regard. She wished for one fleeting, irrational moment that James was still there.

Hawthorne did not comment on the girl, but once Sara had gone, he turned the sickening gray of his gaze on Angelique.

"Since you have returned to London with such alacrity, I assume you got my letter."

Angelique forced herself to breathe deep, but her nerves would not be calmed. They jittered beneath her skin as they had for the last two days, except when James loomed over her in bed.

"I received your note. It was a bit cryptic, Your Grace. I did not understand your meaning."

"Did you not? I thought my lawyer was quite plain. Well then, let me be more blunt. Your interference between me and Arabella Hawthorne ceases as of this moment, or every contract you currently hold with cotton suppliers both in the Empire and abroad will be rendered null and void."

"I have not stepped between you and Arabella. I don't know where she is."

"Do not lie to my face, Lady Devonshire. I know for a certainty that you tried to make me believe, falsely, that Arabella had traveled with you into Shropshire. I know just as well that she did not. I also know that between you and the Lady Westwood, you have made a concerted effort to undermine the rumors I started and fed about Arabella's benighted honor."

"The lies you spread, you mean."

"They were lies when I started telling them, I grant you. But now that she has run off to parts unknown with her old lover, Pembroke, Arabella is a whore in truth."

Angelique would have slapped him for his effrontery, but he was too far away. And like an adder, he was always poised to strike. Angelique did not want to get close enough to feel his fangs close on her throat.

"I don't know what you're talking about," she said.

Hawthorne's gray eyes narrowed. "Do not lie to me. I have taken all the insults from you that I can bear."

"Even if Arabella has fled with Pembroke, it doesn't mean she is a whore. It only means that she does not want to marry you."

"She will do as she is told!"

His voice was like thunder in the small sitting room. Angelique almost expected to hear the crystal on the mantelpiece shatter. She did not retreat but held her ground. She had spent all of her adult life dealing with men like him. She would be damned if the likes of Hawthorne ever saw her flinch.

"Let me be clear, my lady, for I am a busy man with little time to waste. If you do not return Arabella Hawthorne to my side within the week, your shipping contracts will not be worth the paper they are written on."

"You do not have that power."

"I assure you, I do. No man worth his salt wants to come down on the wrong side of this dispute. The Prince Regent may not know that I dabble in trade, but everyone in the City does. I own controlling stock in enough shipping interests between here and the former colonies in America to squelch any deals you currently have and any deals you might make in the future. And don't think of trying to go to India for the cotton you need. I have cut that road off to you completely."

Angelique stared at him. She thought of the men she knew in the cotton trade and of how long it had taken her to get any of them to trust her. Even now, she had a cargo full of rotten cotton in her warehouse, a stunt no supplier would ever have tried on any man of her acquaintance. Since Anthony had left her, the insults had gotten worse. Now, with Hawthorne and his forces arrayed against her, she would be hard-pressed to bring a shipment of cotton into port, much less sell it afterward.

"The cotton mills of Leeds are displeased with your supply as well, you'll find. They'll be buying their cotton from me from now on."

Angelique reeled as under a blow. She did not know what to say. She did not know whether to move forward or back. Her father had been an honest man and had taught her to deal honestly with her business associates. If honesty had been trumped by a duke's power, there was little she could do.

She thought of going to Anthony for help and discarded the thought just as quickly. She thought of asking the Prince Regent for assistance but knew that she would not be able to stand joining the groups of people dependent on him for their living. The only reason she had ever enjoyed her time with the Carlton House set was that she depended on none of them, not even the prince. Not to mention, Hawthorne had the prince in his pocket.

Her finely woven world was unraveling, and she did not know what she would do to stop it.

Hawthorne answered her unspoken question. "Bring Arabella Hawthorne back to London, and I might be persuaded to allow one or two of your old contacts to supply you with cotton. The mills of the North are closed to you, but you might always sell your cotton to me. For half the usual price, of course."

The duke strode toward the door, taking up his walking stick from where he had laid it on a mahogany table. "You will not hear from me again, Lady Devonshire. I tell you now, and for the last time, bring my Arabella back to me."

"She is not yours," Angelique said. "She will never agree to come, even if I ask her."

His gray eyes passed over Angelique like a curse. "You think her consent necessary? I hold the purse strings. Once you return her to London, I will deal with her. Like any bitch, she will come to heel."

He smiled then, and the slime of his gaze made her wish for a bath.

"If by some chance Arabella refuses to come home to me, and I ruin you completely, I'll be happy to take that little piece I saw here earlier under my protection."

"Stay away from Sara," Angelique said.

"Sara...is that her name? She's Geoffrey's bastard, is she not? She has the look of him."

Hawthorne left then, and Angelique stood in his wake, her stomach churning. She shook with the need to be ill, but she forced her bile down. She sat on her purgatorial settee, knowing that she needed to send for Smythe, to make plans, to see what might be done. But before she could ring the bell to call for Anton, Smythe had arrived on her doorstep.

Her man of affairs came into her sitting room after Anton had shown him in, looking as pale as she had ever seen him. He carried a great sheaf of papers, but they were in disarray, as if he had been going through them for days and had found nothing that might help her.

George Smythe stood staring at her from behind his gold-rimmed glasses. "The duke has been here already," she said.

"I am sorry, my lady. I am going to keep trying..."

"But no one will see you. None of my business associates want to deal with you anymore, and by extension, with me."

"No, my lady. I'm sorry."

Angelique sat adrift on an endless sea. She had been her own mistress her whole adult life, since her husband died. She had made her way in a man's world, and now that way had been cut off, with no road forward or back.

One thing was certain. If Hawthorne did not know where Arabella was, he soon would. Arabella would have to leave Derbyshire, and quickly. Angelique needed to go to her and warn her. The duke was an open maw, with an appetite for destruction that could not be sated.

"It's all right, Smythe," Angelique said at last. "You've done your best. That's all anyone can do. Give me a few days. I'll think of something."

Twenty-six

JAMES AND HIS FATHER TOOK A HIRED COACH TO Greenwich, where the family sloop was moored.

"She's not a huge ship, but she's only the first. If this goes well, I'll build the fleet slowly, until we're doing all our own shipping and won't need to depend on others for the quality of the cotton we buy." John Montgomery caressed the rail of the ship he stood on. The crew had been given leave, save for a few left guarding the ship, all of whom stood by the gangplank, and one high in the crow's nest. James took in his father's pride and joy and could find no flaw in it.

"I'm going to buy a ship of my own, Father."

Sir John waved his words away. "Hear me out, son. Leave your money in the bank for now and think. If you come into business with your brother and me, you won't have to establish new supply contacts. We have them all. You only have to step in and take over the shipping. As easy for you as rolling off a log."

"Father…"

"If you won't come in on my say-so, buy into the business then. It's a damned fool thought, since the business is half yours already, or will be when I'm dead, but if it pleases you, give us a few thousand pounds. We'll buy another ship with it."

James smiled. "I need to think, Father."

"I expected you would. Take this ship on its next voyage. A weeklong journey to Aberdeen and back. See how you like the crew. See how she handles. Then, in another week or two, you might take her as far as Malta to pick up a shipment I've got coming in from Egypt. All small potatoes for now. If you find the ship, and the business, to your liking, then you can invest."

"I can't live in Aberdeen," James said without thinking. "My life is here now."

He said that last without thinking either, but as he spoke, he knew it was true.

"I saw that this afternoon. Your mother said as much. Your countess is a lovely woman and worth staying in the South for. You can do your work, and ship out, from here."

"Angelique is not my countess," James said.

Sir John waved his hand in dismissal. "She's yours if you want her. You're your father's son in that regard, my boy, and no mistake."

James laughed. He saw for the first time where his natural arrogance had come from.

"Take the ship out tomorrow morning with the tide. See how she sails. Then decide."

James extended his hand, and his father took it. "Fair enough. We'll try it your way, Father. For now."

John Montgomery beamed. "Your mother will be pleased."

"Which is really all that matters," James quipped.

"When you've been married for over thirty years, boy, you'll see how true that is. Life goes smoother when the women are contented."

"That's why we won't let women onboard ship. They're too much trouble," James repeated the old adage, though he no longer believed it.

Sir John looked at him sideways. "No women? What fun is that?"

❧

Rather than taking his dinner with his family, James came home to Regent Square instead.

Angelique thought of it as him coming home, but she knew he had not. He did not live with her, or she with him. He had a life beyond her, just as she did, and his family was a reminder of that. They had been kind to her, but they could not possibly approve of him taking a mistress. Though the Montgomerys were the opposite of every story she had heard about dour Scots, they still could not be pleased.

James did not mention his family but to say they sent their regards, before he kissed her and poured himself a whisky from his own flask.

"I've asked Anton to acquire some. What is the name of yours?"

"Islay whisky is the only Scotch worth drinking," James said.

Angelique laughed. "Then it will be the only whisky I keep."

James kissed her as a reward, and she tasted the oak-laced flavor of his Scotch on his lips. It was becoming one of her favorite flavors in the world.

She knew she should tell James about her visit from Hawthorne, but she put it off. Maybe after dinner, when Sara was in bed.

When Sara came down to dinner, Lisette's influence was revealed. Her hair was combed back, not in country braids but in a sleek chignon. While not a style that Angelique would have chosen for a girl of thirteen, it suited her fine-boned face.

Her gown was new, simple white muslin covered with blue cornflowers that matched Sara's eyes. The long skirt and high waist suited the girl's thin frame, giving her an air of elegance. Angelique had no idea where Lisette had found such a lovely dress, and on such short notice. Her French maid was nothing short of a miracle worker.

"Lisette has been teaching me some phrases in French," Sara said.

"All clean I hope," James quipped. Angelique shot him a dark look.

Sara frowned. "She hasn't taught me words about cleaning yet," she answered. "But she taught me how to say hello and thank you and *Vive l'empereur!*"

"That last one you can forget," James said.

"She's been reading to me, too." Sara's smile threatened to split her face as she ate her creamed turnips with her salad fork.

"Not Mrs. Radcliff, I hope," Angelique said.

"I do not know that author, my lady. She read *The Lady of the Lake* by Sir Walter Scott. She said I can learn to read poetry in English first, but that the best poetry is in French."

"I am fond of poetry, too. Perhaps tonight after dinner we might sit and read some together."

"I would like that." Sara's smile grew ever wider.

Angelique felt an unaccustomed joy rise in her breast at the sight of Geoffrey's daughter, safe and well, eating creamed turnips at her table. She felt that joy mix with fear. She knew in that moment she would do anything to keep that girl safe, now and every day after.

Her hand shook as she drank her Burgundy, and James reached for her and touched her arm. "Are you all right?" he asked low when Sara had gone to the sideboard to look at the silver chafing dishes laid out for breakfast tomorrow.

"Of course," Angelique said.

She stood then and led them both into the drawing room for tea and cakes. She felt her lover's eyes on her and knew that he would not let the matter drop. How she would keep him from knowing of her disaster, she was not sure. Part of her wanted to throw herself into his arms and tell him everything, though she knew that there was absolutely nothing he could do.

She listened to James read from Sir Walter Scott, his accent from Aberdeen lending the poetry extra credence and lyricism. Angelique tried to lose herself in the wash of sensation, her joy at seeing Sara so happy, the pleasure she felt knowing that the handsome man reading to her by candlelight would soon be in her bed. She did her best to forget the fact that Hawthorne existed at all. And for a few minutes together, she almost succeeded.

❧

"I must leave in the morning," James said.

Lisette had taken Sara upstairs to bed, and he and

Angelique lingered in the drawing room while he finished his whisky. She stiffened at his indelicate declaration, and he tried again.

"My father has a ship, and he wants me to sail it to Aberdeen. I'll be gone a week. And after that, he needs me to pick up a shipment of cotton on Malta."

"He buys his cotton from Egypt then?" Angelique asked, her voice detached.

"He gets a bit here and there under the table," James answered. "It's cheaper than dealing with the East India Company."

She laughed, and her shoulders relaxed a little. "Your father wants you to be a smuggler then?"

"Only on this trip. We deal with the East India Company too, when we have need."

"So you're going into business with your father?"

"I'm thinking about it, very seriously."

She moved to him and kissed his lips. "I am happy for you. If I had a father, I would do the same."

James laughed under his breath. "If your father was with us, not only would he let you nowhere near his shipping interests, he would have shot me already."

It was Angelique's turn to laugh. "Fair enough."

James wanted to take her in his arms there in her drawing room as he once had done in the Blue Velvet Room at Carlton House. He would draw her down onto her delicate sofa and make love to her against its soft velvet cushions.

The alabaster skin of her throat beckoned to him in the light of the candles. He wanted to press his lips there and work his way slowly down to the curves of her breasts, barely hidden by the gown she wore. But

Sara might come downstairs again, or Anton might see. He did not want to humiliate her in front of the people who depended on her.

Instead of bringing her beneath him on the drawing room rug, as he wished to do, James took the hand she offered and led her upstairs to her bedroom suite. He did not take a candle but walked with her up into the dark. His eyes adjusted quickly to the feeble light that came in from the open window at the end of the hall.

The moon was up and shed a little light on them as he climbed the stairs to her bedroom. Angelique walked beside him in silence, her hand in his.

She turned to him and pressed herself against him, not importuning him, not begging him to stay, but in the simple joy of desire, in the warmth of the passion they found together whenever they were alone.

He brought her before the fireplace but did not touch her save for his hand on hers. He stood staring down at her, watching her breasts rise and fall with her breath beneath the blue silk of her gown. He studied it for a moment and found the tie that bound it. With only a few tugs, it fell open, and her breasts were revealed to his gaze in the firelight.

She wore nothing beneath the silk: no stays, no chemise, no drawers. As the royal blue gown fell away, Angelique stood naked before him, wearing only stockings tied just above the knee and jeweled slippers trimmed with diamonds.

The creamy expanse of her skin gleamed in the firelight, but still he did not touch her. He stepped close enough to breathe on her and to watch as her nipples tightened in response. Her breath turned shallow, but she still did not speak.

He ran his hand over her body in the shadowy firelight, his calluses snagging on the smooth skin of her belly, of her breasts, of her thighs. Angelique did not move, but stood still and let him touch her, almost as if she were a goddess accepting worship from a man who had never before seen the divine.

It might be a month or more before he had her again. He planned to make the most of it.

He followed the path of his hands with his lips until he was kneeling before her, spreading her thighs so that he might taste her, so that his tongue might delve into the smooth warmth of her. Angelique moaned when he did that, her knees giving way. He caught her as she slid down to join him on the floor and laid her on the Turkish carpet before the fire.

He ran his tongue over her belly, before delving again between the sweet apex of her thighs. She moaned but would not speak his name as he explored her with his tongue, lips, and teeth. He nipped at her and watched as she bit her bottom lip to keep herself from screaming. He raised one hand to cover her mouth, her breath hot on his palm; he rode her with his tongue until her passion rose like the crest of a wave, her pleasure shuddering through her body like a hurricane hitting dry land.

She wept with the pleasure he gave her, and he wiped her tears away. But still, she did not speak. He raised himself over her then, unfastening his breeches before he slid into her, filling her body completely. Her body clasped him like a fist, flexing around him as he rode her, sliding in and out of her depths, his own pleasure consuming him as it never had before.

❧

Angelique lay awake in his arms all that night. She listened to the evenness of his breathing, which to her ears did not sound like sleep. The hours of the night moved past her as the shore moves past a ship going down the Thames, slowly at first, then quickly as the ship comes to the mouth of the river and moves out to sea.

She had not told him about Hawthorne, and she wasn't sure why.

There was nothing he could do. That was one reason, and it was a good one. And after meeting his sweet family, after watching his youngest sister, Connie, devour her tea tray, after talking poke bonnets with his eldest sister, Margaret, after meeting his bluff but charming parents, she knew that she could not bring the wrath of Hawthorne down on them.

It would take little for the duke to ruin them, as he was ruining her. And she would not have that.

So she stayed silent as he slept beside her.

He rose before dawn to leave her. Afraid that she might do something foolish, or womanly, and ask him to stay, Angelique did not reveal that she was still awake. She kept her eyes closed and her breathing even as James caressed her cheek once, very lightly, his touch as soft as a butterfly's wing, so insubstantial that had she not been completely attuned to his movement, she would not have felt it.

It did not take him long to dress. He was quiet as he moved around her bed, picking up his discarded clothing, but her ears were filled with the whisper of linen as he drew on his shirt, as he tied his cravat.

His bag was packed and waiting for him in the hall. She knew this because she had ordered it done. As he unlatched the door to her bedroom, she listened to the pause in his quiet steps as he saw the bag waiting for him. She did not open her eyes even then, but waited until the door clicked quietly shut.

Perhaps by the time he came home, she would have solved her own problems. As it was, she would do her best to keep him untouched by them. Hawthorne was a formidable enemy.

She missed James with a strange and palpable longing, as if she had mislaid something that she desperately wanted back. Her heart actually ached as she lay alone in her suddenly too-large bed. She knew that if he were there, he would tease her for being sentimental.

She ran her hand over the place where he had slept, burying her nose in the pillowcase that still bore his scent. Cedar and leather filled her nostrils, and she wished for him, though he had not yet been gone an hour.

She was in love with him then. God help her.

&

Angelique and her ward ate together in the sunny breakfast room that overlooked the small town garden behind the house. She buttered her brioche before passing the jam to Sara, who sat beside her. The girl had been uncommonly quiet that morning, looking surreptitiously at the door, no doubt expecting James to walk through it.

"Captain Montgomery has gone away," she said at last.

Sara did not answer but fiddled with her butter knife, smearing bits of broken bread onto her plate. She did not eat anything but stared down at her untouched food.

"Is he coming back?" the girl asked.

Angelique felt the blade of truth press into her heart, taking her breath. She did not lie to the girl or to herself. "He'll be back in a month. Maybe a little longer."

Sara looked at her then, for it seemed she heard the pain hidden in Angelique's voice, the pain she so desperately wanted to hide. The girl looked over her shoulder at the footmen standing by, but neither of them met her gaze or gave any indication that they were listening to the discussion at all. Still, Sara frowned at them before hunching low over the table in an effort to lean closer to her guardian.

"Do you miss him?"

Angelique did not answer, but only took a sip of coffee from her demitasse cup.

"Do you love him?" Sara asked.

Angelique almost choked but managed to set her china cup down. She met the girl's eyes. "Yes," she said. "I love him."

"Did you tell him?"

Angelique smiled. "No, I did not."

"Why not?"

"I'm not sure."

Sara did not speak for a long moment, but neither did she eat her brioche. She tore the bread into little pieces until buttered crumbs were scattered across the porcelain of her plate. "He didn't say good-bye."

The girl's voice was very soft, so quiet that Angelique almost could not hear her.

"He left early, before dawn. The tide was turning, and he had to go."

Sara began to tear apart another piece of bread. Angelique sighed. When Cook saw her good bread wasted, Anton would have a great deal of trouble calming her down. Cook prided herself on her fresh bread.

"My father left me," Sara said. "Before I was born. Before my mam died."

Angelique sat poised as on a knife's edge, not certain whether to move forward or to go back. Geoffrey was a subject she never discussed, not with anyone, not even Arabella. But Sara raised her blue eyes, eyes that were so like his. Angelique swallowed her pain and forced herself to speak.

"Your father left me, too," she said. "I was going to have a baby, and he left me for an opera dancer in London. He died while he was with her."

"Why did he die?" Sara's voice was small and soft, the voice of a much younger girl.

Angelique thought of the pox that had killed him and decided to tell a simpler lie. "The fast carriage he was driving fell over on him."

Sara lowered her gaze, flattening a bit of bread with her fork.

"Where is your baby? Is she at school?"

Angelique swallowed hard. "My baby died, a long time ago."

Sara froze in place as if Angelique had slapped her. She seemed to take in everything Angelique could not say, all the things she could never say about Geoffrey and her daughter in one swift glance. The girl left off toying with her abandoned breakfast, dropping her fork with a clatter as she took Angelique's hand in her own. She squeezed her fingers tight, until the blood was blocked off.

"I will look after you," Sara said, her eyes taking on a fierce and loyal light. "I will not die. I will not leave you."

Angelique felt her throat swell with emotion. For once she did not swallow her tears but let them come. Only two fell. She wiped her eyes with her free hand and smiled at her adopted daughter.

"I am glad to hear it," she said. "We will stick together, you and I. We will look after each other."

Smythe was waiting to speak with her, with more news of disaster. Lisette waited impatiently for Sara abovestairs, ready to teach her daily lessons in reading, writing, and revolutionary French. She knew that they needed to set out for Derbyshire at once, as soon as possible, that they might reach Arabella before Hawthorne did.

Angelique knew all of these things, and she ignored them. She set aside trouble and mayhem, packing and French maids, and called for her pelisse and for Sara's. They took the carriage to the pond in St. James Park carrying the crumbs of bread from Sara's discarded plate to feed the waiting swans.

The rest of life could wait.

Twenty-seven

JAMES WAS GONE TO ABERDEEN FOR ONLY A WEEK, BUT it seemed like a year. Skirting the shore of England and Scotland was nothing like sailing the open sea. It was safe. It was comfortable. He found that he liked it. Perhaps he was getting old.

The journey he would make to Malta would be a good deal more exciting. With the Ottoman pirates still active in the Mediterranean, and with the East India Company to dodge, the voyage promised to be a taste of adventure. His father's sloop boasted three cannons, not enough to hold out in a fight, but the ship was fast and could outrun most things on the sea.

James wasn't worried about his chances between there and Malta. But he did want to see Angelique again.

He called at her house to find Anton there alone. She had gone to visit a friend in the country, a woman friend, her butler had assured him. She had not left word when she would return.

James was tempted to follow her.

But he knew his duty. He had given his father his word, and he would keep it. While he waited to ship out the next morning, he went to visit an old friend living ashore in Greenwich, Captain Albert Franklin.

"Damn my eyes, Jamie, it's good to see you in one piece."

Franklin took his friend in his arms as soon as he saw him, drawing him into his home. The stone house was small, for Franklin had not made much prize money during the war. He had not sold his commission, but was on half pay until his new ship would be ready to sail in two months' time.

For the moment, Captain Franklin lived in Greenwich near the Royal Naval Academy with his wife and infant son. James took in the tiny house with its poky hall and ill-lit staircase that led to the bedroom above. Though the downstairs parlor was dark, it was cheerful and clean. A fire burned in the grate, and the savory scent of stew made James's stomach rumble. Franklin laughed at that as his wife dished up bowls for both men.

"Have you been on the sea all this time, Jamie? I looked for you at the Academy but could not get word of you."

"No, Bert, I've been inland."

"Chasing after a woman, no doubt," Franklin said.

"Something like that."

Franklin stared at his old friend as his wife brought their dinner. She pressed her husband's arm in passing, and he leaned down and kissed her hand. Mrs. Franklin was a steady, capable woman who seemed to be the anchor not only of the house but of Franklin's life. James was not sure why he thought so, other than there seemed to be a silent affinity between the two, an acceptance of what was, and a quiet happiness that whatever time they had together, they would savor, drinking down every drop until Franklin was at sea again.

"I came ashore to inquire after a ship for sale. Now it looks as if I will be going into business with my father's concern, sailing for Malta."

Franklin said nothing but took in James with one measured glance, finishing his first bowl of stew. Without speaking, Mrs. Franklin filled it again with one hand, holding their sleeping son with the other.

James saw the easy way she had with the house and her family, the calm purpose behind every move she made. No great lady, this was a woman who worked from dawn to dusk in the service of her family, seeing to it that they were fed, clothed, and warm. Even as he watched her, she settled the baby in his crib by the fire and took up her sewing.

She continued her work with neat, even stitches, not giving James a second glance. He could tell that she was making a new shirt for her husband. He wondered if Angelique had ever plied a needle in her life. Somehow, he could not imagine it. Still, Mrs. Franklin in no small way reminded him of the woman who rarely left his thoughts.

"Do your eyes follow my wife for some purpose, Jamie?"

"Forgive me, Bert. I did not mean to be impertinent. It is only that she reminds me of someone."

Franklin leaned back in his chair, pushing his empty bowl aside. "Ah. I see."

James felt his hackles rise at his friend's tone, though he could not have answered why, if asked. "What do you see?"

Franklin did not take offense at James's harsh question, but only smiled. "I see a great deal more than you do, my friend. This woman my wife brings to mind, what is her name?"

"Angelique," James answered.

"A Frenchwoman?" Franklin's eyebrows rose, and James found himself smiling in spite of himself.

"Worse. A countess."

Franklin did not answer that directly, but exchanged a look with his wife that James could not read. "Well then. That's your own business, I reckon. But might this countess be the reason for your overlong stay on dry land?"

"She's the reason."

Franklin lit his pipe and smoked for a long moment in silence. James took in the sweet scent of tobacco as it mingled with the scent of the stew.

"There was a time when I ran from a good woman," Franklin said. He and his wife caught each other's gazes, and this time she did not look away but laid her sewing down.

"I fled from my fate. I found that I could not run far enough or fast enough. No matter what shore I came upon, or what port I sailed into, she was always there before me, waiting." He tapped his temple. "I carried her with me, everywhere I meant to hide. I found I could not lose her, though I tried for a year and a day. So at last I came back, when the war was through. And she was here, in her mother's house, waiting for me."

Mrs. Franklin rose to refill Bert's cup of ale. She did this, still silent, and filled James's, as well. But instead of stepping back from the table, she sat down beside her husband. Franklin opened his great palm, and she placed her tiny hand within it.

"You cannot run from yourself, Jamie, or you'll be running all your life. If this French countess is the woman of your heart, you must stand for her and face her. You would not run from battle. You cannot run from this."

"She's out of town."

Franklin smiled, but it was Mrs. Franklin who spoke at last. "Then, Captain Montgomery, you had better go and fetch her back."

❧

Franklin agreed to take the ship to Malta in James's place. The tide was turning, and the sloop would sail the next day. Franklin was the only man James would commit his family's interests to, and on such short notice. He sent word to his father, who had already returned to Aberdeen, and went to drink at White's.

James wondered what Angelique might say if he made her an offer of marriage.

The thought rose into his head as the fumes from his malted Scotch rose into his nostrils. He took a sip of the fiery liquid, but it did not burn and choke him as his own thoughts did.

He was not a marrying man.

But as he sat alone at White's, James remembered the look that had passed between Franklin and his wife. Their quiet affinity and their easy grace. He thought of his parents and of how they still loved each other after almost forty years.

He was musing to himself, lost in his own thoughts, when Viscount Carlyle sat down beside him. Carlyle was drunk off his top, but he was still immaculately groomed and pressed, save for his cravat, which had been knocked slightly askew. He had just come in from the card room and carried a hint of bourbon and smoke on his black superfine coat.

"So they are still allowing captains of the line to drink at White's? I thought the last time I saw you here was an aberration."

James smiled. He heard in Carlyle's tone a hint of humor beneath his genuine ire. "My father is a member."

"Is he indeed? And your elder brother?"

"Yes. They are the bastions of my family."

"And you are the black sheep."

"Perhaps more a mottled gray."

Victor laughed as a footman brought a fresh bourbon, taking his empty glass away. "Bring another for my friend," he said. James nodded in acceptance and the footman moved off to procure another single-malt Scotch.

"I thought you were away with the lovely Angelique Beauchamp on a country idyll. Back so soon, Captain?"

"I thought I told you never to say her name again."

"So you did. I don't suppose you'll shoot me?"

"Not just yet."

"More's the pity." Carlyle drank deep. "Ah, well. I suppose I have no desire to get shot this close to my wedding."

"When is the happy day?"

"Tomorrow morning at St. George's, ten o'clock sharp." Victor drained his second glass of bourbon in fifteen minutes and signaled for another. "And may God have mercy on my soul."

Victor leaned back into the leather of his armchair. "As a friend... though I suppose we are not truly friends, are we, Captain? But who is truly friendly in this benighted world? As a friend, I tell you that if you have come back to shore seeking Angelique, you seek her in vain. She has traveled with the rest of the bored *ton* to the wilds of Derbyshire to see a play."

"A play?" James was sure that Carlyle was either completely foxed or simply trying to lead him astray, but for some reason he waited to hear him out.

"Shakespeare, worse luck. Can you imagine anything more ghastly than *A Midsummer Night's Dream* in Derbyshire?" Victor shuddered as if someone had just danced on his grave.

"I have always preferred *Much Ado About Nothing*," James said.

"Indeed?" Carlyle shuddered again. "I prefer to be shot in the head rather than see or hear one word of Shakespeare. Comedy or no, it is sure to be a disaster."

Carlyle tried in vain to straighten his mussed cravat.

"The Earl of Pembroke is playing Oberon. Can you imagine? Raymond Olivier, a peer of the realm, performing in the market square like a mountebank. Good God." Carlyle drained the last of his bourbon and signaled to the footman for yet another. "I wish I'd thought of it. If I could stand the stuff, I'd have done it myself. Set tongues wagging for a year at least."

Victor downed his last bourbon in one long gulp. "Nothing for it but to marry tomorrow. If I were a praying man, I suppose I'd ask for clemency."

"A stay of execution?" James asked.

"Just so. Ah well, marriage is one bullet we all must

face at one time or another." Carlyle suddenly looked cheerful. "Perhaps she'll die tonight, and I won't have to marry her at all."

"Or perhaps you will, my lord."

Carlyle laughed, and this time his laughter held a tinge of bitterness. "Little hope of that, Captain."

James rose to his feet, bowing to the man who had saved him a week of wasted travel. "There is always hope, my lord. I suppose I must thank you for the information regarding the Countess of Devonshire's whereabouts. But don't mention her name again."

"Ah, no doubt I will forget the beautiful Angelique and all else, Captain. That is the beauty of drink."

Carlyle raised his empty glass in salute as James strode from the room. He was off to his hotel, and then to the livery stable to hire a horse. He could not take Spartacus without Smythe's consent, and he wanted to be on the road too early to consult with Angelique's man of affairs. He hoped to be riding north to Derbyshire before the sun was up.

At the door of the barroom, he took one last glance back at Viscount Carlyle. Victor was still conscious, if only barely. James had no idea how the man hoped to go to his bride at ten the next morning, nor what state the poor woman would find him in.

What the hell Angelique was doing in Derbyshire was a mystery he would soon solve. He did know that once he reached her, he would ask her to marry him.

He had no idea what her answer would be the first time he asked, but he would stand by her, and keep asking, until her answer was yes.

ACT III

"But manhood is melted into curtsies, valor into compliment... He is now as valiant as Hercules that only tells a lie, and swears it."

Much Ado About Nothing
Act 4, Scene 1

Twenty-eight

ANGELIQUE TOOK HER TIME GETTING TO DERBYSHIRE. Traveling with a young girl and a maid, with all their baggage as well as hers, called for a slower pace. She did not know what she might find in Pembroke Village, but she was fairly certain that she could trust Lord Pembroke to guard Arabella at least until Angelique arrived. She knew she was running away from the realities of her shipping concerns. She knew that she would have to deal with Hawthorne and the damage he had done to her business. But for once, she was setting business concerns aside and looking to her friend's safety first.

If Angelique had been a romantic, she would have considered the possibility that Pembroke might offer to protect her friend for the rest of her life. Angelique rarely thought kindly of marriage, for any institution that stripped a woman of all her worldly possessions and left her at the mercy of a virtual stranger bore more of a resemblance to highway robbery than a sacrament.

But her time with James Montgomery had changed her views on marriage. She had begun to think in

their weeks together that it might be possible to know
a man well enough to trust him with her life. Where
this mad idea had come from, she was not certain.
Perhaps it would pass as so many feverish imaginings
did. But as she rode in her well-sprung traveling
chaise with Sara beside her, Angelique found herself
remembering things about James Montgomery that
had nothing to do with madness.

She remembered their affinity in bed. She found
she could not sleep at night for longing for his touch.
But it was the time they had spent together in company that she remembered most. She thought of the
times James had held his glib tongue and let her deal
with Sara as she saw fit. She had never known a man
to support a woman with the silence of his presence.

A few weeks were not enough time upon which to
judge a man. Even if he had offered for her instead of
leaving for the open sea, she could not have married
him. She could not lose control of all her assets, for
too many people depended on her. Even if she were
foolish enough to take a risk with her own life, she
could not risk the vulnerability of her dependents.

And then there was the fact that she loved him. In
the past, love had only served to wound her. Geoffrey
had used her love against her. Anthony had thrown
her love back in her face. She did not expect such
treatment from James Montgomery, but after only a
few weeks in his presence, she could not be sure.

She tried to ignore the love and pain and hope
lodged together in her chest, but James Montgomery
would not leave her mind. As her carriage pulled up
in front of the cottage Smythe had rented for her, she

found herself looking at it as James might have done, wondering if he would like it as much as she did.

Tucked away on a side street just off the main village road, the little stone cottage was set back from the lane. When her traveling chaise pulled up before the front gate, she feared that gate was not wide enough to accommodate her carriage. The bright, cheerful blue of the wood stood out from the gray stone of the wall. When William the footman leaped down to open the gate, it swung wide without a squeak of protest.

It opened to reveal a small house tucked within a garden. The flowers had not been tended in quite a while, but Angelique saw columbine and thyme, rosemary and goldenrod. A profusion of blooms welcomed the kiss of the sun as flowers mixed with herbs along the neat path that led to the cottage's front door. The roof was thatched, and when she stepped into the front hall, she saw that the interior walls were whitewashed. It seemed like a house from another time, an enchanted place where she might live in quiet, filled with the same soothing peace that she sometimes felt in James Montgomery's presence.

She wondered if the cottage was for sale. She would send word on the morrow to Smythe so that he might make inquiries. What she would do with a cottage hidden in the wilds of Derbyshire she was not certain, but something drew her to that place and held her so that as she stepped past its blue-painted door, she found that she did not want to be anywhere else. If there was a place that was the opposite of her false life in London, this cottage was it.

As Angelique stood with the front door open behind

her, beams of sunlight came into the house through the windows, carrying bits of dust. The furniture in the house gleamed, a pair of mahogany chairs flanking the entrance and a tea table and sofa of the highest quality drawn up before the empty fireplace. She recognized a few of the pieces from Mr. Landau in London, from whom she had made purchases before. Smythe had outdone himself in preparing the cottage before her, combining a house from a fairy story with the things she loved most, beautiful furniture and quiet.

Sara came to stand beside her. The small house was nowhere near as grand as Aeronwynn's Gate, but her ward did not seem put off by that. Instead, Sara gazed around the front parlor, taking in the two sets of wide windows that looked out on the gardens both at the front and the back of the house. Through the back windows, Angelique could see an apple tree in bloom.

"It is very pretty," Sara said. "I think my mam and I would have been happy here."

Angelique took the girl's gloved hand in her own. Sara did not pull back but stayed close, looking on the house in silence as Angelique did.

"You and I will be happy here. I will buy it for you, if you wish."

Sara face lit up. "A house of my own?"

"Indeed. A woman should always have her own property."

"Would I have to live here by myself?"

Angelique did not laugh, though for a moment she wanted to. "Certainly not. A gently reared young lady does not live alone. I fear you are stuck with me, at least for the moment."

Sara turned her head so that she could see Angelique past the stiff edges of her own bonnet, which was trimmed in lace and silk flowers. Sara had decorated the bonnet herself, at Lisette's instruction, and had done a fine job of it. Angelique had rarely seen as simple and as elegant a creation when riding among the *ton* in Hyde Park. Sara was unaware of her innate elegance or of her own grace. Her blue eyes were clear of guile as they met Angelique's.

"I am glad to be stuck with you, my lady. Even Mrs. Withers was not as kind to me."

Angelique did not speak, for an odd lump had risen in her throat. Such emotion seemed to rise more and more often where Sara was concerned. Angelique smiled at the girl before she drew her hand from Sara's grasp so that she might walk ahead of her through the house to the back door.

The kitchen was clean and well lit. The cook and housekeeper Smythe had hired, Mrs. Beebe, curtsied to them as they passed but did not stop her work for long. "There will be tea in the parlor in a few minutes, my lady."

"Thank you, Mrs. Beebe. I think we will take tea in the back garden."

"Yes, my lady."

Angelique gave no thought to the dirt of the road that still clung to her traveling cloak. She flung the cape off and laid it over a chair outside, displacing a bit of garden dirt.

Sara did the same, going so far as to take off her bonnet and turn her face to the sun. Angelique knew that she should direct the girl to protect her white

skin, but with a sigh, Angelique did not. Instead, she
drew her own bonnet off, listening with half an ear
while Lisette fussed in French over the wasted goat's
milk that went into preserving her lady's pallor.

"Lisette, sit with us awhile. Take tea. The goat's
milk and our bags will wait."

Lisette silenced her muttered tirade in midstream,
her eyes wide with shock. She stopped gathering up the
traveling cloaks and laid them down on a wooden bench.

Suddenly, she did not seem to mind the brushing
she would have to give those clothes to get the pollen
off them. Lisette brought up a chair to the table that
sat in the back garden, dusting it first with her handkerchief before she sat down. Mrs. Beebe brought
a tablecloth, and a quiet girl, the housemaid named
Sally, brought the tea tray. Fresh cream and scones
melted on Angelique's tongue as she surveyed the
roses along the far wall and took in the scent of apple
blossoms overhead.

"This is paradise, my lady," Lisette said.

"Yes," Angelique agreed. "It is."

❧

In spite of the unexpected peace she found in the
loveliness of her rented cottage, Angelique had not
forgotten why she had come to Derbyshire in the
first place. After tea, once she had bathed her face and
hands, she took her carriage to Pembroke's house on
the hill. Arabella was there, and Angelique could not
truly rest until she had seen her.

As she passed through the village, she saw that
Titania's theatre company was hard at work on the

green. The production of *A Midsummer Night's Dream* would come on Midsummer's Eve, in two days' time, and to Angelique it seemed that the show would not be ready. The actors were clad in bits of costume, some still with their scripts in hand, gesticulating in the throes of their art as she drove past. The set painters still worked with their brushes while Titania's stage-hands set up the lamps that would burn at the foot of the makeshift stage.

They would be lucky if the entire monstrosity did not go up in a blaze of flaming glory. But she had seen enough of Titania's productions by now to know that the woman never did anything by half measures. Even in the country, Titania and her troupe would find a way to triumph. Just two days before the performance, Angelique could not see how, but then she did not have to. Like all good producers, she offered her money quietly and left the rest to the professionals.

Though this week's performance would be given for free as a gift of the Earl of Pembroke to his villagers and tenants, as producer, Angelique stood to make a great deal of money from the rest of the tour that Titania had planned that summer across the north of England. Leeds, Manchester, and York rarely saw London theatre, but like all Northerners and Scots, they loved a good story and would pay in gold to see one. Especially Shakespeare, whom they claimed as one of their own, Stratford-on-Avon be damned.

Many in the *ton* had been bored enough to leave London to see Pembroke play the role of Oberon. Well-sprung carriages and lacquered barouches arrived by the dozen at the houses along the main road of the village. Angelique wondered if people had left their own homes to rent to those aristocrats who would not take rooms in the inn. She thought of the overly fastidious ladies and lords trying to find suitable lodgings in such a small village and laughed out loud.

She would have to spend a bit of time in the village teahouse and catch up on the gossip produced by this latest adventure of the *ton*, gossip that had nothing to do with Arabella and everything to do with the entitled airs of her so-called friends. Her own false life in London had begun to pale in the light of Sara's genuine sweetness and in the aftermath of James Montgomery's passion. Angelique wondered if she might spend less time among London's elite and more months at home in Shropshire.

When she arrived at Pembroke House, Pembroke did not greet her, but his butler did. She followed a housemaid, not into a sitting room abovestairs as she expected, but down into the kitchen. Arabella, she was told, was making a pie.

Angelique stepped into the kitchen at Pembroke House, heedless of the oddity of it. The cook's staff stared at her as if she were an apparition, but she smiled serenely as if it were a common occurrence for a countess to enter their domain. She greeted Arabella with an embrace, ignoring the floury apron her friend still wore, surprised to find a bloom of happiness in Arabella's cheeks. Hawthorne might be threatening her and ruining her reputation among the peers of England and Scotland, but Arabella did not seem to care one fig.

Though Angelique was happy to be reunited with

her friend, and even happier to find her safe and well, it seemed that Anthony and his young wife and baby son were guests at Pembroke House as well. Angelique would have given her left arm to be away from there as soon as she discovered that, but Arabella looked so downhearted when she tried to escape that Angelique simply smiled and gritted her teeth.

Even after a long dinner in Anthony's company, Angelique found herself relieved and more peaceful than she had thought possible as she rode in her carriage back to Pembroke village. Her mind turned from Anthony and Caroline, from Pembroke and Arabella, from Anthony's son, baby Freddie, to her own ward, Sara. She hoped Sara had not yet gone to bed. She and the girl had begun to read together in the evenings, and it was a pleasure she did not wish to forgo.

As her carriage drew through the cottage's front gate, Angelique found herself thinking once more of James Montgomery. She knew he would have been impressed with her calm dealings with her ex-lover and his wife. Angelique did not know why James Montgomery's approval would even occur to her. But she felt an added glow of satisfaction that she had behaved well, and that, if he knew of it, James Montgomery would be proud of her.

The man had changed her life, no matter how short a time he had been in it. He brought her pleasure, even now. He loved her, she was sure, and she loved him. The love between them was a closed circle, a loop that would not end. Whatever the risk to her life as she knew it, she wished that she had told him so. Perhaps she would, the next time they met.

Twenty-nine

WHEN SHE ARRIVED AT HER COTTAGE, ANGELIQUE DID not have long to ruminate over James Montgomery or anything else. As Mrs. Beebe closed the door behind her, she was greeted not by Sara or Lisette but by Titania, a woman who was a force of nature to rival a gale wind at sea.

Titania was tall for a woman, her golden gown completely out of place in Angelique's little rented house. Her deep bronze hair owed nothing to artifice, and while beautiful, the contours of her face were also strong, as were the dark brown of her eyes. Her features were too powerful for real beauty, but lit from within, they glowed with the vigor of her personality, with the glitter of her soul.

She had been on the stage in London for the last ten years, and rumor had it that she had once been a lover of Prinny's. The Prince Regent still came to all her plays, though he slept through most of them.

Titania spoke without preamble, as if they were in the middle of a conversation already. "Your ward has gone to bed. Tired from the drive, country hours, and all that. I spoke to her briefly…she is quite charming. Are you certain she is Geoffrey's girl?"

"There is no doubt of it."

Mrs. Beebe took her cloak. Angelique opened her mouth to ask that tea be served, but Titania had already seen to that and was pouring her friend a cup.

"She is a lovely girl and will grow into a lovely woman," Angelique said. "She is smart and quick to learn. She already loves poetry, and she did not even own a book a week ago."

"You sound very proud of her."

"I have had very little to do with her good qualities, but yes. I am proud of her. And I am happy to see a piece of Geoffrey live on in her."

Titania did not dignify that mention of Angelique's dead husband with a response save for a dissatisfied rumble in her throat, as if she were clearing away something vile. "You've done amazing things with the girl, no mistake. I'm sure she's grateful."

"It is I who am grateful. Sara has brightened my life."

They sat together in the house's tiny parlor, and Angelique sighed with contentment, grateful to be tucked away with her friend. They were often too busy to sit together in London and simply enjoy each other's company.

Titania sipped her own tea. "So you always say, every time you pull someone out of a scrape. You said the same of my first production, *The Tempest*, do you remember? Prinny would never have come to see the play if not for you."

"Anthony had a hand in bringing the Prince to the theater as well as I," Angelique said.

Titania waved away the mention of the Earl of Ravensbrook with one hand. "It was you who financed the piece, and it was you who made a success of it. I would still be working for that moneylender on the boards at Covent Garden if it were not for you."

Angelique drank her tea, embarrassed to have her past good deeds brought up. "How is the current production? Is Pembroke truly standing up as Oberon?"

"And doing a fine job of it, too. I know you think me biased, and I am, but Claridge, my stage manager, has no such scruples and he says that his lordship is a decent actor as well as a fop."

"A decent actor? High praise indeed."

Angelique drew her chair close by the fire and Titania did the same. The weather was warm, but there was something cheerful about an apple wood blaze that Angelique could never resist. The small fire that burned in her rented grate gave off a warmth that seemed to transcend the physical and enter the sublime.

In spite of the fact that she and the Ravensbrook family had made an uneasy peace, her afternoon among Anthony and his family had not been an easy one. She was grateful to be tucked away in this small house, safe from the larger world. She could almost forget her own troubles here, though she knew they were legion.

Several letters had followed her from London, all from Smythe, filled with talk of financial retrenching in the face of lost business associates. She had read them all but had been unable to focus on the problems they presented. Her mind whirled like a dervish, coming up with no solution.

Her reverie was broken by Titania. The actress's voice was grave, in spite of the hint of a smile that still lingered on her lovely face. "Quite a few of the *ton* have come to the country for the amusement of Lord Pembroke's play."

"Is that what you're calling the production?"

"They speak of Arabella and nothing else."

"She is engaged to Pembroke. The banns have been read. Is the protection of his name not enough for them?"

"Indeed not. It may not even be protection enough once they are wed. Hawthorne is putting it about that theirs is an affair of long standing, one that went on behind her husband's back for the whole of her marriage."

Angelique had heard that rumor before, but it still had the power to make her fury rise like a flash fire. She took a deep breath in an effort to keep hold of her temper.

"Pembroke and Anthony have their lawyers dealing with the duke," she said. "But what can lawyers do to save Arabella's reputation? Will she even be received when she returns to London?"

"Perhaps," Titania said. "If Pembroke really does marry her. He is willing, I think. He looked besotted with her in London. The question is, will she marry him?"

"She will. She still loves him, after all this time, and he, her. The wedding is set to take place in three days. It is all but accomplished."

The pain on Titania's face was as vivid as a bruise, pain that her friend could not hide in spite of her ability to act onstage and to dissemble in company. Angelique reached out and took her hand.

It was common knowledge that Titania had been Pembroke's latest mistress and that he had left her for Arabella. Angelique had thought it purely a business matter between them, for she found Pembroke amusing but a man of little substance. She realized now that Titania saw a great deal more in him than Angelique ever had.

Titania took a sip of her cold tea and grimaced. She refreshed her cup, drawing her hand from Angelique's grasp. She took a breath, and a mask of smiling indifference fell into place, hiding all evidence of her distress.

"Hawthorne is lording it over them all as the highest-ranking man in the county, telling tales of Arabella as he goes from house party to house party," Titania said. "Mark my words. The man is a devil who will not be banished at the church door. He thinks Arabella is his to do with as he pleases. I do not see the words spoken by a curate putting a stop to that."

"Nor do I."

Angelique sat with her friend in silence, the only sound the crackling of the fire in the grate. "Perhaps someone will put a bullet through him," she mused.

Titania choked on her tea, setting down the cup as she made an effort to catch her breath.

Angelique went on. "If we manage to save Arabella, who knows what woman will be Hawthorne's victim next? Why do good men stand by and do nothing while a decent woman is ruined?"

"'Valor is melted into curtsies,'" Titania mused, quoting from the Bard's *Much Ado About Nothing*. "Hawthorne does not go long between victims, from all I hear. But there is nothing I can do to help her. As an actress and a member of the demimonde, I am not received myself."

"And I am a notorious widow, bent on seducing good men away from their wives, as all the gossips say." Angelique frowned. "Perhaps I will simply have to shoot him after all."

Titania laughed out loud at that. "Well, you have cause. To change the subject from one unsavory topic to another, I understand that you took dinner with a gentleman of our acquaintance and his lovely wife in Pembroke's house this evening."

"Did Lisette mention that or have you heard it from the village gossips?"

"The *ton* gossips, my dear. When I came offstage to take a bit of cider before my evening meal, it was a favorite topic in the tavern. The whole village is buzzing with it. The only thing as interesting as Hawthorne's disrespectful tattle about Arabella is the fact that people have lighted on you and Anthony as an *on-dit* that is a bit fresher."

"There is very little to it. We met face to face, and everyone behaved well. We were all discommoded to say the least, but we managed not to come to blows. We even made a sort of peace. There was a ghastly moment when I first saw that woman again, but she was graciousness itself. And I have to admit that their child is beautiful. He may be the best reason for me to have lost Anthony."

"My dear, Anthony lost you. He is simply too big a fool to know it. He never appreciated you when you were together, and he still does not have the sense to appreciate you now. Good riddance, I say."

Angelique smiled at her friend's fierce defense of her. She had watched Anthony and Caroline together over dinner. They truly loved each other. She could not begrudge Anthony that. The way he looked at Caroline reminded her of the way that James Montgomery sometimes looked at her.

She smiled at the thought, wondering where he was, how close he was to Malta, and thus to returning home. Titania caught sight of that smile and set her teacup down.

"Ho, ho...well, my dear. And there is a story behind that."

Angelique could not stop herself from smiling more as she poured herself a fresh cup of Darjeeling. "I don't know what you mean."

"That cat-got-the-cream smile of yours...I've only seen it once before, when you first had Anthony Carrington in your web. Might that smile have anything to do with a certain Scottish sea captain I have heard tell of? A certain Captain Jack?"

Angelique laughed out loud to hear the ridiculous false name that Prinny had given him. She set her cup down in case she might spill the lukewarm tea on herself.

"His name is James."

"Much better! Much more dignified."

"Well, I don't know that I would go that far."

"The gossips say he is an Adonis with a brogue, a man of few words but glorious action."

Angelique leaned back against the soft cushions of her chair, smiling into the fire. "I can attest to that. Though with me, he talks quite a bit."

"Well, a lovely change from Anthony on both counts then."

Angelique shot her friend a wry look, and Titania held up both hands in surrender. "You'll never hear a good word from me about your ex-lover, and you know it. He led you a merry chase for ten years."

"That he did."

"A man worth his salt would have the sense to chase you."

Angelique could not stop smiling. "So it seems. James followed me from London all the way to Shropshire."

"Did he indeed?" Titania leaned forward so that her generous cleavage was on display, though sadly, there were no men present to see it. "And where is this paragon of manly virtue and good sense now?"

"Somewhere between Gibraltar and Malta, I imagine."

Titania looked shocked, and Angelique laughed out loud. "He is a man of the sea, after all."

"When does he come back?"

"In a month."

"You should be done here by then."

"I'll be done here within the week. I'll see Arabella safely wed, and then I will go home."

Angelique did not mention her business troubles and the damage Hawthorne had done to her shipping contacts. She would keep producing plays as long as she had the lucre, so there was no need to alarm Titania about Hawthorne's attack on her life. At least, not yet. Arabella was enough to worry about for the moment.

Titania set her cup down, and Angelique thought that her friend would return to her rooms at the inn, leaving her to sleep. But a shadow passed over the beautiful green of Titania's eyes. Angelique felt a frisson of fear as her friend took her hand.

"I have news that will be hard for you to hear. Victor Carlyle was shot and killed the night before his wedding."

"Dear God," Angelique breathed. "Who would do such a thing?"

"I can think of any number of foes. Victor was not one for making friends, but he collected enemies by the dozen."

Angelique felt her mind go numb. Victor was larger than life. She had trouble believing that he was dead. She simply could not wrap her mind around it.

"He was good to me."

"I know. You have always said so. That was why I wanted to be the one to tell you, before you heard the news from some more malicious source. He tweaked the wrong nose at last."

Titania pressed her hand before rising to don her cloak. When Angelique moved to ring for Mrs. Beebe, Titania waved her away. "No, let the poor woman sleep. There is no need to rouse her on my account."

Angelique escorted her friend to the door, thinking of Victor Carlyle and of how he had been her lifeline during the dark days after Anthony left. Victor had been a fool and a blackguard, but she had cared for him.

"So Victor's fiancée is unmarried still," Titania said. "A narrow escape for the young miss, if you ask me."

"Victor would have made her life a misery," Angelique said.

Titania did not speak again but pressed a light kiss to Angelique's cheek before she climbed into her carriage. Her unofficial crest was emblazoned in silver on the lacquered door, the symbol of her company, the Bard's quill pen.

Angelique closed the house and banked the fire in the sitting room. Before she went up the narrow staircase to her bedroom, she remembered the teachings of her mother. She lit a candle for Victor Carlyle and said a prayer for his soul, on the off chance that anyone was listening.

Thirty

JAMES HAD TO PUSH HIS HORSE IN ORDER TO MAKE HIS way to the wilds of Derbyshire before Midsummer's Eve. He was a Scottish baronet's son and no stranger to traveling north from London, but he had always traveled home by ship, never by horse. To be confined to the vagaries of land travel made him chafe against its limitations, but Derbyshire was landlocked, so he rode his rented gelding north.

He carried in his pocket a star sapphire that he had purchased in Mayfair before leaving London. The ring was a delicate platinum band, very plain but for the five-carat stone it bore. Come all the way from India, that sapphire was the only jewel in any shop he had entered that came close to matching the deep blue of Angelique's eyes.

Angelique loved him, he was sure of it. It might take him a week or two to wear her down, but in the end, she would surrender.

She would be his.

James was not certain why he was so confident. Angelique was the least biddable woman ever to be born on the face of God's earth. She would guard her life and her property like a tigress and would fight against marriage and the laws that would make all her property his. James had a solution to that, too, once she deigned to listen to him.

Though he loved her, he had not known her long. But did one ever come to fully know a woman like her? She was a mystery that revealed only as much of herself as she saw fit in any given moment. Angelique might never reveal all of herself to him, but James knew that he would rather spend his life coaxing glimpses out of her. Life with Angelique would never be dull.

What marriage would mean to his career, he could not say. Franklin and his wife had shown him that love and the sea could live together, but he was not certain he could leave Angelique for months on end. There was something about her that drew him in and held him. Though he had tried to escape her pull over and over again, she brought him back to her as inexorably as the moon brought in the tide.

James arrived in the small village of Pembroke to find it overrun with Londoners, just as Carlyle had said. He saw actors eating their lunch on the green and well-dressed ladies perusing the wares of the shops along the village high street. He did not stop at the inn, for he had no doubt that it was filled to capacity and had been for the last week.

A lady he had met at a ball in London smiled and nodded to him as he passed. He tipped his hat to her as he rode on, though he could not remember her name. He hoped Angelique did not listen to village gossip.

He would hate to have her hear of his coming before he had seen her himself.

He turned his horse toward the cottage Angelique had rented. He had remembered the need for a ring, so he had not set off at dawn after leaving Carlyle in his cups as he had planned. He went instead to see Mr. Smythe, who had been very accommodating once again, giving him Angelique's location as well as letters of business for her to read. Smythe had seemed very distracted, almost worried when James had come to see him in his office in London. Of course, had James been tied to a desk all day and night, he might seem nervous, too.

But something told James it was more than that, and when he pressed him, the other man gave way and told him all. The Duke of Hawthorne was not a rival for Angelique's affections after all, it seemed. But he still needed killing.

James pushed away the dark thoughts he had brought with him from London, for he had a plan and would defeat Hawthorne at his own game, whether Angelique wanted his help or not.

Thinking of how spitting mad she would be when he stood up to defend her left a satisfied smile on James's face as he dismounted and opened the blue wooden gate to Angelique's cottage. From the outside, the stone walls revealed nothing of the beauty they held. The flower garden alone made him stop and take in the scent of honeysuckle and roses. The cottage itself looked like a place that had been set under an enchantment, its clean, whitewashed walls and thatched roof like a house in a fairy story.

He knocked at the front door after tying his horse to the post outside. The gelding began to eat the greenery closest to the house, a bit of ivy and bramble that hopefully the gardener would not miss. He had no time to deal with his mount, however, for instead of the housekeeper, he was greeted by Lisette, Angelique's lady's maid.

"Captain Montgomery." Lisette smiled, her light-blue eyes taking him in with a glint of mischief. "I thought we might be seeing you again, but I did not expect you until we returned to London."

"I had a change of plans. I understand that the Countess of Devonshire is here in Pembroke."

"And you came hundreds of miles to woo her and make her your own."

James weighed his options and decided not to lie. "Yes."

Lisette's smile widened but she did not let him in. "You are welcome, but you cannot come in. The house is tiny and the mistress will know you're here. You must surprise her at the play this evening. She is too busy to see you until then anyway."

"Surprise her among her fancy friends? I suppose I might do that. But the inn is full."

"No worry, Captain. We hold a room at the inn for Mr. Smythe. He has letters for the lady, and she expects him within the week. You may take his room."

"I have the letters with me."

"*Très bien.*" Lisette's smile was the warmest he had ever seen it. "Madame has been a bit down since you left, Captain. She is a strong woman, but like all women, she needs a good man."

James knew very well what Angelique would make of that assessment, but he did not correct the maid. "I reckon I'm good enough."

Lisette perused him from his auburn hair in its queue to the dust on his boots and shrugged one shoulder in her Gallic way. "You will do, Captain."

He laughed as she closed the door in his face.

∽

Angelique spent the morning in Pembroke Village while Sara worked on her reading with Lisette and her embroidery under Mrs. Beebe's careful eye. Angelique enjoyed spending time with her ward, but she was restless. Seeing Anthony with Caroline, and Arabella reunited with her Pembroke, had made her hunger for James Montgomery in the dark reaches of the night.

Usually, she kept an iron grip on her imagination, even in her dreams, but last night she could not sleep for remembering his touch on her skin, the way his calloused hands had felt on her naked flesh. She had spent the night in a torment of fiery memory only to fall asleep toward dawn to dream of him as well.

The dream was still with her as she sat and watched the rehearsal for Titania's play. She could not hear much of what was spoken onstage, for her mind was filled with the memory of James Montgomery's voice, the Scottish cadence that came to his lips whenever he was lost to the pleasure that she and her body brought him.

She was lost in thoughts of him when a shadow fell over her where she sat on the village green. It was almost noon, so the shadow blocked the welcome warmth of the sun. Angelique looked up, drawn out of her reverie, to find Anthony Carrington standing beside her chair.

"I do not understand why you have come," Anthony said.

He had never been one to mince words. That had not troubled her when they had been together, for she had been certain that his terse manner had hidden a depth of feeling. She realized now that she had been right on that score, but those feelings had simply not been directed at her.

He had wanted her, though. She wondered idly if he still wanted her now, if he had approached her with rudeness simply to engage her in conversation. Anthony had never been one for games, but perhaps that had changed. He was a man, after all. She turned in her chair to face him, shading her eyes from the sun beneath her lace-trimmed bonnet.

"Indeed," she said. "How kind of you to inquire, my lord. I am an investor in this production. If you object to my presence, feel free to remove yourself and your wife at once."

He did not answer with a snide comment of his own. Instead, he drew a chair up and sat down beside her. "How did we come to this?" Anthony asked.

Silence lengthened between them. The actors onstage kept up with their antics. The rustics were producing the play within the play, Angelique's favorite moment in Shakespeare's romantic foolery. She found that she could not listen to the actors on the boards, though that scene never failed to make her laugh.

She was not miserable as she should have been sitting next to the man she had once thought was the love of her life. She had clung to that notion long after she had lost him, long after he had moved on with another. She realized now that she had given that idea up when she had first met James Montgomery.

"I do not know," Angelique said. "I mean you and yours no harm. I am willing to begin again."

He took her hand in his. For the first time in years, there was no heat between them and no rancor. As she turned to look into his eyes, she found that his deep brown gaze no longer had the power to wound her.

That knowledge made her generous and more forgiving of Anthony Carrington than she had ever been. She knew as she looked into her old lover's eyes that he would never wield power over her again. All that was left was the memory of the love she had once borne him. She discovered, much to her surprise, that the memory was sweet.

"Peace then." She let her hand rest in his, waiting patiently until he let her go.

"Peace."

They sat in silence side by side, her hands folded demurely in her lap, as proper as if she had never been his mistress at all. She felt the eyes of the *ton* on them, as well as the gazes of actors who had stepped off the stage, and she suppressed a smile.

Perhaps she might single-handedly replace all the evil gossip about Arabella with gossip of her own. Within the half hour, every lady and lord in the village would be convinced that the Earl of Ravensbrook had come to Derbyshire not to support Pembroke but to take her up as a lover once more. She felt laughter threaten to rise from beneath her breast and she tamped it down.

"I wonder that I find you here alone. I understand you are quite fond of a young sea captain, the gentleman I met at the Prince Regent's card party. Captain Jack, I believe his name was."

"Do not let him hear you call him that."

"He has heard me call him that already."

Angelique smiled. She no longer wanted this man, but she was surprised as well as gratified to discover that Anthony had kept such close tabs on her love life.

"Captain Montgomery is away at the moment on the sea. I am here alone."

"By choice," Anthony said.

"Yes. Everything I do is by my own choice now."

Anthony opened his mouth only to close it again. Awkwardness rose between them, and Angelique knew that it was for her to dispel it. She bore this man no ill will. She had a life of her own apart from him. She could afford to be generous, in spite of all that she had lost.

"It is forgiven," she said. "If I had anything to forgive you for, Anthony, it is long past. We may let it rest there and bury it."

He did not speak another word but raised her gloved hand to his lips. He stood and bowed formally, as if they sat in her mother's drawing room.

She knew that she was truly over him when she was not even tempted to mention her troubles with Hawthorne. Anthony had steered her into safe waters many times during her early days as a woman of business. He had helped her, and nurtured her, and would have helped her now. But she did not ask him.

He left her alone once more in the warmth of the early-afternoon light. The rehearsal was winding down. Angelique had missed most of the last act, but she had seen enough to know that the show would be a hit.

She kept her eyes politely on the stage even as she listened to the swell of whispers rising around and behind her. She and Anthony made excellent fodder for the gossip mill. She was relieved to be at Arabella's service in that small way. Distracting the gossipmongers from her friend gave the day a sense of satisfaction that it had lacked before. Angelique supposed she had Anthony to thank for that.

She caught Titania's eye where she stood in full costume at the foot of the makeshift stage. The actress offered her an inscrutable smile and gave her a wink.

Thirty-one

WITH ANTHONY GONE, ANGELIQUE STAYED SEATED beneath the trees of the green. She had begun to contemplate how well she and Anthony had learned to handle themselves with each other, and how the fact that he had never loved her no longer had the power to tear her heart out. Every time that old loop of thought rose into the forefront of her mind, the thought of a broad-shouldered Scot with auburn hair replaced it almost at once.

She did not have long to consider this, because Hawthorne loomed over her in the next moment like an ogre in a fairy story. A sick, sinking sense of dread drained into her stomach, but she forced herself to meet his eyes anyway.

So much for finding a haven in sleepy Derbyshire villages. Give her Shropshire and the banks of the Severn any day.

"I am surprised to find you blithely wiling away the hours in Derbyshire when your shipping business burns behind you in London."

Angelique straightened her back, crooking her neck

to the side so that she might give the duke a mocking smile. "Indeed, Your Grace, I do not have as dark an opinion of my business as you do."

"Then you do not know the facts."

"I gather you've already done your worst."

"Then you have deluded yourself twice."

He stared down at her as if he might skewer her on the end of the blade concealed in his black lacquered walking stick. The silver knob gleamed in his gloved hand, and she wished she had a weapon of her own.

Of course, she did.

Her face slid into the lines of her old seductive mask, the one she usually kept for Prinny's benefit. "We might come to a different arrangement," she said.

The duke's gray eyes narrowed, taking on a calculating gleam, as if she were a sum of figures he was trying to add up. "Our current arrangement suits me fine."

"My business is gone, unless I sell my cotton to you, yes?"

She shrugged her shoulder the way her mother always had, so that the shoulder of her gown slipped just a little to reveal a bit more skin.

"It is."

"Perhaps if I were to draw the Earl of Ravensbrook into our discussion, you might see things differently."

Hawthorne seemed to pale in the sunlight. He swallowed hard, and she knew she had struck her mark. She had no arrangement with Ravensbrook, but Hawthorne did not know that.

"You would hide behind your old lover then?"

"To keep from doing business with you, I would dance with the devil himself."

Something caught Hawthorne's eye beyond her, and his focus shifted. "Think on that a while longer, Lady Devonshire. Ravensbrook might be able to help save your business affairs, but he won't give a tinker's damn for Devonshire's bastard daughter. Think long and hard on what might happen to her if you defy me again."

He smiled then and Angelique felt the bile rise in her throat. "Remember our bargain. You keep your shipping, some of it, and I get Arabella."

"I made no such bargain."

"I followed you from London. She's here, and you led me to her."

Hawthorne was gone, his long strides crossing the green, leaving her as abruptly as he had come. She had so many reasons to curse him: the fact that he had called her bluff about her imagined alliance with Anthony, that he had ruined her shipping in the first place, that he had used her to find Arabella without her knowing it. Of course, he might have heard of Pembroke and Arabella's time in Derbyshire from some other source, but his accusation gnawed at her like acid on her skin.

She did not have time to think of the wrongs Hawthorne had done her, or of ways to thwart him, for Arabella had wandered down from the great house and was standing alone on the green. And now, Hawthorne was with her.

Angelique moved quickly and came to her friend's side. She wanted to step in front of her, to block Hawthorne's view of Arabella, but she had the distinct impression that to do so would only draw him deeper into the confrontation. For all their mocking exchange only minutes before, his desire for Arabella went beyond power. He might push her aside and carry Arabella off in front of the *ton* and the village both.

She cursed under her breath, wondering where the devil Anthony was now that he could be of some use.

Arabella was intent on the duke and barely nodded to Angelique. Hawthorne, far from casual about his designs on Arabella, seemed set to devour her friend in one bite where they stood. Angelique could not tell if the gleam in his eye was twisted lust or some kind of true madness. Arabella did not seem flummoxed by it, but spoke as calmly as if she were out for a stroll on a beautiful summer day and had come across an unwelcome acquaintance, not the man who had tried more than once to destroy her life.

"I thank you, Your Grace, for both your kind words and for your concern for my well-being," Arabella said. "As you see, I traveled to Derbyshire without mishap. No brigands greeted me along the road. I arrived quite unharmed."

Angelique blinked at the veiled mention of one of the duke's early threats, that he would have Arabella killed along the roadside as she traveled through Yorkshire to his family seat if she did not toe the line and marry him.

"What good fortune," the duke said. He opened his mouth to speak again, but to Angelique's shock, Arabella interrupted him. Clearly her friend had grown claws and was learning how to use them.

"Indeed, Your Grace. The roads from London to Derbyshire are a good deal safer than the roads in Yorkshire. I stopped here, and I will stay here for the rest of my life."

Angelique was so intent on watching her friend face down her adversary that she did not see or hear Pembroke approach until he came to stand beside Arabella. To Angelique's ears, Pembroke's friendly hail-fellow-well-met tone sounded forced. "Good afternoon, Hawthorne. What brings you to Derbyshire?" Pembroke asked. "Come to see our production, I suppose. I had no idea that you had a taste for Shakespeare."

Hawthorne smiled then, looking down at Arabella as if Pembroke had not spoken. Angelique felt her shudder. She took Arabella's arm as if to help her walk away, but it seemed her friend would not back down and leave Hawthorne in possession of the field. It looked as if Arabella, angry and adamant for the first time since Angelique had known her, was in the mood to confront him head on.

"Hawthorne, it was good of you to come," Arabella said, addressing the duke as a man would, as an equal. "But once you have signed over my property, our business together is done."

"But you have no property rights on the Duchy of Hawthorne," he said. "As soon as you marry another man—this Sunday the banns said"—Hawthorne looked to Pembroke then raised one inquiring eyebrow— "the Hawthorne lands revert back to the estate."

Arabella did not bow beneath his contempt; she did not blink in the face of his implacable will. It seemed she had found her backbone and that she had a will of her own. "You will turn over my money to me directly," Arabella said. "And then you will go back to London, and I will never see you again."

Angelique held her breath, certain that such a

blatant challenge would send the duke over the edge
of reason, but Hawthorne only smiled. "What a
charming story. You sound almost as if you believe it.
But I will not let you go."

Anthony chose that moment to appear from
wherever he had been hiding, and his young wife,
Caroline, followed a step behind, bringing their son,
baby Freddie, in her arms. Angelique wanted to
mutter, "Well, it's about bloody time you showed
up," but she held her tongue.

Freddie, like his father, seemed not at all intimidated
by the foreboding duke. He took one look at the man
before dismissing him, turning to lay his head on his
mother's shoulder, where he promptly fell asleep.

Anthony Carrington did not smile nor did he
speak, but he stepped between Arabella and the Duke
of Hawthorne, staring the man down as if he were a
member of the French cavalry, as if Hawthorne were a
man he meant to kill. Caroline stood at her husband's
back, cradling Freddie, flanking Arabella. Angelique
noticed an equally cold assessment going on behind
Caroline's eyes, as if she might draw a dagger and
carve the duke up like a Christmas goose. Angelique
wondered for the first time if all the rumors about the
Countess of Ravensbrook being addicted to knife play
were actually true.

Anthony's tone was cool, but his calm took nothing
of the menace from his voice. "As charming as it is
to see you, Hawthorne, I know that you will not be
at liberty to attend the performance," he said. "I do
hope you managed to bring the paperwork we spoke
of when I was last in London. The papers that the

duchess needs to sign in order to accept a lump sum in lieu of her widow's portion before she marries."

Arabella swayed a little, and Angelique's grip stayed firm on her arm. Pembroke drew close as if to shield her from the piercing dagger of Hawthorne's gaze.

Hawthorne ignored them all and kept his attention focused on Anthony. "Indeed, Ravensbrook. It is kind of you to mention our last meeting. I have the papers with me. I will send them up to Pembroke House with my man as soon as it is convenient."

Angelique blinked as the men around her took in this absurd statement as if they actually believed he spoke the truth. She opened her mouth to challenge him, but Anthony shot her a quick glance of reproof and she fell silent. Surely these intelligent men knew better than to think that Hawthorne would give up so easily and let his chosen prey go.

❦

Angelique spent the afternoon at Arabella's side and watched as Hawthorne's man did indeed bring papers to the house, and as Arabella signed them, accepting the money he settled on her in lieu of her dower portion. Angelique tried in vain to catch Anthony's eye, for surely he was not naïve enough to believe that the likes of the Duke of Hawthorne could be dispatched with the flick of a quill.

Pembroke surprised her even more, however, when he signed a second document turning over all of Arabella's wealth to his wife-to-be. For the first time in her life, Angelique met a woman who would keep her money intact after her wedding vows were spoken.

Angelique pored over the document, looking for a flaw or a loophole, but found none. She wished Smythe was in the village, that he might go over it as well, putting his lawyer's mind to the task. Anthony looked on, disapproving, and Angelique knew he had counseled Pembroke against such a gesture.

Angelique met Pembroke's eyes with a new respect. "You let her keep her money."

"Yes," Pembroke said. "I don't want her for her money. I want her for my wife."

Angelique felt a lump rise into her throat, and she swallowed it down. Arabella took Pembroke's hand, raised herself on her toes, and kissed him gently. "Thank you, my love. It is the best wedding present a woman could ask for."

Anthony harrumphed and turned his back on the scene. Caroline went to his side and touched his arm once, and his look of censure softened. Still, he was not best pleased. Angelique swallowed her laughter, if not her smile. She could see the wheels in her old lover's head turning: If men started letting their wives keep their own property, what was the world coming to?

Angelique left for her cottage to dress for the play, musing over the wonder she had just witnessed. If the Earl of Pembroke broke with law and precedent and let his wife keep her own money, perhaps Angelique might make the same arrangement, if James Montgomery ever offered for her.

Why she kept harping on thoughts of marriage when she had barely known the man a month, she was not sure. Still, the thought lingered as long as the midsummer twilight.

Thirty-two

ANGELIQUE STOOD STARING INTO THE FULL-LENGTH
looking glass that Lisette had insisted they pack in
one of the three trunks her groom Sam had driven up
from London in the baggage cart. Her midnight blue
gown gleamed in the lamplight. The sun still coming
in through the bedroom window caught the sheen of
silver along the bodice and the hem.

"You are a vision, madame."

"Thank you, Lisette." Angelique turned, taking in
the curve of her hip beneath the silk, watching the fall
of the bodice pulled tight over her generous breasts.
"You don't think it too much for the country?"

"*Mais non, madame.* I say, let us give them an
eyeful," Lisette said.

Angelique laughed, her eyes meeting her maid's in
the glass. "Indeed, why not?"

She walked to the village green accompanied by
Sam. She knew better than to walk out alone, though
a part of her longed to. With Hawthorne lingering
somewhere nearby, she would be a fool to take a
chance like that, even in this quiet, bucolic place.

Sara had asked to come down to see the play, and Angelique had been forced to refuse. She could not keep an eye on the girl herself, and with Hawthorne loose in the village, she could not vouch for her safety. Sara had gotten that stubborn, wall-eyed look that Geoffrey had often worn, and she had glowered even more when Angelique told her she looked like her father.

Angelique met Arabella and Caroline walking toward her beneath the great trees before the stage, and Angelique nodded to Sam, who took a few steps back. He moved a discreet distance away, but she knew that he would keep his eye on her, his pistol under his coat. He had served under her father's command on the *Diane* many years ago, and now in his retirement from the sea, Sam watched over her.

"Well met, Lady Devonshire," Caroline said, shifting baby Freddie on her hip. "I hope you will sit with us. The vultures are circling, and we need another woman with her wits about her to keep them off."

"Nonsense," Arabella said. "There are a few people here from London, but they have come to see the play. They don't care a fig about me."

Arabella smiled as if she had not a care in the world. She glowed with the certainty of a woman in love that all would indeed be well.

Angelique exchanged a look with Caroline over Arabella's head. They both could hear the whispers. It was time to give the *ton* something else to talk about.

Angelique smiled warmly at her old enemy, going so far as to lean close and kiss her cheek. If Caroline was startled by her sudden show of loving kindness, she did not show it. Anthony's wife did not even blink as she kissed Angelique back as if they were French peasants. Angelique heard the tide of whispers rise almost to a crescendo, and she smiled.

The Carlton House set, along with the rest of the London elite, considered the two of them to be mortal enemies. All knew how they had fought each other for the love of Lord Ravensbrook. Caroline had won that war, and the fact that she now stood casually and calmly so close to her old rival caused a great stir of gossip. That news, on top of the talk of Angelique and Anthony's meeting that afternoon, would go a long way to distracting the poison mongers from Arabella altogether.

Angelique walked on one side of the oblivious Arabella as Caroline paced beside her friend on the other. Like a guard of honor, they escorted Arabella to her seat before the stage, flanking her on either side. Angelique wondered where the devil Anthony was. It was not like him to leave his wife alone even for the space of fifteen minutes. They might use him to fan the flames of scuttlebutt.

Angelique, never one to shrink in the face of public notoriety, reached across Arabella and took baby Freddie onto her lap. The baby cooed and cried out with joy to see her, wrapping his fat fists in the necklace at her throat. She pried her diamonds out of his grasp, turning to smile over the assembled company as if holding her ex-lover's child was the most natural thing in the world. The tide of whispers rose again in a great wave, and Caroline laughed under her breath.

Anthony appeared in that moment, stepping out of the public house where he had been speaking with Pembroke. Like his wife, Lord Ravensbrook did not shrink from gossip, but neither did he acknowledge it. Anthony strode across the village green as if he were Mars crossing a field of war. He looked neither right nor left but sat down beside his wife, kissing her on the lips for all to see.

An audible gasp rose from the assembled ladies, and the local villagers applauded to see the earl greet his wife with such open affection. Anthony did not acknowledge the approbation of the locals, but Caroline smiled and waved to them as if she were a queen greeting her court.

Angelique laughed under her breath, keeping her focus on baby Freddie. Anthony did not look at her even to glower at her. She was disappointed, hoping that leading the Londoners to think the three of them had begun some kind of bizarre *ménage à trois* would throw Hawthorne's destructive plans into complete disarray. No one would care what a widow might do, a staid widow who showed no sign of wildness save that she loved the Earl of Pembroke. As colorful an *on-dit* as a fallen widow made, a torrid affair between Anthony, Angelique, and Caroline was far tastier.

As she listened to the talk all around them, Angelique feigned fascination with the baby on her lap, who had started babbling at her in earnest as if he were imparting knowledge of great import. He really was quite handsome and had more charm than any baby on earth should. If he played his cards right, when he was grown, Freddie might rule the realm with a smile and a wink without half trying. The House of Lords would never stand against him. Prinny had better look to his crown.

In the next moment, a tall, well-built man came to sit at Angelique's side. She felt the length of his shadow pass over her in the torchlight, and she knew before she turned that James Montgomery had come back. She took in the smell of the sea on his clothes, along with the sweet smell of cedar, and felt for one blessed moment that she had come home.

She gave him a sideways glance and a smile. If it was possible, he was more beautiful than she remembered. She felt as if it had been longer than two weeks since she had seen him. His long auburn hair was tied at the nape of his neck with military precision, and his Royal Navy uniform gleamed dark blue and gold in the slanting sunlight.

Aware of the company around them, and not wanting to fully acknowledge their relationship in public, Angelique nodded to him somewhat coolly, raising one eyebrow. "Good evening, Captain. I see that you have left the sea behind yet again. I thought the tide was turning and that you must needs be gone."

"The tide is always turning, my lady. Wait twelve hours, and it will turn again."

His voice was deep and sweet, like mulled cider with honey mixed in it. Angelique shivered against her will at the sound of it, and she wished all those around them, her friends and foes alike, might disappear and leave them alone.

She had been so worried about Arabella for the last weeks, even more worried than she was about her own shipping business. But with James Montgomery present, all her recent worries, Hawthorne included, were momentarily swept away.

A wave of pleasure in the sound of his voice rose to swamp her, and she clutched baby Freddie closer. The child frowned at her but did not cry to return to his mother. Instead, he settled close to her ample breast and leaned his head against her.

Angelique spoke to him, keeping her voice low so that no one else might hear. "Shall I introduce you as Captain Jack of Trafalgar fame?"

He laughed softly, the heat of his arm close to her body. She breathed deeply to try to stave off the heat that rose from within to consume her.

Arabella gave her a questioning look, but Angelique retreated, ignoring both her and James in favor of the baby on her lap. She found in that moment that she did not want to introduce him as just another lover she had taken, another lover she would one day discard. James Montgomery was different, and sitting there so close to her friends, she saw at once how true that was.

Caroline peered down the row to smile warmly at their new acquaintance. Though Anthony had met James at Prinny's card party, he managed to ignore him completely.

James, however, refused to be ignored by anyone. "Forgive the Countess of Devonshire," he said. "She is a noble savage with no manners but those used to seduce a man."

It was all Angelique could do not to laugh out loud at that. She turned her gaze on him but found that he was focused on Arabella, the center of their little group.

"Allow me to present myself," he went on. "I am Captain James Montgomery, formerly of His Majesty's Navy, at your service."

Arabella's warmth was palpable even from where Angelique sat. Her friend was one of the kindest, most loving women Angelique had ever known. Angelique might have brought a guttersnipe to her table, and Arabella would have welcomed him with open arms.

"Good evening, Captain Montgomery," Arabella said. "Any friend of Angelique's is welcome in our circle. I am Arabella Hawthorne, and there you see the Earl and Countess of Ravensbrook."

Anthony had the civility to nod, though he did not spare a glance for James. Caroline seemed of the same opinion as Arabella, that any fine-looking man brought around by Angelique was worth welcoming. "Good evening, Captain. What brings you to Derbyshire?"

Angelique turned her head to face James as baby Freddie made another grab for her necklace. She drew the diamonds from the baby's fat fingers once again, as her tongue loosened just a little. No doubt her eyes were dancing with pleasure, but her voice was relatively smooth. "Indeed, Captain. What brings you here?"

James Montgomery smiled and the setting sun seemed to surround her, driving away the shadows of twilight. "Why, Lady Devonshire, like the rest of London, I am here to see the play."

She swore under her breath at that ridiculous, blatant lie. Freddie looked at her questioningly, but fortunately Arabella and the rest of the company did not hear her lapse in civility, for the play had begun. James did hear her swear, and she turned her shoulder to him in an effort to keep a straight face as the warmth of his chuckle spread out over the skin of her bare shoulder like warm honey.

She was fortunate in that the production was a good one, for she could almost keep her mind and thoughts focused on Titania, Oberon, and the young lovers. The rustics were a welcome relief as they always were when she saw this play staged, and she found herself laughing as heartily as she ever had in the past. As she listened, though, James's laughter filled her ears, and she found herself distracted from the production, falling silent as she listened to the music of that laughter.

She caressed the baby in her lap in an effort to keep her mind from the beautiful man beside her. Freddie snuggled close, his eyes drooping a little as a bit of drool escaped his lips and stained the front of her gown. She was distracted again by the thought of the apoplexy Lisette would experience when she discovered the lingering stain.

If someone had told her even two months before that not only would she have adopted her husband's bastard daughter as her own, but that she would be cradling Anthony and Caroline Carrington's child in front of all the *ton*, she would have mocked them for a fool. But here she sat, a baby clutching her close, a warm, heavy burden in her arms, drool running down her breast, James Montgomery at her side. As odd a picture as this little tableau painted, she found that she would not change one moment of it.

The play ended, and Pembroke and Titania took three ovations, bowing to the crowd with smiles wreathing their faces. Angelique knew that word of this production would spread through the north, and that their bookings in Leeds, Manchester, and York would be filled to capacity within a se'nnight.

Shakespeare was always a hit in the north, as long as one stayed far away from the history plays. This comedy would take the northern towns by storm.

The sun had almost set and the local villagers had lit the Midsummer bonfire. Angelique stood to walk with her friends to see it, enjoying James Montgomery's presence as he clung to her side like a burr.

The sight of the Scottish sea captain no doubt had already confused the gossips all around them. Angelique wondered if any of the fiction she had hoped to create regarding herself and Anthony's family had been able to hold at all. She felt the weight of James's regard like hands on her skin, and she hoped that for once in his life, he would hold his tongue until they were alone.

James dogged her steps as she and Arabella walked with Caroline toward the Midsummer celebration. Their party had grown now, with Anthony flanking the women on one side and James Montgomery on the other. Baby Freddie, fully awake again, was cooing at James as at a long-lost friend. With a barely civil nod, Anthony moved to Angelique's side and lifted his son into his arms.

James took the opportunity to draw closer to her, taking her into the shadows with him. He held her a step back from the others, and Angelique watched as the rest of her escort moved away into the crowd of villagers toward the fire. Music was playing, and laughter filled the rising darkness.

Arabella seemed safe, for Hawthorne had not shown his face once all evening, but Angelique was not sure he would stay gone. He was a menace and a bully, and like a dog with a bone, he was unlikely to let either Arabella or herself go.

"Angelique, I must speak with you." James pitched his voice low, the sound of it making her shiver yet again.

"Here?"

A muscle in his jaw leaped, but that was the only evidence of his irritation.

"Not in front of this country village. Come with me."

He took her arm and drew her into the darkness of the trees that lined the green. Sam stepped forward as if to stop them, but she waved him back. Angelique knew that she should not follow James into the darkened wood. All the *ton* would see her leave with him, and her well-placed gossip suggesting that she and Anthony had come together again, and brought Caroline into their bed, would vanish like so much smoke.

But then she looked into James's eyes and knew that she no longer cared what the damned *ton* thought. Arabella would be married on the morrow. Let Pembroke keep her safe, since he was sworn to do it.

With her hand in James Montgomery's, standing on that village green in the middle of nowhere, Angelique realized that there was no place she would rather be.

She knew that she was being a fool. Arabella might be safe from Hawthorne, but Angelique herself was not. Still, her business troubles seemed very far away. As she took in the scent of James Montgomery's skin, the rest of the world receded into the distance, Hawthorne included.

Angelique let him take her hand and followed him into the woods.

Thirty-three

HE HAD FOUND HER IN THE MIDDLE OF NOWHERE IN Derbyshire, just as her man of business had said he would. Instead of running into the unknown on the word of a drunkard like Carlyle, James had spoken with Smythe as well, who had a great deal to say about a certain duke who had threatened her livelihood, cutting her off from her cotton suppliers and from the mills who bought her wares in the North.

Just the thought of it made James's blood boil. He had thought to call the bastard out, but when he inquired for the duke at Hawthorne House in town, he had discovered that he was not there.

Like the rest of Angelique's so-called friends, save Prinny himself, Hawthorne had gone to Derbyshire to see a play.

The play wasn't bad, which was a pleasant surprise. But James was tired from travel, and tired of thinking of all Angelique hadn't bothered to tell him. When he saw her again, looking luscious in a dark blue gown, sitting only a few seats down from her ex-lover

Ravensbrook, and Hawthorne hiding only God knew where in the shadows, he found himself annoyed.

The sun had set completely, and night had risen from the ground, filling in the spaces between the trees. James heard other couples slipping away from the Midsummer fire, seeking privacy and pleasure in the dark.

Angelique did not speak, but stood with him beneath the spreading branches of a great oak and let him move close beside her.

The moon was rising, but it was a mere sliver in the dark. In the distance, he could see the blaze of the great bonfire shedding its light into the copse of trees. The light was far away. James stood with her, safely wrapped in shadows.

"I am happy to see you," she said.

He pulled her toward him, his arms light around her, his hands resting on her hips. The sweet scent of her orchid perfume filled his nostrils, and the warmth of her breasts rose against his chest. Despite the wool of his clothes and the silk of hers, he was as aware of her as if she were naked. He took a deep breath and drank her in.

"We need to talk, Angelique," he said for the second time that night, trying to keep his mind on the business at hand, on the things she had not told him, of the dangers she had faced, alone, until he discovered them.

"I need to go back," she said.

"To Anthony Carrington? Have you and the earl arranged an assignation for later tonight, once his wife and child are safely abed?"

He heard the jealousy in his own voice and the idiocy of his own words. She did not taunt him with them though, but answered honestly, as they both had agreed to in her bedroom the first time he had made love to her.

"I am not meeting Anthony," she said. "It was over between us long ago."

He relaxed, the muscles of his shoulder beginning to unknot. She raised her fingers behind his head, where she began to toy with the ribbon that bound his hair.

"I take only one lover at a time," she said.

"Is that so?" He was breathless. She pressed the curves of her beautiful body against him, and he shuddered with sudden need.

"You are my only lover," she said.

"At the moment," he quipped, trying to stay in control of his lust, in a vain effort to keep the upper hand. If he had ever had the upper hand with this woman, he had never known it.

"You're the only man I want," she said. "You were gone for weeks, and I wanted no other."

"Neither did I."

"No nubile girls in Aberdeen? No sloe-eyed beauties in Malta?"

"I did not go to Malta," he answered. "I came looking for you."

He kept his touch gentle but inexorable as he drew her even closer, and turned until her back was against the oak tree. Her lips were soft beneath his as he kissed her, feather light, as he explored the contours of her mouth. He dropped kisses along the edge of her lips, to her jaw, down her throat. He pressed her back against the tree, and the bark no doubt dug into her back. He tried to stop, he tried to rein his lust in, but his need for her rose like a flash tide, a wave of desire that threatened to make him forget everything else.

Her skin was like heated silk beneath his fingertips as they slipped beneath the scooped neck of her gown, delving beneath her stays and shift until he found the soft curve of her breast. He stroked her then, very lightly, a caress that was intended to be more tempting, more intoxicating than if his hand had tried to devour her. It must have worked, because she opened her mouth beneath his.

James dove in, drawing her tongue into a slow dance with his. He was careful with her, gentle, as if she was made of spun sugar and might melt if he heated her too quickly. But he could feel his control stretched tight, a thin thread that might break at any moment. Angelique began to tremble, and she pulled away, turning her head to the side to escape him.

James felt cut off, adrift. His breathing was harsh in his own ears. He remembered where they were then. He knew that he did not want to make love to her up against the trunk of an oak tree in the middle of nowhere in the middle of Derbyshire.

He stopped moving his fingers against the softness of her flesh, but they stayed within her bodice, as if in rebellion, as if they did not want to let her go. James drew his hands away from her and found they were shaking, as he was.

"I didn't mean to molest you in the woods," he said.

Her sultry laugh made his blood heat a second time. He did not want to leave her, but he took one step back.

"You need to tell me about Hawthorne," James said.

"Here in the woods of Derbyshire, where anyone might hear?"

She did not sound reluctant to discuss her affairs. James wondered what the hell he was doing out there. He needed to take her home.

The light from the bonfire caught her eye then, and he saw her smile. "Not here. At your cottage, where Lisette is no doubt waiting for us."

"She'll be angry that you've ruined my silk gown, pushing me up against trees."

James laughed. "Ravensbrook's son ruined it already by drooling on it. Not that I blame him."

Angelique laughed with him, taking a moment to smooth her dress, to refasten one of the pins in her hair. She looked as if she had been thoroughly kissed, but then, no doubt so had every woman present.

"I'm sorry I dragged you away from your friends," James said.

"I'm not. It's been too long since you had your hands on me."

James almost swallowed his tongue, but he kept a tight grip on his control as he took her hand gently and walked with her back into the circle of light on the village green.

The rest of her friends had gone, but the Duke of Hawthorne stood waiting.

If Angelique was surprised, she did not look it. James smiled to see her stand and face her foe as a man might have done. She was one amazing woman.

"I thought you had gone, Hawthorne," Angelique said. "Ravensbrook seemed to think you left for London as soon as he dealt with your solicitor."

"And good evening to you, Countess. You seem to know as much about my affairs as I know about yours. I suppose you are still Ravensbrook's light o'love after all."

James tensed on hearing that insult, his hand tightening into a fist as he tried to draw away from her. She clutched his hand in both of hers, no doubt knowing that if she did not, he would strike the duke down.

"Speak that way to her again, and you'll have my fist down your throat."

Hawthorne turned his cold gray eyes on James. "Indeed? Captain Jack, is it?"

"My name is for my friends. My words are for you. Stay away from Angelique."

Hawthorne laughed and James wanted to kill him on the spot. He had known men like this all his life, bastards who would burn your ship and take your cargo, but only if they didn't have to get their hands dirty. James had dealt with cowards like this before by putting a bullet through their brains.

Maybe he would do the same for Hawthorne.

The duke ignored him as if he hadn't spoken, but James knew that Hawthorne was aware of him. James cased the crowd and found three men lurking at the edges of the firelight, ready to move in and slit James's throat if the duke so much as raised a fingertip.

James waited and watched. He wouldn't be much good to Angelique dead. And he couldn't take three of them and still keep her safe.

Hawthorne turned away from James as if he were not there, focusing his attack on Angelique, his original target. "I have a bit of information about the bastard you have taken into your home."

"I would thank you to hold your tongue where my daughter is concerned."

"Your daughter, is it? It seems the chit has come up in the world. But then, who better to train a future whore than Angelique Beauchamp?"

James felt the world go white. His hand came up in a fist, but it did not connect with the duke's smirking face because Angelique hung onto it.

She stepped between the two men, turning to James, taking his face between her hands. She pressed herself against him, staring up into his eyes, as if willing him to draw his glare from Hawthorne and to turn it on her.

"He is not worth it, James. Let him go. Please. For me."

When the word *please* passed her lips, James met her eyes. She pressed her lips to his, heedless of all those watching. Her lips touched his once, gently, and the world seemed to shift. When she drew back, he was staring down at her. His fist was still clenched, but he lowered his arm.

"Only because you ask it," he said.

Ravensbrook's voice broke in between them then, and James wanted to turn his wrath on him. Angelique knew too many smug men, himself included.

"A very moving scene," her old lover said. James looked around for his blonde wife, but it seemed she had vanished. "I would expect such theatrics from the Countess of Devonshire, but not from you, Your Grace."

Hawthorne sneered, not noticing that Anthony had placed himself between the duke and Angelique. James tensed under her hands, ready to strike at both men and take his chances, but she pressed herself against him again, silently pleading with him to stand down.

It would have been the perfect moment to strike, because Hawthorne was focused solely on Anthony as the only threat. James stayed still because the duke's men still lingered, their hands inside their jackets. No doubt they would not fight like men, but draw guns and shoot him down like a dog in the street.

James took Angelique by the hand and led her away. He kept his eye on Hawthorne's men, but they did not move to follow. Let Ravensbrook deal with him, if he was so keen on it. James had had enough of Angelique's so-called friends for one night.

"That's the bastard who's trying to ruin you?" James asked.

"That's the bastard who has ruined me," Angelique answered.

"He hasn't reckoned on me."

Thirty-four

ANGELIQUE WALKED TO HER COTTAGE HAND IN hand with James Montgomery. Sam kept pace behind them, watching their backs as if the Duke of Hawthorne or his minions might spring out of the dark. No one followed them, though, and no assailant appeared. They entered her silent garden, the sliver of a moon bright overhead. The night wind shifted the roses in their bower so that Angelique caught their scent. Their sweet perfume seemed to reach out to draw her in, and James Montgomery with her.

She knew that she was being fanciful, but she still did not let go of his hand.

Sam took a long look at his mistress with her lover, and sighed. "If you are both well settled here, I'll take myself back to the village tavern for a pint."

Angelique forced herself not to look at the man beside her. She nodded, her lips forming an absent smile. "Thank you, Sam. I will see you in the morning for the walk to church."

"Yes, my lady." He doffed his cap to her and bowed,

nodding to James before he walked away, closing the garden gate behind him.

"You're going to church tomorrow? It's a Saturday."

"Tomorrow is Arabella's wedding day."

"I would have wished her happy had I known. But that brings up another thing I want to talk to you about."

Angelique felt her heart accelerate, and she did not look at him.

"Come upstairs with me;" she said. "Let's leave all talk for tomorrow."

The silence stretched between them, unfurling like a long, endless banner, a scarf to wrap around them both, cocooning them from the world. Angelique knew that this was an illusion.

"Marry me," James said.

Angelique's heart stopped abruptly, as did her breath. "What?"

"Marry me," he said again. "I'll protect you from Hawthorne."

"I don't need protecting."

"Your man Smythe seems to think you do."

She felt a frisson of anger and tamped it down. "You spoke with Smythe?"

"I did. He's at his wits' end."

"He knows better than to speak to anyone about my business affairs, ever."

"I'm not anyone, Angelique. I'm the man you're going to marry."

"No."

To her surprise, he did not keep sparring with her. Nor did he stop and woo her, drawing her down to sit on the bench beneath the maple tree. Nor did he bring her into the apple orchard where the flowers had just begun to fall. He took her one inexorable step at a time into the small stable where her four grays kept company.

Her horses were asleep, all but for the lead gelding, which stared at them from behind the door of his stall and blew at them hopefully, asking for a treat.

Angelique knew where Sam kept the dried apples, but before she could reach into the barrel, James pulled her to him, backing her against the stable wall.

"Is there a groom asleep in one of these stalls?" he asked.

"No. Bart sleeps in the attic. Sam looks after the horses at night."

"He's the one who went down to the pub?"

"Yes."

Angelique was breathless, taking in the scent of bay rum and cedar on his skin. Her anger had fled, along with the dirty feeling she had gotten from fighting with Hawthorne on the village green. Standing alone with James, she felt clean. A light-headed giddiness rose in her, as if she were intoxicated, though she had not so much as a glass of wine since dinner.

James did not speak again but pressed close, his lips on hers. She felt him taste her cheek, her temple, moving down to her throat until he reached the low neck of her gown. He unlaced the gown and made short work of the stays, not asking permission this time, but freeing her so that both gown and stays fell away. She stood in just her shift, backed against the wall of her rented stable, her horses awake now and watching them.

"Captain Montgomery."

He did not answer. Indeed, it was as if he could not hear her. His eyes were fastened on the generous rise of her breasts where they pressed against the fine linen of her shift. The hand he still kept behind her bunched the material in the center of her back, so that the thin linen was drawn tight against her breasts. He leaned down and took one nipple into his mouth, his lips and tongue playing over her flesh, wetting the soft shift between them.

She moaned and pressed closer in spite of herself.

"James," she said. "I have not said yes."

He drew back and met her eyes.

"Are you saying no?"

The heat in his blue gaze was like a scorching brand, a fire so hot, it seemed as if it would never go out.

She pressed herself against him, taking his head between her two hands, drawing his lips up to meet hers. He did not hesitate then, but unfastened his breeches with one hand as the hand behind her drew up her shift, sliding beneath the smooth skin of her bottom. His erection freed, he lifted her with both hands, using the wall behind them to brace himself as he plunged up and into her.

It had been only a couple of weeks, but it seemed like so much longer. She had dreamed of him, and now her flesh sang at the familiar feel of his body against hers, her body welcoming him in as if it were she who was coming home. The feeling overwhelmed her even as the pleasure did, rising to swamp her so that she cried out. James did not silence her this time, but groaned himself, the air echoing with their cries, startling the horses. She could hear the grays shifting in their stalls, so that even as tears came down her cheeks, she laughed a little.

That was what life was, she supposed. Moments of laughter and tears mixed together, if one was lucky.

James withdrew from her but held her close still, suddenly gentle. He stroked her hair, which had fallen from its pins and now drifted past her shoulders in a curtain of midnight curls. "Did I hurt you?"

She shook her head, swallowing her pain. "I am all right."

But she could not stop crying. It was as if a dam had broken. She had shed few tears over Anthony. After the first few days, she had locked her pain away, tamped it down, and gone on with her life. But now, in the arms of this man, it was as if all the pain of her life rose to fill her at once, her father's death, her mother's loss, her aborted marriage, her buried daughter, Anthony's betrayal, and now the loss of her livelihood. She did not know how she would solve her current problems, how she would mend her fate. Time and again she had risen from the ashes, but this time, she just didn't know how she could.

James drew her down onto a bale of straw, careful to keep her soft flesh from the prickly golden mass. He held her on his lap, stroking and soothing her, murmuring to her, saying nothing and everything, offering comfort, offering the first sense of peace she had ever known.

Angelique stopped crying. She knew her face must be swollen like uncooked mutton. She moved to wipe her eyes, but James offered her a large handkerchief that smelled like him. She breathed that scent in deeply, until it almost made her weep again. She stopped herself and blew her nose, wiping the last of her tears away.

"I do not cry," she said.

"No? My sisters always do. They say it does them good."

His voice was calm, as if they were discussing the weather. His tone held no judgment, nor did he seem to think her weak. He was matter-of-fact, as he was about so many things.

She felt the temptation to be ashamed slide away. She wriggled down from his lap and gathered up her stays and gown. She did not bother with the stays, but she drew the gown back over her head and tied it loosely, so that she might make it back to the house without it falling off.

"We are not done, Angelique."

They stood together in the light of the night lamp. The horses watched them, chewing their oats, a rapt audience to their drama.

She rubbed her hand over her eyes but forced herself to look at him. "I am done for the night, James. Come up upstairs with me and sleep."

"I won't sleep in your bed until you agree to marry me."

She laughed, the last of her tears wiped away. "Are you serious? Is this *Lysistrata* in reverse?"

James smiled then, but the set of his eyes was serious. "I'll make love to you wherever and whenever I can. But we won't settle into the luxury of your bed until you wear my ring."

"You'll give in," she said.

"No." He smiled, as if he had all the time in the world. "You will."

His dark auburn hair was mussed from where her fingers had woven themselves into it. His ribbon was lost somewhere in the woods, and now his hair fell around his broad shoulders like a highland warrior's.

She could still taste him on her tongue. A part of her wanted to agree to anything he asked, if he would just come upstairs and make love to her again.

"I'll say good night," she whispered.

"Good night, Angelique. I'll see you at the church tomorrow. Think on what I've said."

"There's no need to think," she answered. "I'm not the marrying kind."

But her own thoughts of marriage pressed in on her. She remembered the paperwork she had perused just that day, letting Arabella keep her money even after she wed. She and James might draw up similar paperwork, if she could figure out a way to save her sinking ship, if she could find a way to shield his family from Hawthorne's wrath.

As if he could read her mind, James drew her close and pressed his lips to her brow, just above her eyes. "We'll talk tomorrow. We'll deal with Hawthorne together. Sleep tonight, and dream of me."

His words gave her comfort, though she had no idea why. She went upstairs alone. She thought she would miss him in her bed, and she did, but not as she had when he was away at sea. Something real lay unfinished between them, and she knew it.

Something had changed inside her. Some great

boulder had shifted; some heaviness had lifted from her heart since she had cried in his arms. He had held her while she wept, and not mocked her, and now she was a different woman. The world was a different place.

But she could not face that now. It would be dawn in a few hours. She knew that she must sleep so that her looks would not frighten the whole village when she stood up with Arabella on the morrow.

She slept deep and dreamed of James.

Thirty-five

JAMES STOOD WAITING FOR ANGELIQUE AT THE CHURCH door. He had not been to a service since Christmas. His mother always made him attend with the rest of the family when he was home in Aberdeen, sitting in the Montgomery pew, his sisters chastened into stillness and silence for fear of his mother's wrath. Once the matter of marrying him was settled with Angelique, he needed to take her home to meet the rest of his family. He had been too long away.

He did not wear his Navy uniform, as that would draw too much focus from the bride. He wore a simple dove gray coat and waistcoat, his black breeches neatly tucked into his boots. He had not slept the night before but had called for wash water early and had bathed and combed himself into civility. He had been waiting at the church door for an hour already, getting to the chapel even before the curate came out of his parish.

The round, small man smiled at James but asked no questions, simply passing through the church door to prepare for the service. James did not move but waited for Angelique.

As the morning wore on, James began to feel like a misplaced usher. He nodded to people he did not know as they passed him on their way to claiming a seat within. He watched as Lisette stepped into the church on Sam's arm. The Frenchwoman winked at him, and he could not help but smile at her. If Sam and Lisette were here, Angelique could not be far behind.

Sara came finally, and Angelique with her. The young girl was dressed in a sprigged muslin gown and bonnet trimmed in silk roses. James bowed to her and offered her his arm before he turned to take in the woman he had come for.

Angelique stood swathed head to toe in midnight blue silk. The indigo silk was so dark, it was almost black, but the severity of its color was relieved by its cut. The silk was draped over her soft curves as if her body were a package wrapped especially for him. The low-cut gown made his hands itch. Had they been anywhere else, he would have ripped it off her.

He took a deep breath, raising his gaze to her eyes in an effort to get control of his breathing. But even then, he failed, for she stared back at him, not the lacquered, shielded woman he had first met in London, but the woman who had wept in his arms in the dark of the night. He wanted to reach for her now, to shield her from the burdens she carried, to shield her for the rest of her life.

James forced himself to breathe again and to smile at her. He could not propose to her again here on the church steps before the duchess's wedding. He must hold his tongue and bide his time. The next time he asked her, she would no doubt refuse him. Not that her refusal would signify. He would simply ask her again.

Sara tugged at his arm, so with a bow, he left Angelique standing with the bride, whom he did not spare a glance. Sara led him gently down the aisle to a pew on the bride's side of the church. James sighed, waiting with impatience for Angelique to reappear. Music rose from the church organ, and before long the bride came down the aisle and Angelique followed.

The duchess had dismissed the need for maids to follow her with flowers but had wanted a friend to stand up with her instead. Where she had gotten this mad notion, James could not guess, but the people of the village seemed to like it, just as the few guests from London sneered down their noses.

James barely noticed the murmurs of the nobility or the Duchess of Hawthorne. All he could see was Angelique. All he could think of was how beautiful her midnight hair looked caught in the sunlight streaming in from the windows behind the altar.

He did not hear a word of the ceremony, though Sara was so moved by it that she had to borrow his handkerchief to dab at her eyes. He did not take his gaze from Angelique. Toward the end of the service, Angelique turned to walk behind the bride and groom out of the church. Finally, only then, did she look at him and smile.

Angelique stayed at the wedding-breakfast-turned-garden-party until midafternoon, and James Montgomery stayed with her. Arabella was radiant in her happiness, speaking to all, nobles from London, actors, and villagers alike. Everyone was welcome at the great feast Pembroke had planned. All the locals seemed to take satisfaction in the union, pleased to see their lord happy at last.

Angelique had slipped into Pembroke House to get a moment's peace when James came up behind her.

"You won't escape me that easily," he said.

"I wasn't trying to escape you."

"Weren't you just?"

He drew her into a small sitting room tucked behind the back stairs. No doubt it was the house-keeper's room, though that good lady was too busy with the wedding breakfast to take her leisure.

James closed the door behind them and turned the key.

"Do you think to ravish me in the housekeeper's parlor?" Angelique asked, raising one brow.

"Have I ever needed to ravish you anywhere?"

James smiled, and the glint in his blue eyes made her blood heat. She felt her heartbeat skip in time to her breath, and she started to back away.

When she did not answer him, he moved closer. "I like a willing partner."

"And I am that? It's the middle of the afternoon in the middle of my best friend's wedding."

"What better time for a bit of delight, then?"

The lilt in his voice made her hands shake. She wanted to touch him so badly she thought she might swallow her tongue. She tucked her hands behind her and stopped, finding herself against the white plaster wall.

"We've been here before," James said.

"In a housekeeper's parlor?"

"With you up against a wall."

He kissed her, plunging in as into a deep pool on a hot summer day. Her lips opened beneath his even as he wrapped his arms around her and drew her clasped hands out from behind her. He raised them up and over her head, wedging one large thigh between both of hers.

She shuddered at the pleasure of the heat of her center touching the heat of his flesh through his wool worsted trousers. She writhed against him, unable to stop herself. When she drew back to see if he was enjoying her surrender, she saw no mockery or self-satisfied expression on his face. Only lust.

"I love you, Angelique."

His lips were hot on hers, trailing down her throat. His thigh moved between her legs, and she shuddered with pleasure. He did not stop his relentless motion, even as she writhed on top of his thigh, shaking, trembling, as he lifted her to the tips of her toes, driving into her.

She spiraled so quickly, she had no time to think, no time to do anything but feel. She was up and over the precipice of her own pleasure before she took her next breath, and still he pressed his thigh into the heated core of her, rubbing her, letting her pleasure spiral out, until it was spent, as she was.

"Dear God," she said.

"No," he answered. "Just James."

She did not have any particular belief anymore, but she swatted him for his blasphemy anyway. Of course, there was not much force behind her hand, and her palm glanced off his shoulder without making much of an impression on him. He drew back then and grinned down at her.

"Wouldn't this be more fun in a bed?" he asked.

She slapped at him again, and this time, her palm connected with his shoulder with more force. He did not seem to feel it but kept smiling down on her like a man who knew that, in the end, he would get what he wanted.

He kissed her again before drawing back and helping to right her clothes. She felt as limp as a cut flower. She found herself leaning on his arm as they went to Pembroke and Arabella to say their good-byes.

❧

When they were riding back to her rented cottage, James said, "You haven't told your posh friends that we'll be marrying."

"That's because we won't."

"I beg to differ, Your High and Mighty Ladyship."

Angelique ignored his words. "Will you stay for supper? It will be a cold dinner, just a bit of meat and bread and a little fruit."

He smiled at her, and she felt as if she might warm herself by the light of his smile for the rest of her life. She toyed with the idea, trying it on as she might a new bonnet. She was surprised to find that it fit.

"I will," he answered.

His large hand covered her, the warmth of his palm draining into hers. The leather of his glove and the smooth kidskin of hers did nothing to hold back that heat. She felt a little breathless and shivered as a bolt of pleasure spread up her arm. He could make her want him with just the touch of his hand on hers. She did not know how she was ever going to recover from this.

"And you will be marrying me," he added.

She laughed at his tenacity and let him hand her down onto the clean white gravel in front of the cottage she had fallen in love with.

She had sent word to Smythe, and he had written back that the house was indeed for sale. In spite of her business worries, she would buy it and put it in Sara's name. Every woman needed a home of her own, a refuge from the world. Aeronwynn's Gate was hers. This place would be Sara's.

They took supper out in the back garden, and Hawthorne and his threats, her shipping business and London, all seemed very far away. Mrs. Beebe laid the table with fresh flowers and honeysuckle. Soft white bread was left in a basket sitting on the white tablecloth beside bowls of strawberries and cream. Some cold mutton lay on each plate, warmed by the sun as it slanted into the garden, shedding its golden light on them all.

Lisette retired to her room early. Angelique had seen the looks that had passed between her and Sam, and was surprised at Lisette's condescension at flirting with a mere coachman, no matter that he was a strong, good-looking one. Perhaps it was true love between them, though no doubt Lisette would have rolled her eyes at the notion.

Sara retired next. Her ward had warmed up to James over milk and bread, but she shot him a look of warning as she left him alone with Angelique. He stood when each of them left, as if they were great ladies. Lisette winked at him, and Sara managed a smile, even as she sent a worried glance at Angelique.

"Good night, Sara. All will be well."

"Yes, my lady."

The girl curtsied as if she agreed with her, but she knew Angelique well already. She looked miserable as she climbed the stairs to her room.

"I find that I do not want to fight with you this evening," Angelique said. "Can our usual rough-and-tumble wait awhile longer? Until sundown?"

"That won't be until nearly midnight," James said, his smile lighting his face.

She did not answer that.

He sighed in mock sorrow. "What will we do, if we're not making love in your bed, if we're not fighting for dominance like a pair of apes?"

"Let's sit in the garden and listen to the wind."

He rose and drew his chair close to hers. The wicker kept them a decorous distance apart, and he did not try to draw her onto his seat with him or onto his lap. Instead, he took her hand in his and held it. They had discarded their gloves in order to eat, so his great hand swallowed hers with nothing in between them.

Angelique sighed when he touched her, as if a piece of the puzzle of her life had just fallen into place. She knew that this was an illusion, but it was one she could keep, at least until the sun went down.

She had not slept much the night before, so she found herself drifting off, her hand in his. He did not speak a word but watched over her as she slept.

Thirty-six

AFTER THE SUN HAD SET, THE AIR BEGAN TO COOL. James listened to the cicadas in the distance, singing beneath the oaks and hawthorns. He picked Angelique up from her wicker chair and carried her into the house, placing her on the settee in the sitting room, leaving the door to the back garden open behind him. The fire had died down, and he built it up again as she slept on. He found a bottle of Burgundy and poured a glass of it, bringing it back to the fire to warm it. He turned to her then and saw that her eyes were open and watching him.

"I'm glad you slept," he said.

"So am I."

Her voice was hoarse but beautiful, like a layer of raw silk. He wanted to run his hand over the soft curve of her cheek. He wanted to reach out and touch the curls that had slipped from their pins to fall around her shoulder. He did neither but brought her the warmed glass of wine instead.

"Drink this," he said. "And I will ask you to marry me again."

"I am not changing my answer tonight," she answered him.

"You may yet." James did not smile but pressed the glass into her hand. "Drink."

She did as he said, and as he watched, the color returned to her cheeks. She drank the wine down, and he took the empty glass from her and refilled it for himself. He drank deep, as if to seal a bond between them, as she had done the first night she had brought him home, before he set the empty glass aside.

He stood between her and the door as if he feared she might bolt. He knew that she would not run from any room, much less from one in her own house, but he took the precaution anyway. He would not have her slip away before she heard him out.

"I love you, Angelique." He spoke with no pre-amble. "I know no poetry to use to woo you. I am not an educated man. I love the sea, as I was born to, but I love you more."

Angelique did not speak but sat huddled on the wooden settee. She held a pillow over her heart, as if to ward off his words. She had kicked off her slippers, and her feet were drawn up beneath her gown.

"My father owns a ship and looks to own more. My family carries cotton from the colonies to the factories in the North and makes a tidy profit at it. Bring your ship into alliance with ours, use our contacts, work with our company, and keep all the profits your ship brings in. You will be free of Hawthorne and free of all the fancy people you call friends. We can live in London, or Shropshire, or wherever you wish."

She blinked at him. He paused, to give her the

opportunity to interrupt him, as she was always so eager to do. But this time, she said nothing, only gazing up at him in the firelight with those clear sapphire eyes.

He reached into his coat pocket and drew out the ring he had been carrying with him all the way from London. He bent down on one knee to take her hand in his, and he slid his ring onto the fourth finger of her left hand.

"I will leave the sea for you. Or I will return to it, if you go with me. Marry me, Angelique. I would have you for my wife."

⨏

The next moment passed like one in a dream, but a dream that changed in mid-thought, as a stream sometimes did, coursing over stones. Angelique lost her breath as soon as he spoke the word *love* again, as he slid the most beautiful ring she had ever seen onto her finger. She knew that this time, she would have to answer him and mean it.

But before she could, before she could even gather her thoughts, James grunted once as if in pain and slumped to the floor at her feet. Horrified, she watched him fall. Rising to her stocking feet as quickly as she could, Angelique managed to keep his head from striking the oak floor. There was blood on the back of his head, clumped in a mass at the base of his skull.

She looked up then and saw the Duke of Hawthorne step out of the shadows to stand over them.

"That was a moving scene," the duke said. "I was almost sorry to interrupt it. But we have unfinished business, you and I. That one cannot stand in the way of it."

Angelique saw that his arm was in a sling, that he had been wounded in the shoulder and that his wound had been dressed by a surgeon. In his other hand, he held a pistol, its grip coated with James's blood. As she watched, Hawthorne turned the pistol so that it was now pointed at her.

She drew her handkerchief from her sleeve, pressing it to the gash on James's head, her mind whirling as she thought of Sara asleep abovestairs. She wondered how she might get the duke to leave the house and her charges in peace.

There was a gleam of madness in his gray eyes, the same gleam she had caught a glimpse of when he came into her home in London. Only now, he seemed to burn from within with the light of that madness, as if Arabella marrying another had pushed him over some internal edge no one had known was there.

Angelique stood very slowly, her hands held in front of her where he could see them. She did not move her arms but stepped away from James in the futile hope that she might be able to draw all of Hawthorne's focus to herself. Unlike Anthony's young wife, she knew nothing of combat, nothing of self-defense. She had Sam for that, though the need had never arisen. Now Sam was down at the pub in the village, where he could do her no good.

"Your sweet-faced friend ruined my life," Hawthorne said.

Angelique took one more step closer to the fireplace, where the poker lay close to the blaze. She stopped her progress when he gestured wildly with the pistol. He had not fired a shot from it yet, and it was double-barreled. He could shoot her, then turn the gun on James without even reloading. Angelique stopped moving and stayed where she was.

"Arabella would have married me," he said. "She would have had no choice. But you and Pembroke and Ravensbrook ruined that. You took her from me. I cannot strike at either of them; they are too powerful. I can strike at you."

"Because I am a defenseless woman?"

"Because you are a whore. Because no one cares when a whore is dead."

He raised the pistol, not as if to shoot her but as if to strike her with it. She shrank back, her heart rising in her throat, but she had the sense even still to take one step closer to the poker.

Then she heard Sara shout, and her heart went into her throat. She had not even heard the girl's step on the stairs, and now she was there, in danger, and there was nothing Angelique could do to save her.

"No!" The girl threw herself at Hawthorne, as a puppy might throw itself at a mastiff. Hawthorne took Sara by her night braid and lifted her high, brandishing her as he might a rabbit he meant to kill. Her feet went out from under her as she clutched his hand, her toes barely touching the floor. Angelique had the horrible notion that he might rip the girl's hair away from her head.

"Your husband's bastard. Born of an opera dancer who died birthing her. But your demon husband didn't have the sense to let the chit die in the dirt she was born in. He brought her to clean country, to that woman at that benighted inn. And now you've taken her in and think to make a lady of her. I might as easily make a thoroughbred out of a mule. We are born what we are, Lady Devonshire. Not even your wiles and connections can change what this girl is."

Angelique felt her ire rise to join her fear, and she struggled to push it down, struggled to keep her head clear in the face of her enemy. "I don't care who her mother was. Sara is mine now. I am the daughter of a sea captain, a man who built his own fortune, and his own life, and lived by no one else's leave. Sara will have the chance to build her own life, or I will die trying to give it to her."

"She'll die here, and now, as you will."

Hawthorne raised the pistol toward her daughter then, and Angelique reached for the poker. But before he could fire, James rose from behind him, hitting him once over the back of the neck and once at the wrist.

The pistol flew, striking the floor and sliding across the oak boards. Angelique leaned down and took it up. She leveled it at the mad duke even as James pulled Sara away from him.

Hawthorne stood straight, not caring that the gun was pointed at his chest. "You think to best me, to shoot me with my own pistol? You do not have the mettle. You are nothing but a whore."

Angelique knew that she would never see the end of this man. If he did not kill her here and now, and Sara with her, he would be back another day, or he would send a minion to do his killing for him, and she and Sara would die then.

She tuned out the sound of Sara's weeping. She

disregarded the sound of James's voice as he tried to speak to her. In her mind, the room was suddenly silent, and there was only herself and her enemy, staring back at her.

She did not hesitate, but fired.

The smell of smoke and sulfur filled the sitting room. Angelique heard Sara cry out, and Lisette screaming from above, first in French and then in broken English.

"Stay upstairs," Angelique called to her maid and Mrs. Beebe. "We are all safe here. I will tell you when to come down."

She listened as Lisette and Mrs. Beebe spoke in high-pitched horror at the sound of the gunshot below, each babbling in her own language, for in times of stress, Lisette always lost her English.

Angelique turned her mind to the task at hand and to the man who lay dead on her rented rug.

She had aimed for his chest, but the kick of the gun had sent her shot higher into Hawthorne's forehead, the lead ball exiting in a fist-size hole through the back of his head. His brains and blood lay everywhere, on the rug, on the floor, on James's coat, on the wall behind him, in Sara's hair. Angelique took in the carnage before her, beginning to shake, the gun, suddenly heavy in her hand, falling to the floor.

Sara ran to her then and clutched her, getting the duke's blood all over Angelique's dark blue gown. Her arms were around her daughter, holding her close, the girl she had saved, the girl she would never let go of.

"I will hang for this," Angelique said. "But it was worth it."

"You will not hang," James said. "We will say that I did it."

Before they could get into an argument, a sharp knock sounded on the front door, and Titania's voice called to her.

"My lady! Was that the prop gun I heard go off? I knew I should not let you borrow it for a lark. Let me in."

Angelique laughed, hearing the edge of hysteria beginning to enter her voice. She did not move, but still clutched Sara close while James passed into the hallway to open the door. Titania came quickly into the sitting room and took in the scene with one glance before turning to Angelique.

"What a shame. It looks as if the Duke of Hawthorne fell to a robber's pistol along the road. I wonder what he was doing there all alone in the dead of night? Nothing good, I imagine."

Angelique blinked, thinking for a moment that Titania had lost her wits. Her friend was as calm as a lake on a windless day. "No one else has seen this?" Titania asked.

"Only you, and the three of us," James said.

"Good then. My people and I will set him by the road." She turned to look down at the duke as if he were a pile of refuse to be removed. "This death was too good for him. The evil do flourish, don't they?"

"This one no longer will," Angelique answered.

Titania nodded. "And we have you to thank for that." She turned to James. "Give me the gun. I'll lay it by him. It looks as if the highwayman shot the duke with his own pistol."

Angelique sat on the settee, and James stood between her and the door. She had changed out of her bloody gown and had helped Sara do the same. Their clothes, along with James's bloodied coat, had been taken into the kitchen until Sam could build a fire in the yard the next morning and burn them all to ash. Sara, her hair freshly washed, would not lie down with Lisette but slept next to Angelique on the too-small settee.

Titania had brought her two strongest men back from the inn, and they had wrapped the duke in the bloody carpet and loaded him into a wagon in the stable yard. They drove quietly into the night with the duke's body in tow, the hooves of the mule muffled in cloth. "We'll burn the carpet in a bonfire of our own when we reach the next town," Titania said.

Angelique rose to her feet, carefully covering Sara with a blanket. The girl did not wake.

"I can never repay you," Angelique said.

Titania drew her close. The heavy scent of the actress's perfume engulfed her just as her arms did.

"There is never any need to speak of payment between us."

Another shadow loomed in the dark of the doorway, and Angelique jumped at the sight. James moved without a word between her and that shadow, so that she had to peer around him to see Anthony Carrington standing in the doorway of her sitting room.

"Captain Jack, isn't it?" Anthony raised one eyebrow, taking James in, as if sizing him up for a thrashing.

Unlike any other man she knew, James did not retreat at the sight of Anthony's narrowed gaze.

Instead, he took a step forward, blocking her from Anthony completely, as if he would stand between her and her old lover, between her and the rest of the world.

"The name's Montgomery," James said. "Captain James Montgomery. And Angelique Beauchamp is mine."

Angelique felt the blood rise into her cheeks, and beside her, Titania smothered a laugh in her velvet handkerchief.

Anthony smiled, a small quirk of his lips. "Captain Montgomery it is then." He turned to the center of the room, where the rented rug was missing. The expanse of bare floor had been scrubbed clean of blood, as had the walls behind him. Anthony's eyes ran over the surface, looking for traces of the murder she had committed less than an hour before.

"I understand there is news of Hawthorne's demise," Anthony said.

James did not answer but stared him down. Angelique reached for him, and he seemed to feel the weight of her gaze, for he left off blocking Anthony from the room and came to stand beside her. She took James's hand just as Caroline slipped in, passing her husband in the doorway like a cat.

"Good riddance," Caroline said.

"I understand a highwayman took him down with his own pistol," Anthony said.

Angelique felt gratitude rise in her chest. If the Earl of Ravensbrook backed their story, then it would hold, even in London. No man called Anthony a liar. Not twice.

"It might have been that Hawthorne killed himself after the loss of Arabella," Titania mused. "Or perhaps he was shot over a debt of honor as Carlyle was in Town."

Angelique tightened her grip on James's hand.

"Two blackguards dead in the same week," Anthony said. "That may be a record."

Caroline raised an eyebrow at her husband, her disgust plain on her lovely face. "I thought you had killed Hawthorne already, Anthony."

"I had him escorted out of town last night and set his carriage on the road south. I am no murderer."

"I am," Angelique said. "And I would do it again."

Heedless of the people around them, heedless of Anthony's eyes on them, James took her in his arms. Angelique responded at once, as if waking from a nightmare to the light of a clean morning. She pressed herself against James, drawing up on her toes to take his lips with hers. He did not disappoint her, as he never did in this. He kissed her, and she felt his heart in it.

"What is your answer, Angelique?" he asked. "You're still wearing my ring."

The absurdity of the fact that James was pressing his suit for the second time the same night she had killed a man threatened to overwhelm her. She felt her laughter bubbling up beneath her heart, her stomach beginning to writhe with it. She opened her mouth to let it come but found that she made not a sound.

It was as if the rest of her life fell away, save for her daughter and the weight of the duke's death. Angelique felt lighter as she looked at James, but she knew she would carry the weight of the Duke of Hawthorne for the rest of her life. But she would carry it gladly, as the price of keeping Sara safe.

She looked into the clear blue of James's eyes. He did not seem flustered by her hesitation, but stared down at her as if he knew her answer already. His bedrock certainty felt like a haven, like a shield against an uncertain world.

With Hawthorne dead, the Montgomerys were safe, and she would be free to rebuild her business one contact at a time. She would give herself over to what she truly wanted; she would yield at last and face whatever came after.

"Yes," she said.

"To marrying me?"

"Yes."

The tension drained out of James, and he sat down in an armchair by the fire. He had allowed her to dress his head wound already, but she saw that the blood had begun to flow again and to darken the white gauze bound around his head. She moved with him and sat on his lap, not caring that Anthony, Caroline, and Titania still watched them, as if they were in a play of their own.

"Derbyshire is lovely this time of year, Angelique. But let's go home."

She kissed him. "We'll leave tomorrow for London."

"No," he said. "Let's go home to Shropshire."

Angelique could not answer him, for tears clogged her throat. Caroline, ever watchful, took Anthony by the hand to lead him away. The Earl of Ravensbrook seemed to hesitate by the door, and Angelique met his eyes. She found her voice, swallowing the joy that blocked her speech.

"Thank you, Anthony. You hold my life in your hands."

It was not Anthony, but Caroline, who answered her. "We will not break faith with you," Anthony's wife said.

Titania raised one hand before she let herself out the front door, into the night. Angelique knew she should see her guests out, but she was too tired to think, too tired to move. It seemed as if she had been running all her life, and only now had come to this place where she might stop and catch her breath. Her place, it seemed, was not Shropshire, or on the open sea, or even at Aeronwynn's Gate, but in James Montgomery's arms.

Neither of them spoke for a moment. Neither was much for poetry, it seemed, or romantic murmurings in the dark. But James's arms were warm around her, warmer for the fact that she could stay within their circle for the rest of her life.

"'I love nothing in the world so well as you,'" James said.

She finished the quote for him. "'Is that not strange?'"

He kissed her, and his lips lingered on hers, not asking to make love, only savoring the taste of her. When he drew back, she laid her head on his shoulder.

Tomorrow she would look to Sara's welfare, to Mrs. Beebe, and to Lisette. Tomorrow she would call on Smythe to draw up the proper papers to make her lands her own, whether she married or not. But for tonight, sitting with James in the firelight was enough.

She leaned against him and sighed, relaxing against him as he stroked her hair.

"You are the most stubborn woman I have ever known," James said, his voice soft, musing, as if he had murmured an endearment.

"And you are the most arrogant man I've ever met," Angelique said. "Between Anthony and the Prince Regent, that is saying something."

"I like a stubborn woman."

"I find I enjoy an arrogant man."

"We should get on well together then," James said.

Angelique kissed his throat where his heart beat beneath her lips. "Yes, we will."

ACT IV

"I do love nothing in the world so well as you."

Much Ado About Nothing
Act 4, Scene 1

Epilogue

"Jamie!" Constance shrieked. "She'll make the most beautiful bride!"

His youngest sister ran to him from the carriage, leaping into his arms. Constance was followed by Maizie, who was nine, and by Emma, who was eleven. All three girls surrounded him, wrapping their arms around his waist. His older sisters, Margaret and Sarah, followed more sedately, but they did not wait their turn to embrace him, but pushed their little sisters out of the way.

"We came by ship again," Constance cried.

"I got sick three times," Maizie said in her quiet way. Her soft blonde hair blew about her head in tufts and ringlets, fighting the pins her mother had placed them in.

"I helped clean it up," Emma said proudly, pushing against his leg in case he might not listen otherwise.

"Yes, girls, you all did very well. Now step back, and give Jamie room to breathe," Margaret said, the voice of authority that everyone but Constance heeded.

James set his youngest sister down, caressing her

brown hair as he let her go. His mother was in his arms then, and he held her close, careful not to squeeze her plump form too tight or to muss her fashionable curls.

"We came up the river Severn to Aeronwynn's Gate," she said, her voice almost as breathless as Constance's. "Who knew it was so wide?"

His father came to him and took his hand. "Indeed, who knew?"

He smiled at his son and drew him into a bear hug. John Montgomery felt no concern about crushing him.

James turned to watch as Angelique's ward, Sara, sat down with his own sisters, Sarah and Emma. Maizie and Constance ran in circles around the threesome, grabbing sweets off the tea cart even as Sara tried to pour for her guests. Used to the antics of the twins at the inn at Wythe, Sara did not blink an eye but kept talking to her two new friends as if she had not a care in the world. And he supposed, for the first time in her life, she did not. Thanks to Angelique.

His wife-to-be was wrapped in his mother's arms. Angelique did not shy away but stood in the older woman's embrace, as if taken back to another time and place, as if wishing for her own delicate mother and her soft touch. But all hints of sadness and loss were blasted away by the joyous cacophony of his family, all of whom were intent on making her theirs, just as he had been.

Angelique met his eyes above the fray and gave him a dazzling smile. She did not look like the elegant society woman he had first met onboard her ship. Nor did she look like the sultry countess he had waltzed with at the Duchess of Claremore's ball. She looked like

Angelique, the daughter of a sea captain, the woman who loved him. The woman who, in a few days' time, would be his wife.

His mother let her go, and he crossed the room to stand beside her. Still nodding at whatever Margaret was saying about her new bonnet, Angelique took his hand. James sat down with her, content to be silent and let his sisters' conversation, and the noise of his family, wash over him like an incoming tide.

Angelique was his anchor, his ballast, in the midst of the sudden storm of family. He watched them all with love, the warmth of the woman he loved beside him.

❧

Their wedding day dawned bright, without a hint of clouds.

The summer sun had risen early, and the dew on the grasses of her garden had long since been burned away. Angelique walked with Sara and his youngest sisters, Maizie and Constance, as her attendants. The rest of his family and hers watched as she walked to him up the gentle rise beside the river Severn.

The field of white Queen Anne's lace lay all around them, its pristine purity broken here and there by the dark blue of irises, a dark blue that matched the color of her gown. She had tossed aside the bonnet she had considered wearing. Instead, she wore white roses from the garden in her hair and let the sunlight kiss her.

James waited for her in the deep blue of his Navy uniform. He stood with his father beside him and watched her come to him, smiling as if he had known all along that they would end up here, making their vows in the sunshine together.

Her daughter lay buried less than twenty feet away, but Angelique did not feel the sorrow of her loss that day. She felt almost as if her child stood beside her, as old as James's sister Emma was now. She felt as if her daughter blessed her and wished her happy.

She looked at James Montgomery with tears in her eyes. He spoke his vows in front of the vicar, and she did the same, but the truth of what they promised lay behind the old worn words.

James kissed her, and suddenly, he was all she could see. The rest of the world, their families included, receded, and it was only the two of them, standing in the sunlight.

"I will love you 'til I die," he said.

"I'll love you beyond death," she answered.

"You always have to top me," he said.

She smiled at him and pressed closer, thinking of their bed. "Not always," she murmured.

He leaned down, and kissed her again.

⚜

A week after their wedding, after his family had all gone home, Sara, James, and Angelique took a sailboat out on the river Severn.

Through the clever machinations of Smythe, James had been presented with an agreement that signed away all rights to Angelique's property, and her rights to his. Smythe had been a bit shocked by the idea, and the solicitors had charged double to draw it up, certain that no court in the country would uphold such an outrageous document. A man's rights over his wife's property were sacrosanct. James heard these arguments as he sat by Angelique's side. He had nodded and listened again, and then against all legal advice, he signed anyway.

Angelique took the document into her gloved hand, the document she had paid a fortune for, the papers that had taken her solicitors three weeks to draw up. She cast them into the fire.

"Your money is yours. Your ship is yours," James said.

"I know. And I am yours."

A week after she and James had been married, Angelique reclined in a small skiff as James sailed it down the Severn. Sara sat in the bow, the wind catching her hair beneath her bonnet until the ribbons finally came untied, and her bonnet flew away.

"We'll make a new one," Angelique promised her.

"But the sun will make me freckle," Sara protested.

"There are worse things," Angelique answered. "A few freckles will not mar your looks. You are beautiful as you are."

Sara's smile was bright with joy. Angelique took off her own bonnet and cast it to the wind. Her dark curls came loose and billowed in a cloud around her head. She shook them behind her, so that she could take a look at her husband. James, his hand on the rudder, watched the bending of the river and followed it unerring. She wanted to see him stand like that on the deck of her ship, the *Diane*, where they had first met.

"I would have married you even if your name was Jack," she said.

James came back to her, away from his obsession with the water they sailed on. He laughed, leaning close in the small skiff to kiss her once, hard, a promise of what would come later.

She leaned back, lifted her face to the sun, and smiled.